IRON HORSE CLAIM

On the Dakota Frontier

By
CK Van Dam

Iron Horse Claim

Published in the United States in 2025 by Pasque Publishing

www.ckvandam.com

Cover design by Douglas Moss

Pasque
Publishing

Dedication

The women who came West followed their dreams.

They dreamed of being independent.

They dreamed of being leaders and builders.

They dreamed of creating a world that fit them – rather than fitting into someone else's world.

This book is dedicated to the women who tamed the frontier … and to the women who lead the way today, creating a world for tomorrow's leaders and builders.

Windmills teach us many life lessons.

To be reliable and to press on.

That gentle breezes can help us fly.

And to always stand tall against the sky.

Table of Contents

Chapter 1 – June 1872

Drought

A handful of black dirt trickled like dust through Lizzy Ward's fingers. Ever the farmer, she checked her fields for the corn and wheat she'd planted last month. The rich, loamy soil should have been clumping in her hand, but it had been a dry spring — too dry. She scanned the skies in vain, hoping to see a rain cloud.

Over the hill, she saw her son, Max, coming up the ravine from the creek. Scout, the family dog, bounded ahead of the boy. Max carried a fishing rod, but no fish were on his stringer.

"No luck today, Max?" Lizzy asked.

"Nope." Max shook his head. "The creek's dry."

Max, named after Lizzy's brother, who died during the war, was tall for seven years. Suspenders held up his knee-length britches, preventing the pants from falling off his skinny frame. A straw hat partially covered his thick red hair and shaded his green eyes. As always in the summer, Max was barefoot.

The creek being dry was news to Lizzy. She'd driven the cattle from the south pasture to the creek just yesterday. There had still been a trickle of water in Medicine Creek, enough to satisfy her growing herd of beef cows.

In the nine years that she'd been farming in Dakota Territory, she encountered all sorts of weather, from blizzards and floods to tornados and prairie fires. Although there were occasionally dry spells, this felt different. It was too early in the season to be this dry.

Lizzy had farmed for as long as she could remember. As soon as she could walk, she followed her father out to the fields on the family farm in Missouri. She was only sixteen when her father died in a farm accident — and her mother had already been dead for five years — but her age hadn't deterred her from taking over management of the farm. Lizzy's sister, Charlotte, managed the household chores even though her real interest was in medicine.

Together, the two sisters and their younger brother, Max, kept the farm and household operating. Then, the War Between the States erupted. Missouri was a battleground state, split between Confederate and Union forces, as well as Bushwhackers and Jayhawkers. Neighbors fought against neighbors. Brothers fought against brothers.

When their brother joined the Union Army, Lizzy and Charlotte agreed to take action to bring the youngster back home. Charlotte, disguised as a man, enlisted and followed Max into battle. That left Lizzy alone to manage the farm.

It was Lizzy's ability to see the big picture, to plan and to act, that had helped her run the farm in Missouri — and now, her own farm in Dakota Territory. It had been Lizzy who suggested that – in the middle of the Civil War – she and Charlotte leave Missouri and journey to Dakota Territory. In 1863, the sisters staked claims through the Homestead Act on land just west of Yankton, the territorial capital. After five years of hard work and perseverance, both women had proved their claims. Now, the land belonged to them.

Lizzy was accustomed to making decisions about her farm, but she didn't make decisions that would only benefit her and her family. She believed in the importance of community and understood that neighbors needed to support one another. So, when Max said the creek had dried up, Lizzy worried about the effects on her land and her neighbors' farms.

"I saw the water was down yesterday, but it was still flowing," she said to her son. "Let's go take a look."

Max leaned the fishing rod against the barn door and whistled to Scout. Lizzy went to the house and returned with her shotgun in case they roused a coyote, wolf, or other wild beast. She had learned that it was best to be prepared for any event.

Medicine Creek, named by the Lakota people who camped nearby, flowed into the Missouri River. During a good year, the creek watered farms as far south as the Nebraska border. In a dry year like this one, the creek was narrow enough to jump across. That's what Max did when they arrived at the creek bed.

"Goodness!" Lizzy exclaimed. "There's not enough water to fill a teacup." She studied the now-dry creek bed. "But this just doesn't make sense. Let's walk upstream." She motioned to Max and Scout to follow her.

She wished they had saddled horses for the walk, but soon enough she found what she had suspected — a dam. Someone had dammed the creek, and Lizzy suspected that someone was her neighbor Elias Crawford.

Elias and his wife had staked their claim several years ago. Lizzy had welcomed them to the community, but the Crawfords kept to themselves, so Lizzy allowed them their privacy until now. Damming the creek was certainly not a neighborly thing to do.

"Well! We'll fix this!" Lizzy fumed. She and Max began pulling the logs and lumber out of the creek bed. After they had removed about half of the logs, the water from the creek did the rest, freeing the log jam and allowing the creek to flow again.

"What do you think you're doin', missy? I put them logs there for a reason," Elias Crawford boomed at Lizzy.

Elias was an unkempt man. He wore a wide-brimmed felt hat that was no cleaner than his greasy, brown hair, which hung in strands to his shoulders. His homespun trousers and shirt needed patching and washing. Lizzy suspected he smelled as rancid as he looked.

"I'm opening the creek, Elias," Lizzy retorted. "The water flows through all our lands. You don't have the right to bottle it up."

"I say I do. It's on my land, and that gives me the right to do what I want with it," he argued. "Now you and your young'un will put them logs back where you found 'em."

"I don't think so, Crawford," said Stan Walker, a neighbor on the other side of Crawford's claim.

Elias was startled at the voice coming from behind him. Lizzy had seen Stan ride up and was amused that he took Elias unaware.

Crawford peered down at Elias from his horse. "I rode down here to figure out why the creek was filling up when we haven't had a lick of rain. I should've known that you had something to do with it, Crawford."

Elias scowled. "You should be happy that you and your cattle have more water, Walker. You should be *paying me* for the water."

Stan just laughed at the outrageous statement. "Nope. The dam stays busted. We all need water this year. If we find you've dammed the creek again, you'll be explaining it to the sheriff."

He dismounted from his large, gray stallion and led the horse to where Lizzy and Max stood. "Now, I'll be escorting Miss Ward and her son back to their farm."

Elias huffed in response before turning away from them.

The three followed the creek south and out of sight of the Crawford claim.

"Thank you for your support, Stan," said Lizzy. "But you know, I didn't need you…"

"…you didn't need me to rescue you. I know it, Lizzy. You're a force to be reckoned with, and Elias Crawford just doesn't know it yet."

"He does now," she said with a half-smile.

"He does, indeed," Stan agreed.

Max stifled a chuckle. "Would you have used the shotgun, ma?"

"I don't think it would have come to shooting. But we'll never know, will we," she answered.

"You know, it's only a matter of time before the creek dries up on its own this summer," Stan said.

Lizzy chewed on her lip. "I've been thinking about that."

"I know that look," Stan said. "You've got a plan."

"It's the beginning of a plan," Lizzy admitted.

"Clara and me, we've known you and Doctor Charlotte for a long time. Heck, you and your sister were our first neighbors," Stan said. "Crawford, he doesn't understand that neighbors watch out for one another. You and Charlotte have helped us more than a time or two. I still recollect how relieved Clara was when she was birthin' Bear and Charlotte arrived. I was pretty durn relieved, too."

"Char and I have always counted you and your wife as good friends." Lizzy looked at her son. "And who would Max get in trouble with if he didn't have Bear to pal around with?"

That got Max's attention. "Hey, now that the creek is open again, Bear and I should go fishing."

Lizzy smiled. "I'd like some fresh fish." She turned back to Stan. You've seen us clear of Crawford's land. Thank you for that. We can get home on our own. Say hello to Clara for me. I'll stop by soon for coffee."

Stan Walker tipped his western hat at Lizzy, mounted his horse, and rode north, making sure to skirt the Crawford claim.

When they arrived home, Lizzy saw a visitor waiting by the well. Nellie Jameson's buckskin quarter horse was drinking from the water trough while Nellie herself enjoyed a dipper of cold water.

"It's going to be a hot one today," Nellie said when she finished drinking.

"Hot and dry," Lizzy said in agreement. "We were just at Elias Crawford's claim. He tried to dam up the creek."

"He hadn't counted on Ma," Max said with a chuckle.

"Max…" Lizzy cautioned her son. "We — Stan Walker and I — explained that damming the creek wasn't a neighborly thing to do."

"And I'm sure he was just pleased as punch to share what little water is flowing," Nellie said with more than a hint of sarcasm. "Still, if we don't get any rain soon, I'm going to have to move my horses to new pastures. Trouble is, I don't know where I'm going to move them. It's too early in the season to be this dry. Every drop of water is precious."

"We all need water," Lizzy said. "I might have an idea, but I need to talk with Hank Johnson. You're welcome to ride into town with me. Give me a minute to tidy up. Breaking up dams is dirty work. Max, please fetch my horse while I clean up."

Lizzy disappeared into the sod house. She splashed cool water on her face and wiped off a couple smears of mud. She brushed her thick blonde hair, plaited it into a long braid, and tied it with a blue ribbon.

Before the war, the neighbors in Missouri had called Lizzy the "pretty Ward girl," thanks in part to her striking hazel-colored eyes and long lashes. But it was Lizzy's dimples that people remembered. Her dimples were deep set and appeared on her rosy cheeks whenever she broke into a smile. She was still attractive and was thankful she'd kept her curvy figure and slim waist. Taking one last look in the mirror, Lizzy told herself, *That will have to do.*

When she returned from the house, Max had her horse saddled. "Thank you, Maxie. I'll be home for supper."

"Yes, ma'am," he replied.

"Tell you what," Lizzy continued. "I'll ask Aunt Charlotte if your cousin Will can come back with me and stay a few days."

"That would be swell, ma!" Max exclaimed.

Lizzy smiled to herself. Like all mothers, she knew that while two boys could get into twice as much mischief, they would also watch out for each other. She mounted her mare and trotted out of the farmyard with Nellie.

As they rode side by side, Nellie said, "So tell me about your plan."

"Windmills," Lizzy said. "I read in the *American Farmer* how windmills are helping to pump water on dry land. I don't know how to build them, but I'm guessing that Hank Johnson might know."

"What would the town banker know about building windmills?" Nellie asked.

"Hank's a smart man. Besides, he was in the engineering battalion during the war."

The women caught up on each other's news during the ride into Shady Bluffs. They'd been friends since Nellie's parents sent her north to live with her brother, Luke Jameson, during the war. Instead of staying with Luke, Nellie had accepted Lizzy's offer to live on the Ward farm. The two women had grown very close over the years.

Nellie's family owned and operated a horse ranch in central Missouri. Her brothers teased Nellie that she could ride before she could walk. She loved horse ranching as much as Lizzy loved farming. When Nellie turned twenty-one the previous summer, she had immediately staked a claim for 160 acres right next to Lizzy's farm. With the help of her brother and father, Nellie purchased her first string of horses and began building a reputation for breeding and training fine horses.

Like most frontier towns, Shady Bluffs' streets were muddy in the spring and dusty in the summer. This year, the dust kicking up from horse traffic was especially thick — enough that some riders and folks on the boardwalks wore scarves over their mouths and noses. Nellie followed suit, pulling her neckerchief up over her nose. Lizzy wished she had thought to bring a scarf.

The two women dismounted at the Shady Bluffs Savings and Loan and tied their horses to the rail.

"Can I help…" Hank Johnson started to say when he looked up from his accounts register. He paused before breaking out in a laugh. "Nellie Jameson, you look the part of a bank robber with that mask! But your copper red hair is a dead giveaway."

Quickly, Nellie pulled the kerchief down. "Sorry, Mr. Johnson. It's just so dusty out there!"

Despite being six and a half feet tall, Hank Johnson moved with grace and economy of movement that belied his massive frame. He rose from his desk and went to a side table that held a pitcher of water. Pouring glasses of water for them, he said, "This might help."

"Thank you, Hank," Lizzy said. She gestured to the glass. "This is why we're here, or at least why I'm here. I want to talk about bringing more water to my farm."

Hank poured himself a glass of cool water and sat with the women. "How can I help?"

Lizzy pulled out the tattered copy of *American Farmer* from her handbag and pointed to an article. "What do you know about windmills?"

Hank scanned the magazine article. "Windmills have been around for a while. It looks like this man

Wheeler has figured out how to make them practical on the prairie." He looked up from the magazine and smiled. "So what's your plan, Lizzy? I know you have a plan."

"I'll need to borrow some money for the windmills," she said. And since you were an engineer during the war, I thought…"

"You want me to build you a windmill," Hank finished for her.

"Wind*mills*," she repeated. "I'll need more than one to water my cattle and crops. But let's start with one and see how it goes."

Hank laughed. "I can't say 'no' to you, Lizzy Ward."

When Lizzy and Hank began to work out the details, Nellie rose from her chair in the corner and said, "Thank you for the refreshment, Mr. Johnson. I'm going to stop in and say hello to my brother."

"I'll catch up with you when we're done with our business here," Lizzy promised Nellie.

Nellie was glad to leave Hank and Lizzy alone. Once the two of them started talking to each other, it was as if they had forgotten Nellie was there. She had suspected for a while now that Hank was smitten with Lizzy. Some in town wondered why the bachelor banker had not courted Lizzy.

She walked around the corner to where her brother's blacksmith shop was located. Above the double doors of the smithy, a sign read "Luke Jameson, Blacksmith." Inside, Nellie could hear the sounds of metal hitting metal. As Luke worked the bellows, the forge blasted out waves of superheated air.

When the clanging paused, Nellie called out, "Luke, can you take a break?"

Luke finished shaping a red-hot horseshoe and dropped it into a bucket of water. The water sizzled and steamed. He put down his hammer and tongs and grabbed a cloth to wipe his sooty face. Luke was tall. He wasn't as large as Hank Johnson, but blacksmithing had given him a muscular build. He had a thin face and a long, bushy mustache, and he wore his hair — the deeper chestnut color than Nellie's — on the long side. Although he wore a long, leather apron as protection from sparks and flying metal, his arms and torso were bare.

"Nellie! What brings you to town? Did your horse throw a shoe?"

"I'm fine. My horse is fine. I rode into town with Lizzy. She's talking with Hank Johnson. Anyway, I'm still thinking I want to learn blacksmithing." She said this as she poked through Luke's piles of hammers and tongs and tried on a pair of his large leather gloves.

"Put those down! You're always messing with things," Luke said.

Nellie removed the huge gloves, put them on the wooden workbench, patted them, and then smiled at her big brother, knowing the whole time that it would just aggravate him all the more.

"Hmmm. I'd need smaller gloves," she mused.

Luke just shook his head. "Nellie, you are exasperating!"

"That's just part of my charm," she replied. "So, how are my niece and nephews?"

"They're growin' like weeds. Will is going to be taller than Charlie in a couple of years. Eliza can't wait to start school this fall. And Linc went from learning to walk to learning to run in the blink of an eye." Luke chuckled as he talked of his boisterous, growing family. "I can't believe that Charlie and I are the parents of that brood."

"Reminds me a bit of our family back in the day," Nellie said. "Except there were twice as many of us! How did ma and pa do it?"

"You've got me," Luke said, shaking his head. "Three children have been plenty. You should stop by the house and see everyone while you're in town."

"I will. In fact, Lizzy wants to take Will home to keep Max company for a couple of days."

"I'm all for that! And I'm sure Charlie will agree."

News of the Day

***The Chicago Tribune**, **Chicago, Illinois, January 15, 1868**

Headline: Western Patents

The following patents were issued from the United States Patent Office for the week ending December 31, 1867, as reported by G.L. Chapin, patent solicitor, Chicago, Ill:

Weeding Machine – G. Hess, Chicago, Ill.

Snow-sweeper for Streets – W. Smith, Chicago, Ill

…Windmill – W. Peck, Rockford, Ill

Chapter 2 – June 1872
Land Survey

On the way into town, Lizzy and Nellie had been busy chatting about Nellie's horses and how fast Max was growing. On the way back home, however, Lizzy took a hard look at the tinder-dry prairie. Prairie grasses were brown, and fields of flowers were barely in bloom. The lack of rain in April and May resulted in a dry and dusty June instead of the normally lush green prairies.

"Lizzy. Lizzy!" Nellie whispered in a low voice. "There's a stranger on your land." She gestured to their nephew Will to halt his horse.

Nellie pointed to a man standing behind a tripod instrument. He was peering through some sort of telescope and then making notes in a book.

Lizzy, Nellie, and Will watched as the man, with his back to them, moved the equipment to a new location and began the procedure again. Finally, Lizzy told Nellie and Will to stay back while she investigated. She knew that Nellie had a shotgun ready if the stranger became aggressive.

"Excuse me, sir," Lizzy said as she trotted up to the man. He was dressed formally in a dark gray frock coat over a maroon vest and collared white shirt. There was even a pearl pin in his striped tie. Lizzy took in the man's attire and thought to herself, *all that's missing is the top hat.* Then she saw the tall, black hat sitting on a camp table with more books, pens, and an inkwell.

The man turned from his equipment. "Madame, my apologies. Am I on your land?"

Still in her saddle, Lizzy looked down at the man. Ignoring the question, she asked, "Would you explain what you're doing here?"

"Ah, yes. I am Adam Danbury of the Frontier Railroad Company," he said as if that clarified everything.

Lizzy's hazel eyes narrowed, and she pursed her lips. "And that means what, exactly?"

"Well, I'm surveying this land, of course. For the railroad."

"I would assume you need permission for that," Lizzy countered.

He gestured in the direction of Lizzy's house. "I stopped at the sod house back there to speak with the landowner, but he wasn't there. In fact, there was no one at home when I stopped. I was hoping to run into him while I was working."

Lizzy assumed that Max had gone fishing after he had finished his chores, and she wasn't concerned by his absence. But the fact that Mr. Danbury assumed the land was owned by a man irritated Lizzy. She called out to Nellie to join them.

"Nellie Jameson, this is Mr. Danbury of the … what was the name of the railroad?" she asked him.

"The Frontier Railroad Company, ma'am," Adam replied.

"Yes…the Frontier Railroad Company. Mr. Danbury stopped at the soddy to ask the landowner for permission to survey, but *he* wasn't at home."

"He wasn't?" Nellie said in surprise.

"Uh, do either of you ladies know where I might find the landowner?"

"Yes, I do," Nellie said with a snort. "Mr. Danbury, this is Miss Elizabeth Ward. She owns this land. I reckon she's the landowner you're looking for."

Mr. Danbury's cheeks flushed red as he turned to Lizzy. "Oh, my apologies again, ma'am. I assumed…I shouldn't have assumed."

"It's a new world out here, Mr. Danbury," Lizzy said. "Thanks to the Homestead Act, many women have staked and proved their land claims. Now, tell me what you're doing on my land."

"Frontier Railroad has approval from the government to lay tracks from Sioux City to the Black Hills. I'm surveying potential routes for the railroad."

"I see. And if the tracks are on private property?" Lizzy inquired.

"Of course, the railroad will reimburse landowners as needed. Generally, however, we rely on land grants from the government."

"So, you'll pay me to run a locomotive across my farm?"

"Yes…but that will depend on the route we take. This is all very preliminary." He smiled at Lizzy and Nellie.

"Of course," Lizzy repeated Danbury's words. "And what would make this a good route?"

Danbury looked at his notebook. "Well, topography and terrain are important. Flat stretches of dry land are easier and more economical to lay track on. And we look for water sources for our tanks since the steam engines need to refill along the route. I see there is a creek over yonder." He motioned to Medicine Creek, which bordered Lizzy's farm.

"Water is precious in these parts, Mr. Danbury," Lizzy said. "We need it for our cattle and crops."

"Of course, of course, Miss Ward. The railroad would build a pumping station and tank for that purpose. But, as I mentioned, this is very preliminary. Perhaps, after I've finished my surveying later this week, I could call on you with my findings?"

"That would be acceptable, Mr. Danbury. Now, we need to get home."

Lizzy, Nellie, and Will rode on briefly, and then Nellie turned south toward her horse ranch. "Let me know if the railroad man calls on you." She paused, then asked Lizzy, "Would you allow a railroad on your land?"

"I'm not real keen on it. The Hannibal and St. Joseph Railroad was finished just before the war. It was loud, sooty, and scared the cows," Lizzy said. "Of course, it made sending cattle to market much easier."

"Hmmm," Nellie said. "Tradeoffs."

"We're getting ahead of ourselves," Lizzy said. "Mr. Danbury said these are preliminary surveys to determine the least expensive route."

She noticed that Will had ridden off toward the creek. "I think Will spotted Max. I'm going to check on the boys. I'll let you know what I find out about the train. And if Mr. Danbury wanders onto your land, let me know." Lizzy steered her mare toward Medicine Creek.

When she reached the creek, Lizzy saw that her son's fishing trip had been more successful this time. Stan Walker's son, John Running Bear Walker, known as "Bear," had joined Max for the afternoon. Bear was named for his grandfathers on both sides of the family.

The boys had stringers of shiny, white bass and perch.

"Looks like you boys are bringing home dinner tonight," Lizzy said when she saw the stringers. "Bear, you'd best be on your way home. And take care to stay off Elias Crawford's claim."

"I will, Miss Lizzy," Bear replied. "Pa warned me to ride clear of Crawford's claim before I left." He waved to Max and Will, hopped on his pony, and started for home.

"Come on, boys," Lizzy said to her son and her nephew. "We're having fresh fish for dinner. Max, you can ride with Will."

As the three rode toward the sod house, Lizzy looked for likely spots for her first windmill. While this part of Dakota Territory was fairly flat, there were some slight hills scattered over the farmland. She and Hank had decided that building the windmill on high ground would allow her to use gravity and irrigation furrows to bring water to her fields. When she found the highest hill on her property, she nodded and said to herself with satisfaction. *I didn't even need surveying equipment for that.*

Lizzy was thankful she had brought her nephew back to the farm. Not only was Will eager to do farm chores, but he was also a good companion for Max.

Both boys were seven years old. Max celebrated his birthday on Valentine's Day since Lizzy was uncertain of her son's actual birth date. He was only a few weeks old when Lizzy found the infant. He and his mother had been trapped under a collapsed building in the aftermath of a buffalo stampede through Shady Bluff's Main Street. The baby's mother and father were both killed in the stampede.

The young family had been passing through Shady Bluffs when bank robbers caused a buffalo stampede that destroyed half the buildings in town. Lizzy, Charlotte, Luke, and Hank had searched for the family's identity, but there was nothing to determine who the parents were or where they had come from. In the weeks after the stampede, no one stepped up to claim the baby.

Lizzy immediately fell in love with the tiny bundle. Everyone agreed that she should adopt the infant. After a while, no one even remembered that Lizzy's son had been orphaned. It seemed Max had always been Lizzy's son.

Will was born in the summer of 1865, just a few months after Max. The two cousins were inseparable.

On the way back to the homestead, Lizzy listened as Will recounted the meeting with the railroad man.

"He surely looked like a city slicker, Max, with his fancy coat and vest," Will said. "I wish I could have gotten a better look at the scope he was using. Maybe when he comes by, he'll let us look through it."

"He's coming back?" Max asked.

"I think he's trying to make amends to your ma. After all, he didn't get permission to be on Aunt Lizzy's land."

"It has been a day for unexpected events," Lizzy said, diverting the conversation from the boys' gossip. "Max, you and Will can clean that stringer of fish while I start dinner."

"Can we have a campfire after supper and then sleep outside?" Max asked.

Lizzy laughed. "Yes, but don't wander out of the farmyard. And keep Scout with you. He'll watch for coyotes and other critters."

Scout, of unidentifiable parentage, was a large, yellow dog with long fur and floppy ears. He had wandered onto the Ward farm several years ago and had immediately proved his worth as a watchdog. Max, only a toddler at that time, was playing on a blanket when a large bullsnake began to slither toward the boy. Scout had seen the snake's movement and barked until Lizzy found a large stick to fling the snake out of the farmyard. Ever since then, Scout had been Max's companion and protector.

The following day, Lizzy and the boys were moving cattle to fresh grass when Adam Danbury paid a call. Still dressed as a dandy, Adam was riding a palomino horse with a white mane and tail. *That horse was as "showy" as Danbury was*, Lizzy thought.

Adam waited at the edge of the pasture until Lizzy rode over.

"Do the cows return to the barn at night," he asked when Lizzy reined in her mare.

"No, these are beef cattle, not milk cows, Mr. Danbury. They'll stay here until the grass gives out. Then, hopefully, we'll find fresh pastures for them," she explained.

"What do you mean, 'hopefully'? How many acres do you have on your farm?"

"We're in the middle of a drought, Mr. Danbury. As I said yesterday, every drop of water is needed for my cattle and my crops. Even the pastures are drying out."

"What will you do then," Adam asked.

Lizzy assessed the man. He seemed genuinely interested in her farm and her cattle. She decided to give him the benefit of the doubt and politely answered his questions.

"My original claim was 160 acres, as was my sister Charlotte's claim. When we staked the claims, which are next to each other, we built two houses connected by a common room. It's unconventional, but the claims agent in Yankton said it was legal as long as each of us had a dwelling on our own claim."

"Unconventional, perhaps, but efficient," Adam commented.

Lizzy smiled. "Yes, exactly, Mr. Danbury. We were able to share household chores and keep each other company."

"Please call me Adam," he said.

Lizzy nodded. "If we're to be on a first-name basis, you may call me Lizzy."

"Lizzy," Adam continued, "I have the initial surveying reports and I was hoping we might review them together. That is, if you have time today. If not, I can return at a more suitable time."

"Now is as good a time as any," Lizzy replied. "Let's go back to the house."

When they approached Lizzy's house, Adam observed the mirrored construction of the residence. Adam said, "I see what you mean about the design of the house – or is it 'houses'? Does your sister still farm?"

Lizzy laughed. "Char never wanted to be a farmer. We worked the land together, built our homes, and proved our claims. But she always wanted to be a doctor. Now, she's the town doctor in Shady Bluffs."

As they entered the double-wide house, Lizzy continued. "Charlotte married Luke Jameson about a year after we arrived in Dakota Territory. Luke is the town blacksmith. Together, they have three children: Will, Eliza, and Linc. She'd already staked the claim in her name before marrying, so the land is hers. Charlotte pays me to farm the land. It's an arrangement that works for us. So I guess you'd say I farm about three hundred twenty acres. And right now, it's three hundred twenty acres of very, very dry land."

"Have you ever thought of building a windmill?" Adam suggested.

Not wanting to share her plans just yet, Lizzy gave Adam her best, dimpled smile. "That's an interesting idea. Now, let's have some tea while you explain what a railroad survey is."

Adam rolled out several long sheets of drawing paper at the kitchen table. Each sheet showed different topographical features, including elevations, property lines, and water sources.

"There's Medicine Creek." Lizzy pointed to the prominent stream that bordered her land. She saw that Adam had indicated landownership on the map. "How did you get everyone's name?"

"I started at the claim office in Yankton," Adam explained. "Mike Mathews was very helpful. His plat maps were very accurate. After that, I needed to survey the land for elevations and land formations that weren't on the plat maps.

"Before coming to Dakota Territory, I did some surveying for the Northern Pacific in Minnesota. The lakes, bogs, and swamps make laying track much more difficult up there. But here in the south, Dakota Territory was made for railroads. It's extremely flat and, as you said, dry. That's good for the Frontier Railroad Company.

But we'll also need sources of water for our steam engines."

Lizzy considered her next question. "So, if and when you choose a route, what's next?"

"The federal government wants railroads to connect the country. The government realized how important trains were during the war. Now, the U.S. General Land Office is authorized to grant public lands to railroad companies," he explained.

"By 'grant,' you mean 'give'?" Lizzy asked.

"Yes. By granting public land to the railroads, we'll own land where we lay tracks, and we can sell surrounding parcels to pay for the construction. After all, the railroad companies are providing the men and materials to build the tracks."

"Then why are you surveying my land when the government has already given your company public land?" Lizzy asked.

"An excellent question," Adam replied. "We need to ensure that we are choosing the most optimal land for construction. That means I must survey various routes before Frontier Railroad chooses the best option."

"What would make my land the best option?" Lizzy asked.

"Well, in addition to routes that are relatively flat, we look for potential water sources, as I said before. Our steam engines can go a hundred to a hundred fifty miles between water stops. And then we need to refill our water tenders. Each steam locomotive has a water tank that carries several thousand gallons of water. A water tender forces water into the boiler, creating steam. And that's what moves the locomotive!"

Lizzy knew she didn't need to understand the mechanics of steam engines. But she understood that the trains would compete for water on her land.

"I see," Lizzy replied noncommittally. Her mind was racing ahead, weighing responses.

"That's why I was interested in Medicine Creek," Adam said.

"But if the creek dries up?" Lizzy prompted.

Adam frowned. "Not a problem. We would build a windmill and water tower."

Lizzy chewed her lip while she considered the conversation.

Just as she was about to ask Adam what he knew about windmills, there was a knock on the door of her common room.

Lizzy was surprised to see Hank Johnson at the door. Hank occasionally came to the farm for dinner or to help with harvest, but he didn't show up unannounced — until today.

"I didn't realize you would have company, Lizzy," Hank said. "I've made some inquiries about that..."

Before Hank could continue talking about the windmill project, Lizzy interrupted him. "Hank, please come in and I'll introduce you to my guest."

Even though Hank was the town banker, he dressed more like a cowboy than a businessman. He wore his curly brown hair a bit long but kept his brown beard and mustache neatly trimmed. Brass buttons adorned Hank's navy blue work vest that stopped at the six-shooter on his hip. Standing at his full height, Hank made an impression when he entered any room.

Hank followed Lizzy into the kitchen and saw the dandy standing at Lizzy's table.

"Mr. Adam Danbury, this is Mr. Hank Johnson," Lizzy began the introductions. "Mr. Danbury is with the Frontier Railroad Company. Mr. Johnson owns the Shady Bluff Savings and Loan."

"Mr. Danbury, good to meet you." Hank reached out to shake Adam's hand. Hank's huge hand swallowed the other man's in the grip.

"Hello, Mr. Johnson. I've been meaning to stop in the Savings and Loan and introduce myself," Adam said.

"Mr. Danbury was showing me the railroad survey maps," Lizzy explained to Hank. "Oh, are they supposed to be confidential, Adam? I am so sorry if I was speaking out of turn."

"No, no, no, Miss Ward," Adam said as he rolled up the sheaves of paper. "But I've taken up enough of your time today. Thank you for the refreshments. I should be on my way."

Adam packed up the maps, collected his hat from a side table, and headed for the door. Lizzy followed him outside.

"Thank you for explaining the process, Adam. It was very interesting to learn how railroads — and locomotives — work."

"My pleasure, Miss Ward. My pleasure," Adam replied. "It was a delightful afternoon."

Lizzy and Hank watched as Adam rode out of the farmyard.

"Can I just say that you don't see a lot of men dressed that fancy in these parts," Hank said with a chuckle. "He looks like he's going to a funeral — or a wedding."

"I think those are his work clothes," Lizzy replied. "That's how he looked yesterday when I came upon him with his surveying equipment. I think I surprised him. That's why he called on me today: to apologize for not asking permission to be on my land."

News of the Day

The St. Cloud Journal, St. Cloud, Minnesota, January 4, 1872

Headline: Selection of Depot Grounds – What Has Been Done

The St. Paul Press makes an extended notice of the railroad progress of Minnesota during the year 1871. Grading and tracklaying have been done on eleven different lines. The length of track laid during this year was 451 ½ miles, making with what was previously constructed a total of 1,550 ½ miles of railroad in the State.

Minnesota has now about one mile of railroad to every 360 inhabitants – a greater ratio than any other State except Nevada, which happens to be traversed by the Central Pacific. …The present year will add at least five hundred miles more, making a grand total of over two thousand miles of railroad in a State which emerged from a territorial condition but about fifteen years before.

Chapter 3 – Summer 1872
Windmills

"I expected the railroads would be coming to Dakota Territory soon," Hank said as he and Lizzy returned to her kitchen. "I just didn't think it would be *this* soon."

Lizzy relayed her encounter with the surveyor the day before.

"There he was, frock coat and all, surveying my land by Medicine Creek," she said. "I'd read about the railroad expansions in the papers, and I assumed they'd need to cross the Territory to reach the other side of the country. I just didn't think they'd be crossing *my* land.

"When Char and I staked our claims, there wasn't much out here — except the Lakota, of course. Max and I still visit the Lakota camp by Medicine Creek."

Lizzy and her sister had arrived in Dakota Territory as unmarried women. In accordance with the Homestead Act, they each staked claims as "head of household." Luke Jameson had followed Charlotte to Dakota Territory with the very intention of making her his wife. They married the next year. Theirs had been a turbulent courtship, but Charlotte and Luke's marriage was one of equal partners.

When she was younger, Lizzy had assumed she would marry and start a family, just as her older sister had done. Then she adopted Max, and Lizzy's plans changed. Farming and raising a son consumed her life. She didn't have time to think about marriage. Besides, not many men were keen on raising someone else's child.

Lizzy, however, was content with her life.

Max brought a unique kind of love into Lizzy's life. She had been smitten with the squalling infant the moment she rescued him from the collapsed building. Over the years, she had learned to meet the challenges of raising an energetic young boy.

And there was Charlotte, her best friend, who lived in town with her growing family. The sisters had a special relationship. Each woman had always relied on the other for advice and support.

Lizzy had also made many friends in Dakota.

Stan and Clara Walker, their son Bear, and three younger children farmed a section north of Lizzy. Just as Stan had been there for Lizzy during the encounter with Elias Crawford, Lizzy had helped the Walkers when they were in need. Lizzy believed that neighbors had to look out for neighbors.

Then there was Isabell Vaughn in Shady Bluffs. Isabell owned and operated the town's general store, Vaughn's Mercantile. Isabell was one of the first townsfolk to welcome the sisters to Dakota Territory. Lizzy admired the businesswoman and understood the challenges she faced.

And there was Nellie Jameson. Nellie was, as her family in Missouri called her, "a force of nature." She quickly gained a reputation in the region for breeding and training quality horseflesh on her ranch. Lizzy was extremely proud of Nellie's accomplishments. Nellie's homestead claim was directly south of Lizzy's farm. The two women visited each other often.

In addition to Lizzy's circle of female friends, there was Hank Johnson. Lizzy would often stop in the bank to say hello to Hank when she was in town. She considered Hank one of her closest friends and advisors. That's why she had come to him for advice about the windmill.

Now, at Lizzy's kitchen table, they discussed where and how to build the windmill that Lizzy wanted.

"I think I found an option that would work for you," Hank said. He unfolded a copy of the Weekly Ottumwa newspaper and pointed to a story about the county fair.

"Windmills have been around for a long time, but this fellow from Indiana, Leonard Wheeler, has patented a windmill that works in all types of winds," Hank said, the enthusiasm building. He talked about the gears and the mechanisms that made the Eclipse different from earlier windmills. Even though Hank now spent his days as a banker with ledgers and loans, his experience as an engineer during the war drove his excitement for mechanical inventions such as windmills.

"And, Lizzy, we can order kits from the company!" he concluded.

"Hank, that sounds like exactly what we … what I need." She paused, "But can I afford it?"

"Windmills are going to change how farmers work the land. We're in this together," Hank declared. "We need to show other farmers why this is the future. The bank will loan you the money for a windmill."

"Windmills," Lizzy corrected him. "I think I'll need three to start." "I'm going to change into a riding skirt, then we'll do some surveying of our own."

"Right, windmills," he amended.

Dressed in a navy blue split skirt and pale blue blouse, Lizzy strode to the barn and saddled her horse. Over her shoulder, she continued talking to Hank. "There's a hill…okay, it's more like a rise or a mound, in the west pasture. The windmill should catch the wind there."

On their way to check out the first location, Lizzy told Hank what she'd learned about the railroad's plans.

"Adam — Mr. Danbury — said the steam engines require water stops along the route. I'm afraid he's looking at Medicine Creek, and I don't have any water to spare."

Hank considered that information. "You're getting ahead of yourself, Lizzy. The Frontier Railroad may not choose a route that's near your land. Of course, if they do decide that your land is the best option, we can turn that to your advantage."

"How?" she asked.

"We could stipulate that the railroad must build a windmill and allow you to use a portion of the water. But, like I said, we're putting the cart before the horse. Let's wait and see what happens. In the meantime, I think I see the 'hill' you were talking about." He pointed to a slight mound on the ever-so-flat prairie.

"Yes, that's the first spot," Lizzy confirmed. "What do you think?"

"It's a fine location for a windmill. It's well-situated to catch the prairie winds. You can dig irrigation channels to feed water into nearby fields."

"That's exactly what I was thinking," Lizzy said excitedly. "I can water several fields from this location alone! The next location is south of here, where I graze the cattle."

Hank and Lizzy rode toward the next location. "This land isn't as easy to plow," Lizzy said, "so I've been putting the cattle out here."

Hank nodded and studied the landscape. "This might work if we build a stock tank next to the windmill."

"I'm thinking that eventually I could fence off sections of the grazing land and then rotate the cattle from pasture to pasture."

"Good idea," Hank said. "Have I ever told you that I believe you're the smartest farmer in these parts, Lizzy Ward?"

"That's the nicest thing anyone has said to me all day." She laughed to cover her embarrassment at the compliment.

"I mean it. I admire your imagination and your vision."

Before they could continue the conversation, they heard the distinctive sound of a rebel yell in the distance.

"What in tarnation! I haven't heard that sound since the war," Hank said with a shiver.

"There are some things we'll never forget," Lizzy said. She scanned the horizon in search of the source of the high-pitched battle cry. "It's coming from just beyond that ridge." She spurred her mare toward the sound, and Hank followed her.

They found Nellie racing an impressive bay horse in a large figure-eight in a grassy meadow. The horse's black tail was flying, and so were Nellie's copper-colored braids. Her rebel yells were mixed with encouragement to the bay.

"That's it, boy! Woo hoo!" she called to the horse, oblivious to the riders now watching the spectacle.

When Nellie reined in the horse from a gallop to a canter, she saw Lizzy and Hank laughing and applauding her performance.

"Howdy! How long have you two been spying on me?" she asked as she trotted toward them.

"We thought war had broken out again!" Hank said with a laugh. "I haven't heard that rebel yell since Spotsylvania."

"I'm sorry, Mr. Johnson. I was just so excited. I grew up in the middle of Missouri — that was secesh country — and I heard a lot of Rebel yells back home,"

Nellie said. She patted her horse's withers. "But isn't Thunder a beauty? He's got speed, strength, and stamina!"

"He is a beauty," Hank agreed. "I'm in the market for a new ride. Is Thunder for sale?"

Nellie shook her head. "I've got plans for Thunder. I'm going to get some great colts and fillies from this horse."

"You will, indeed," Hank said. "But keep me in mind for a good, strong stallion or gelding. I'm not fussy about the coloring, but I sure do like the look of this bay."

Nellie nodded. "What are you doing this far south?" she asked Lizzy.

"We're surveying my farm for places to build windmills," Lizzy replied.

"If this drought continues, we'll all need to be pumping water for crops and livestock," Nellie said.

"There's one more spot to check out," Lizzy said to Nellie and Hank.

"We'd best be going," Hank said. He turned to Nellie and said with a wince, "Could you wait till we're out of earshot before you start up with those rebel yells again?"

Nellie laughed. "My apologies again, Mr. Johnson. You'll hear no more rebel yells from me."

The third destination was on one of the east sections. Hank noted that the land was particularly flat. "I don't know about this one, Lizzy," he said. "Will it catch enough wind to pump water?"

"It has to. I plan to plow these fields next year, and the crops will need water," Lizzy said. "Besides, have you ever been on the prairies when there's been no wind?"

"Not often," he admitted.

"It's either here or back at the house," Lizzy said.

"You know, a windmill at the house would make your life a lot easier, Liz," Hank said. "Water for cooking, cleaning, washing…not to mention water for the pigs and horses."

"Maybe that's not such an extravagance," Lizzy pondered. She nodded as the idea took root. Pointing to the spot she had marked for the third windmill, Lizzy said, "This will be windmill number four. After all, I won't need it until next summer."

"Good plan," Hank agreed.

The sun was dipping into the western sky by the time they returned to the homestead.

As they rode into the farmyard, Lizzy nodded her head at the soddy. "That's my next big project — after the windmills are producing water."

Hank tilted his head, looking confused.

Lizzy explained, "I want a real house instead of one that I share with all manner of bugs and snakes." She shuddered. "Oh, don't get me wrong, it's warm in the winter and cool in the summer. But I don't want to live in a house with dirt floors, dirt walls, or dirt ceilings. I want a proper house like the one my family had in Missouri. A wooden house with real doors and windows."

Lizzy assessed the double-wide soddy that she and Charlotte had shared.

"We built the soddy on the property line so each of us could abide by the Homestead Act. Char proved her claim and has no need for a house on the land now. I'm working the land, and I want a proper house for my son."

"You shall have a proper house," Hank said. "I'll help…but let's tackle one project at a time. I'll order the windmill kits when I get back to town. I expect we'll have to ride into Yankton to fetch them."

"Thank you, Hank. I…." Lizzy said.

She was going to say something more, but just then, Max and Will burst from the barn.

"Ma! Marigold is calving. I think she needs help," Max called out.

"Never a dull moment around here," Lizzy said to Hank as she dismounted. "Want to help?"

"Tempting offer, but I'll pass," the banker said. "Besides, I'd best get back to town. I'll let you know when the windmill kits arrive."

He nodded and trotted out of the farmyard toward town.

Hank enjoyed the ride into Shady Bluff. It gave him time to review the day's events, plan for tomorrow's events, and think. Sometimes, he thought about Abigail.

A lifetime ago, Abigail had been Hank's wife. Abigail Edison's family attended the same church as Hank Johnson's family. Hank proposed to the quiet young woman right after rebel forces attacked Fort Sumter. That was April 1861.

The wedding was a rushed affair, just as many weddings were during those turbulent war years. Hank had initially joined the cavalry, but when his superior officers learned of Hank's talent for building, he was transferred to the U.S. Engineer Battalion attached to the Union Army of the Potomac. Hank's unit was responsible for building and destroying transportation networks, as well as constructing defensive and offensive placements.

Even though they were Army engineers, Hank and his unit saw more than enough combat at Antietam and Gettysburg, among other battles. While Hank was fighting for his country, Abigail was at home in New York, waiting for Hank to return.

Hank *was* able to return home on leave from time to time. During one of those brief visits, Hank and Abigail started their family. In November 1861, Abigail wrote to Hank that she was expecting their first child. Hank was thrilled at the prospect of becoming a father. That gave him one more reason to return home safely.

He wrote faithfully to Abigail each week. The letters included anecdotes about his fellow soldiers, complaints about the food, and weather reports. He downplayed the danger of the war and never included details of the battles he fought.

Abigail also kept her letters to Hank light and happy. She updated him on the crib her father had made, her favorite baby names, and the progress of her pregnancy. In June 1862, just after the Battle of Cross Keys in Virginia, Hank received a letter from his father-in-law, Louis Edison. Eager to learn if he was the father of a boy or girl, Hank tore open the envelope.

Instead of a joyous birth announcement, Louis wrote that Abigail and her child had died in childbirth.

Hank was shattered. As a soldier, he lived with the threat of death every day on the battlefield, but he could not deal with the death of his wife and child. Hank immersed himself in his work. He rose through the ranks, eventually managing an engineering unit. That was where he learned the basics of money management and realized he had a talent for it.

When the war ended, Hank did not return to New York. He didn't want to live in a community with daily reminders of Abigail, so he traveled west to Dakota Territory to start a new life.

Hank hadn't shared his story about the loss of his wife with folks in Shady Bluffs. As far as they were concerned, Hank Johnson was a confirmed bachelor. He did admit to himself that he was attracted to Lizzy, but he was not ready to go down the matrimonial path again.

News of the Day

The Ottumwa Courier, **Ottumwa, Iowa, August 22, 1872**

Headline: Wapello County Agricultural Fair

Already the stalls are almost full of the finest stock that has ever been exhibited on the grounds of the society....Russell & White are on hand with one of the Sandwich (Ill.) Enterprise Co.'s windmills, an open buggy and farm wagon.

Jno. R. Shepherd, an agent for the "Wheeler Eclipse Windmill" is now engaged digging a well and erecting one of these machines on the ground. T.K. Shepherd also has a windmill in operation.

Chapter 4 – Summer 1872

Farrier

A feeling of isolation was common on the wide-open frontier. There were stories of men and women who went insane with prairie madness. For some, it was the constant winds that caused the insanity. Other homesteaders complained about the silence and loneliness on the great frontier.

Nellie Jameson was *not* among those people. Having grown up in a family with six older siblings, Nellie was used to the commotion of some sort in the Jameson household. As a "girl homesteader" in Dakota Territory, Nellie gloried in the simple sounds of nature, from the whistling winds to calls of meadowlarks and hawks. Her favorite sounds, though, were from her corral. The nickers and neighs of her horses were music to her ears.

When she needed to talk to another human, she would mosey up to Lizzy's house or ride into town. During the war, violence from Bushwhackers and Jayhawkers in Missouri was increasing, and Nellie's parents decided it was safer for her to live in Dakota Territory with Luke. Before staking her claim, Nellie had lived with Lizzy and Charlotte. Now, Dakota was Nellie's home.

The July morning had dawned hot and sunny — like most days this summer. Just like Lizzy, Nellie was worried about the increasing drought. She would never be the farmer that Lizzy was, but Nellie made her living on the land, too. Of course, she had a good-sized kitchen garden with peas, carrots, beans, potatoes, beets and herbs. Like most settlers, she also had a small number of cows and sheep and a few chickens. But it was Nellie's stable of horses that consumed her energy.

Nellie had grown up on the family horse ranch in Missouri and would often tell folks that she could ride before she could walk. While that might have been a bit of an exaggeration, it was close to the truth. She knew as much about horses as Luke did. Now, Nellie wanted to learn more about blacksmithing, which Luke knew plenty about.

She considered riding into town in her work clothes — trousers, a man's shirt, and a broad-brimmed hat — but decided a trip to town merited fancier duds. Nellie stripped out of the grubby trousers and shirt. She took a quick sponge bath, making sure to clean her face of the inevitable dirt and smudges. Her moss green split riding skirt was clean, and she found a white hand-me-down blouse from Charlotte that she hadn't worn in ages. After trying to coil her thick, copper-colored hair into a bun, Nellie gave up and let the hair hang down her back.

Deciding that Thunder could use some exercise, Nellie saddled the horse. Besides, she wanted to show off the impressive stallion to her brother.

Shady Bluffs was a typical frontier town. Main Street, running north to south, was a collection of wooden buildings. In the rainy season, wagons might sink to their axles in the muddy mess. Pedestrians would cross the sloppy, mucky streets by walking on boards. This year, however, dust from the roads blew through the town, collecting in piles at the corners of buildings.

Many of the stores, shops, and offices had been rebuilt after the buffalo stampede seven years ago. There was Vaughn's Mercantile, a stagecoach station, several saloons, the post office, and a handful of churches.

Down the street from the general store was an office with a large wooden sign that had "C. B. Jameson, Doctor & Surgeon" painted in white letters. The "C. B." stood for "Charlotte Blanche." Charlotte had gotten her start as a doctor in the Union Army during the war. That's where she met Luke, who was a patient in the field hospital. Later, when Shady Bluff's doctor died from pneumonia, Charlotte became the town's physician.

The blacksmith shop was across from the doctor's office on a side street, next to a large livery stable. Unlike the other buildings in town, Luke's blacksmith shop looked more like a barn than a store or office, with a large, double-door entrance onto the side street. Nellie tied Thunder to a hitching post in front of the shop. The double doors to the blacksmith were open, and she could hear the clanging of metal on metal from inside the building.

When she entered the shop, heat from the forge hit Nellie like a physical wave. Luke stood by the hearth, pumping the bellows with the lever overhead. He was shirtless, with a thick leather apron covering his torso. Sweat and soot clung to his biceps and face. When the fire was sufficient, Luke pulled the metal shaft from the coals and began hammering and molding it into a farm tool.

"Hey, big brother," Nellie said when Luke stopped hammering. He swiped a fairly clean cloth across his forehead, then wiped his sweaty neck.

"Howdy, Nell," Luke said. "What can I do for you?" He peered out the door of the shop and saw the stallion. "Is that your new stallion? Hank said he was a sight to behold."

Luke put down the tongs he was holding and walked outside to get a better look at the horse. "What's his name?"

Nellie beamed. "This is Thunder. He's going to be the sire for my new line."

Luke ran his hand over Thunder's hind quarter and down the horse's left thigh. "Nice conformation," he said appraisingly. "Where did you find him?"

"I was in Yankton for a horse sale a few weeks back. Saw this one and knew he had to come home with me. She laughed. "You've got to ride him. He's so fast…and so smooth," Nellie urged Luke. She handed the reins to him.

"You don't need to ask me twice, Nell," Luke said. He swung into the saddle, trotted the stallion down the street, and galloped into the countryside.

While she waited, Nellie poked around in the blacksmith shop. Her father had done some blacksmithing, so she was familiar with the process and the equipment. Luke's operation in Shady Bluffs was

45

much bigger than the make-shift forge and bellows on the Jameson ranch in Missouri. But in addition to fashioning horseshoes, Luke produced and repaired farm tools, such as shovels, axes, and hammers. He also mended pots and pans and other household goods. Homesteaders couldn't afford to replace broken farm equipment. They depended on blacksmiths to repair valuable tools and equipment needed on the farm.

Nellie didn't think she would be interested in that side of the business. She was focused on work for her horses: shoes, harnesses, and the like.

She was experimenting with the bellows when Luke and Thunder returned.

"Are you looking for work?" Luke asked as he entered the shop.

"I wanted to talk to you again about learning how to be a blacksmith," Nellie answered. "But I don't want to do all that other stuff — the hammers, nails, pots and pans, and such." She waved at the pile of household items in a corner of the shop. "I want to strictly work with horses."

"It's the plows, pots, and pans that keep this shop in business," Luke replied. "There aren't enough horses and mules in Shady Bluffs and hereabouts to pay the bills. Still, if you're interested, I can teach you the basics of blacksmithing.

"You know," Luke continued, "maybe you're better suited to being a farrier. I worked with a farrier in St. Louis who made his own horseshoes. That's what you really want to do, isn't it?"

"Yes!" Nellie exclaimed. "That's exactly what I want."

Nellie had always been fascinated with the work of farriers. Her father had relied on the skills of a farrier to shoe the Jameson horses in Missouri. Every few months, Mr. Lawson would arrive to inspect the horses' hooves and legs. He would trim the hooves, then fit and shape iron horseshoes for each horse.

Luke nodded. "I thought so. I can teach you how to fit horseshoes. I still have the small anvil that pa gave me when I started out. When you're ready, we can set up a forge and bellow at your farm…"

"My ranch," Nellie corrected him.

"At your ranch," Luke amended.

"Thank you. So, what did you think of Thunder?" she asked.

"He's a beauty, and he'll sire a strong line of horses. You know your horses," Luke said approvingly.

"As much as I'd like to continue receiving your adoration…" Nellie began.

Luke snorted, as any older brother would do.

"As I was about to say," she continued, "did Hank talk with you about Lizzy's idea to build windmills on her farm?"

Luke nodded. "I heard about it. Sounds like a fine plan. Lizzy's always been one to take action and solve problems."

"That's a fact," Nellie agreed. "She's not one to shy away from making a decision. Just look at how she's grown that farm."

The brother and sister walked outside to the hitching post where Thunder was tied.

"Leave him here," Luke said. "I'll take care of him while you're shopping and gossiping."

Nellie ignored the teasing, stood on her tiptoes, and kissed her brother on his cheek. "Thunder thanks you."

Nellie made her way to Vaughn's Mercantile. She didn't actually need anything, but Isabell always had the latest news about town happenings.

Isabell was dusting shelves when Nellie entered the mercantile.

"This dust will be the death of me," Isabell muttered to herself as she shook out the cleaning cloth. "It collects everywhere, I declare!"

Isabell Vaughn was a well-endowed, middle-aged woman with streaks of silver shot through her pale blonde hair. Isabell once confided in Lizzy and Charlotte that she and her husband, Lawrence, had arrived in the Territory in the 50s. Lawrence had died, leaving Isabell to start the general store by herself. Now, in 1872, Vaughn's Mercantile was an institution in Shady Bluffs.

The shopkeeper turned to greet her customer ."Nellie Jameson! I haven't seen you in an age! What can I get you?"

"It has been a while since I've been in the mercantile," Nellie agreed. "I didn't bring a list, but I could use some flour, sugar, and coffee. Oh, and soap. My ma would be disappointed that I don't make my own, but I just don't have the time or the knack for it."

Isabell's eyes sparkled. "I just got in a shipment of soaps." She pointed to a display on a nearby shelf. "There's lilac, rose, and lemon scents."

Nellie sniffed the wrapped soaps and chose two bars of the lemon soap. "The lemon smells nice."

"Suits you, Nellie. But I'm going to add a small bar of the lilac soap, just in case you have a gentleman caller."

Nellie threw her head back and laughed. "Mrs. Vaughn! You are such a jokester. There aren't any eligible bachelors hereabouts, even if I were interested."

"Apparently you haven't met the newspaper editor," Isabell teased. "That's right, Shady Bluffs has its own newspaper now!"

"Well, that's news!" Nellie responded, partly in pun. "Tell me about him. Uh, not that I'm in the market for a man, you understand."

"Of course not! Men are good for reaching things on high shelves, but ladders work for that too," Isabell said with a laugh. She wiped her hands on her snowy white bib apron. While she gathered the dry goods that Nellie requested, Isabell filled in Nellie on the newcomer.

"His name is Gregory Collins. He came out here to start a newspaper. He used to work at a paper somewhere in Iowa…or was it Illinois?" Isabell shook her head, trying to recall the details. "There's no sign on it yet, but the office is next door to Charlotte's clinic."

"Oh, really?" Nellie said.

Isabell nodded. "But the *real* news, Nellie, is that Mr. Collins is a bachelor. He's been in the store several times. If I were a younger woman and in the market for a husband, well, I'm just saying…"

"Of course, I'm not in the market, Isabell."

"Of course, Nellie. Everyone knows that."

Nellie didn't know how to respond to that comment. Deciding to leave it alone, Nellie said, "A newspaper! Shady Bluffs is certainly becoming a real town. I'd best be on my way. Have a good day."

"Same to you. Say hello to Lizzy for me when you see her."

Nellie gathered up her purchases and promised to send greetings to Lizzy.

Outside on the boardwalk, Nellie decided to visit her sister-in-law. Nellie opened the doctor's office door and heard the familiar tinkle of the bell announcing her presence.

"I'll be right out," Charlotte called from an inner room.

"It's just me, Char. Don't stop if you're busy."

"I always have time for my youngest sister," Charlotte said as she entered the front office.

Charlotte Jameson, formerly Charlotte Ward, was taller and much slimmer than her sister Lizzy. Her chestnut brown hair was braided and pinned on top of her head in a large bun. She was dressed in a practical, brown twill skirt and a peach and brown striped blouse with sleeves unbuttoned and rolled up to her elbows. A bibbed apron, much like the one that Isabell wore, protected Charlotte's skirt and the front of the blouse.

"What brings you to town?" Charlotte inquired.

"I wanted to talk with Luke about teaching me to be a blacksmith," Nellie answered.

"Hmm, I haven't heard of any women blacksmiths. Wait, there were two women blacksmiths — sisters, I think — who came through here a couple of years ago. They were headed to the gold fields. They stayed in Shady Bluffs a couple of nights. Of course, their first stop in town was Luke's shop. Those were two very interesting women." Charlotte appraised her sister-in-law and nodded. "You could do it, if you've a mind to."

"Luke had a better idea. He said I should become a farrier. I'm good with horses, and the only reason I wanted to be a blacksmith was to shoe horses."

"That's an excellent idea!" Charlotte exclaimed. "So, how does one become a farrier?"

"It's basically an apprenticeship," Nellie explained. "I can learn most of it by working with Luke. He worked with a farrier in St. Louis during the war. I already know how to take care of the animals. Luke will teach me how to shape and fit the horseshoes."

Charlotte hugged Nellie. "How exciting!"

"So, that's my news. What's new with the Jameson clan of Shady Bluffs?" Nellie asked.

"You're probably caught up with Will. That boy spends more time at Lizzy and Max's house than he does here. But, between you and me, I'm fine with that. He likes helping at the farm, and it keeps him out of trouble here in town. You'd be surprised how much trouble seven-year-old boys can get into."

"I have four older brothers. Nothing surprises me about boys," Nellie said.

"Right. Eliza is my good student. She loves to read, just like her Auntie Lizzy. We've been working on school clothes for her. She's also a big help with Linc."

"And how is my youngest nephew?" Nellie asked.

"Lincoln Jameson gives new meaning to the phrase terrible twos. I'm having second thoughts about naming him after President Lincoln," Charlotte said in a whisper.

Just then, the red-haired toddler raced into the room, followed closely by Shadow, the family German shepherd.

"Auntie Nellie! Daddy said new pony!"

Nellie laughed. "That's right, Linc. Would you like to meet Thunder?"

"When?" the little boy asked.

"Patience, little one," Nellie said. "Patience. My new pony is waiting for me at your daddy's shop. We'll go over there in a bit."

Linc had already lost interest once he heard that the horse was not nearby. He drifted over to a corner of the doctor's office where a pile of color blocks had snagged his attention.

"Isabell said you have a new neighbor," Nellie said to Charlotte.

"He's very handsome," Charlotte said. "And he's single."

"Isabell mentioned that he was a bachelor."

"Perhaps you should see for yourself," Charlotte said as she pushed her sister-in-law out of the doctor's office.

Finding herself on the boardwalk, right next to the newspaper office, Nellie gathered up her courage and entered the newspaper office.

It was still a bare-bones room, with a single, large desk near the front door. A door at the back of the room led to a "back room," whatever that might be.

A young man sat at the desk with his back to the front door. "Welcome to the *Dakota Dispatch*," he said as he swiveled in his chair to face Nellie.

The young man's face had a look of surprise. "Uh…can I help you?" He stood up from his desk.

Nellie was dumbstruck. Charlotte had said he was handsome, but this — well, this was more than she expected. The man was tall, with a thatch of dirty blonde hair poking out from under his flat cap. He wore a navy blue vest over a collarless white shirt. Garters held his sleeves in place, protecting the fabric from ink stains.

But Nellie didn't notice what he was wearing. All she saw were his sky-blue eyes while her heart thumped loudly in her chest.

News of the Day

The Advertiser, **Brownville, Nebraska Territory, April 11, 1872**

Headline: Stock Horses

Frank Fergus, of Humboldt, dropped in on us one day last week, and after "how d'ye do," went to talking horse. Frank declares that when he gets on the subject of horses he goes wild. In that case, there is "method in his madness," for he knows exactly what a good horse is, and won't have a poor one.

Frank keeps three horses for stock purposes this season: Louis Napoleon, Black Stranger and Young Louis. The first named horse is well known in this section, and for draft purposes is not excelled, if equaled, by any stallion west of the Mississippi river. This horse can show more A No. 1 colts than any horse that ever made a season in Nebraska. Black Stranger is a horse of fine appearance and shows some very fine colts. Young Louis was sired by Louis Napoleon, which at once bespeaks his qualities.

Those who desire to raise good stock will do well to examine these horses.

Chapter 5 – Summer 1872

First Windmill

"Can I help you?" the newspaperman repeated to Nellie.

The question jolted Nellie out of her daze. "Uh, actually I just wanted to welcome you to town," she improvised. "I'm Nellie, Nellie Jameson."

She held out her hand.

"It's a pleasure to meet you, Miss Jameson," he replied as he shook her hand. Collins wasn't used to shaking hands with attractive young women but decided that must be common on the frontier.

"Is it 'miss?' My apologies for assuming. I'm Gregory Collins."

Nellie smiled. "Yes, it is Miss. Nice to meet you, Mr. Collins."

"I've only been in town a few days. Are you related to my neighbor, Doctor Jameson?"

"Charlotte is my sister-in-law. She's married to Luke, the town blacksmith."

Gregory nodded. "Do you live in town, Miss Jameson?"

"No, I have a claim a few miles east of here. A horse ranch," she clarified.

"I don't know any of the farmers and ranchers in the country yet," he said.

"Well, now you know one," Nellie said. "What's the name of your newspaper, Mr. Collins? There's no sign outside yet."

"There will be a sign soon. My boss is calling the paper the *Dakota Dispatch*. I was a reporter for the *St. Paul Dispatch* until the publisher shipped me… uh, offered me the opportunity to run this paper as part of the *Dispatch* company. I'm the editor, reporter, advertising manager, and until we get a compositor, I'll be setting type."

"A jack-of-all-trades, then."

Gregory laughed. "You could say that."

"When will the first issue come out?" she asked.

"I'm still waiting for the printing press. It will go in the press room." He indicated the back room. "It should be here in a week or so. Until then, I'm putting out the word that the *Dispatch* is taking advertisements. Of course, the most important responsibility for a local newspaper is to print the legal notices, land deeds, minutes of government meetings, and such. As Benjamin Franklin said, 'There is no such thing as public liberty without freedom of speech.'"

"You certainly have a way with words," Nellie said. "That must be what drew you to newspapering."

Collins looked abashed. "Sometimes I forget and get on my soapbox. Beg your pardon, miss."

"Nope...no, I found it educational," Nellie protested. Feeling she had covered most topics appropriate for a casual meeting, she said, "My, look at the time. It has been very nice talking with you, Mr. Collins. Again, welcome to Shady Bluffs."

Just as when they introduced themselves, Nellie and Gregory shook hands. With that, Nellie exited the *Dakota Dispatch* office.

Nellie made one more stop before heading back to her ranch. Lizzy had requested that Nellie ask Hank about the status of the windmill order. When she entered the Shady Bluffs Savings and Loan, Nellie saw that Hank was talking with another customer, so she waited until they were finished with their business.

"I can guess why you're here," Hank said to Nellie. "You can tell Lizzy that the first of three Eclipse windmill kits arrived by freight wagon yesterday. I was going to ride out and let her know, but I'll let you give her the good news."

"That's wonderful, Mr. Johnson," Nellie said.

"Nellie, how long have we known each other?" the banker asked.

"About seven years, I think," she answered.

"I know your ma and pa raised you to be respectful to your elders, but we've known each other long enough to be on a first-name basis, I believe. Besides, when you call me 'Mr. Johnson,' it makes me feel like an old man." He laughed to ease the tension and show that he wasn't scolding the young woman.

"You're right, Mr..." she paused, then started speaking again. "When I was a child, my parents taught me to address adults as Mr., Mrs., or Miss. But I'm a grown woman now. Thank you ... Hank." She tried out Johnson's first name as if it were a foreign word. Both of them chuckled at her hesitancy.

"It will feel more natural the more you say it," Hank assured her. "Now, back to business. Tell Lizzy that I'll bring out the windmill the day after tomorrow. Oh, and I'll bring a couple of hired hands to dig a well and erect the windmill. Tell her to start cooking and baking!"

"I will, Hank. Thank you!"

She was about to leave but turned back. "I wanted to tell you my news. Luke is going to teach me how to shoe horses! I'm going to be a farrier!"

"Congratulations, Nellie. You'll be a dang good one. Excuse the cuss word..."

Nellie just laughed and skipped out the door.

Lizzy was thrilled to learn that the first windmill was going up in two days.

"You and Scout will be in charge of the house while I'm out on the west pasture with the crew, Max," she said. "I don't want you wandering off to the creek tomorrow, even if Bear Walker begs you to go. Understand?"

"Yes, ma," the boy replied.

Lizzy knew she was asking a lot of the seven-year-old boy, but children on the frontier grew up early. At seven years old, Max could skin a jackrabbit with his hunting knife, and he understood the basics of the family shotgun — not that Lizzy let him use it yet. Max was allowed to fish at the creek by himself as long as she was at the homestead, but Scout was always by his side.

"Can I come out and help the workers, ma?" he asked.

"We'll see. I'll ride in to fetch lunch and check on things. Maybe you can come with me if you get your chores done."

"Yes, ma," he repeated.

On "windmill day," as Lizzy called the momentous event, she packed a picnic basket with muffins, cookies, a pot of coffee, and several jugs of cold well water for the crew. The morning dawned cloudy, but Lizzy didn't expect any rain. For once, she was glad for the clouds; it would make the day cooler, and the work would go easier.

When Lizzy arrived, Hank and two other men were already at the work site. Armed with picks and shovels, they had begun the task of digging the well. This would be the most strenuous part of the project. Still, with four of them — Lizzy included — digging and hauling away dirt, Lizzy hoped they might be able to strike water sometime today.

"Morning, Lizzy," Hank greeted her.

"Good morning, Hank. And good morning to you, Jerry and John," she said to the two men who were already waist-deep in the hole. Thank you for helping today." Jerry, who had done other work for Lizzy, was married to Betsy Tomlinson. Betsy was the owner of Betsy's Place, the best restaurant in Shady Bluffs. John was Betsy and Jerry's teenage son.

"Howdy, ma'am," both Tomlinsons said.

Lizzy climbed down from the wagon. "I've brought coffee and water, and there are muffins and cookies in the basket." Years ago, Lizzy traded dresses and skirts for trousers and split riding skirts. Today, she wore trousers, an old plaid shirt, boots, and a sturdy hat with a wide brim.

The Tomlinsons worked in the hole, digging and filling buckets with dirt that were hauled to the surface and then emptied. Hank and Lizzy were on the bucket brigade.

"How's it going down there, Jerry?" Hank asked. He estimated the hole was nearly twenty feet deep.

"The dirt's getting clumpier," Jerry replied. "We're getting close to the water table. Just a few more feet and we should have a well."

"I'll go fetch lunch," Lizzy said. "How about we take a break when I get back?"

"Sounds good," Hank said.

By the time Lizzy and Max returned to the work site, Jerry's prediction was true. The Tomlinsons had climbed out of the hole using the bucket rope. The well was filling up with cold water.

"Work goes fast with a good team," Hank said to Lizzy as she handed him the lunch baskets from the wagon.

Max was already peering into the deep hole. He threw a rock into the well and heard the satisfying sound of a splash.

"Did you come out to help us build the water tower?" Hank asked the boy.

"Sure did, Mr. Johnson," Max replied.

"First, we're going to have some lunch," Lizzy said. "I brought roast beef sandwiches, Mrs. Schneider's potato salad recipe, sliced beets, and cherry pie. There's lemonade in the jug. Help yourself, gentlemen."

Everyone except Lizzy had seconds of everything.

"And now the fun begins," Hank said as he unrolled a blueprint. He had already laid out all the parts for the windmill. "We'll start with the wooden braces."

Four long, wooden legs were constructed and then reinforced with cross-braces. The legs formed a pyramid, narrowing at the top of the tower. Jerry and John dug narrow, deep holes to anchor the legs to the ground.

"Okay, that was the easy part," Hank said. "Next, we'll start building the platform for the gearbox and weather vane. After that, we'll call it a day."

The sun was low on the western horizon when the crew stopped working.

"I'm making chicken for dinner, boys," Lizzy said. "Come back to the house, clean up, and we'll have supper."

"Thank you kindly, Miss Lizzy," said Jerry. "But the missus is expecting me and John for supper. Besides, we've got chores waiting for us. But we'll be back tomorrow morning to finish the job."

"Say hello to Betsy for me," Lizzy said. "And tell her I'll have another delivery of smoked hams and side pork for the restaurant in a couple of weeks."

Jerry tipped his wide-brimmed straw hat to Lizzy, then he and his son turned their horses to the west toward Shady Bluffs.

Before Hank, Lizzy, and Max rode toward the homestead, Lizzy surveyed the men's progress that day. She was more than satisfied. She was thrilled! The well was dug and filling up. The legs and braces for the frame were completed. Tomorrow, Hank and his team would install the platform, vanes, and gearbox.

And then she would have water for her crops and livestock. Life-giving water.

Riding beside the wagon, Hank said to Lizzy, "That was a good day's effort. Those Tomlinsons are hard workers. After we get the windmill working, you'll need to set up a stock tank to catch the water."

"I've been thinking about that," Lizzy said. "Square or round?"

"A square tank would be easier to build." He stopped to consider options. "If it were my water tank, I'd build the sides of wood but pour a cement bottom."

"Good idea," Lizzy said. "I'm glad I have you around."

Before Hank could respond, Lizzy clicked her tongue, letting the horses know to pick up the pace.

Over the meal of fried chicken, biscuits, fresh greens, and more cherry pie, Hank and Lizzy discussed the water tank and how to get water from the tank to the fields. Hank's experience as an engineer in the war proved useful. He had several suggestions for watering the fields and cattle.

At the end of the evening, Lizzy said, "Hank, you're welcome to sleep in the spare bedroom on Charlotte's side of the house. There's plenty of room. It would save you from riding into town and back in the morning."

"It might save *me* a round trip, but it wouldn't save *you* from clucking tongues, Miss Ward," Hank replied.

Lizzy laughed. "People think of me as an old maid. I'm not worried about my reputation."

"No, I won't put you in that position, Lizzy. I'd best head back now."

Lizzy gave him a hug. "What would I do without friends like you, Hank Johnson?"

"I'll see you in the morning," Hank said as he went to his horse.

The summer stars were twinkling on Hank's ride back to town. Usually, he never tired of finding the constellations overhead. But tonight, all his thoughts were muddled by Lizzy.

He thought about how much he wanted to kiss Lizzy when he left. With her blonde hair framing her face and her dimples showing as she smiled, he felt the familiar tug of how much he wanted to be more than her friend.

Hank recalled the first time he'd met Lizzy. It was right after the buffalo stampede. Lizzy had been holding Max after digging the baby out from the rubble. Even though she'd been covered in dirt and grime, there was something about that woman that got his attention. Oh, she was a looker, but it was Lizzy's grit and compassion that Hank remembered about that moment.

He knew there was talk in town about the "bachelor banker" and more than one young woman in town had set her cap for Hank. Instead of courting one of those eligible young women, Hank would manufacture reasons to stop by Lizzy's farm, hoping that it might spark some interest from her.

It was always Lizzy that his thoughts came back to. Then he thought of her last words tonight, "What would I do without friends like you, Hank Johnson?"

Friends. Lizzy considered Hank a friend. Nothing more.

I would have made a darn fool of myself tonight, he thought. *Lizzy thinks of me as a friend or a brother.*

Maybe if Lizzy knew how he felt about her? What was holding him back from declaring his feelings? It had been ten years since his wife and unborn child had died. He'd made a new life for himself on the frontier. He'd built a business and was part of a new community. He'd left the War years behind him, hadn't he?

Maybe it was time to move on from Abigail, he decided.

Back at Lizzy's homestead, she planned tomorrow's lunch meal. Leftover chicken and biscuits, she decided. While she busied herself with meal preparation, she thought about the evening with Hank.

Elizabeth Ruby Ward, what were you thinking — inviting Hank to sleep over, she thought. *I am so foolish. Hank has never shown any interest in me. He thinks of me as a friend.* She shook her head. *It's like I said to Hank, everyone thinks of me as an old maid. Probably even Hank.*

Lizzy had suitors before the War. Four young men had competed to buy her box lunch at a church social, she recalled fondly. She had always thought she would fall in love, get married, and have children, like most women did. The War had changed everything. Lizzy was so busy managing the farm, and with all the eligible men fighting, she hadn't given a thought to romance — much less marriage!

But she yearned for the companionship that Char and Luke had. Someone to share her troubles and her triumphs. And, yes, someone to hold her in the dark of night.

66

She wiped a tear away when Max bounded into the kitchen. "Ma, that was fun today. Can I help with the windmill tomorrow? Hank is so smart. I didn't know he was an engineer in the war. Did you know?" The boy's questions continued without Lizzy needing to respond to the endless chatter. Finally, Max wound down and yawned.

"Yes, you can help tomorrow, but it's off to bed with you now," Lizzy said. "Wash your face and brush your teeth. I'll be in to hear your prayers in a bit. Good night, sweets."

Lizzy took a deep breath. This was her life. She'd chosen it, and for the most part, she loved it.

No more tears, Lizzy, she said to herself.

She went to tuck in Max and hear his prayers. The sight of her son with Scout on the floor next to his bed nearly brought Lizzy to tears again, but these were tears of happiness.

This is what it's all about, she thought. *Max is the man in my life.*

The next day at the work site went smoothly. Hank, Jerry, and John constructed the platform and tipped the frame upright into the four holes the Tomlinsons had dug yesterday. Hank mixed up a batch of cement and poured it into the holes to secure the windmill in place.

"Good job, men," Hank encouraged the team. "While I build the gear mechanism, you all can work on the holding tank."

He explained how he and Lizzy wanted a square tank. "It will be about 'yay big,'" he said, using a phrase often employed by Yankees in New England. Hank indicated the rough dimensions of the tank. "We'll use twelve-foot planks, so let's figure the holding tank will be twelve-by-twelve. When you've got the spot dug, we'll pour a cement floor to hold the water."

"Sounds good, boss," Jerry said. He handed a shovel to his son. "Let's get to it."

Hank turned to Lizzy. "For now, all we have to do is install the pumping mechanism. I'll ask Luke to help with the stock tank boards. We can do that next week, if you're in agreement."

"That's wonderful, Hank. And then I'll have water out here!" Lizzy was so excited.

The Tomlinsons finished digging the hole for the holding tank before Hank had completed assembling the pump.

"Thanks for the help. Go home and enjoy the rest of your weekend. We'll settle up at the bank next week," Hank said to Jerry and John.

"Take a couple pieces of chicken for the ride home." Lizzy forced food on the two workmen. It didn't take much convincing for them to accept the fried chicken and biscuits.

While Hank finished constructing the pump, Lizzy walked the area around the windmill, trying to visualize how she would irrigate the fields. Max and Scout played fetch nearby.

"There, the linkage is attached and the motor is ready to mount behind the vane," Hank declared. "I'll climb up and install it. Then we're done for the day."

Lizzy watched Hank climb the thirty-foot structure using the foot pegs on one of the legs.

"That looks like fun, ma," Max said. "Can I go up it when Mr. Johnson comes down?"

"No, you may not," Lizzy said firmly. "You'll give me a heart attack!"

Hank stood on the platform opposite the wind vane. He pulled a wrench from his back pocket and made the final adjustments to the mechanism.

"That's it!" he called down to Lizzy and Max. But he didn't anticipate how quickly the vane would catch a gust of wind. The windmill's vane turned and knocked Hank from his perch.

To Lizzy's horror, Hank plummeted to the hard ground. She rushed to his side. "Hank! Hank! Can you hear me? Talk to me!"

Hank wheezed and tried to catch his breath. Finally, he said, "I think my leg is broken…broken bad."

Lizzy saw the blood seeping through Hank's pant leg. "I'll try to get you back to the house, but I'm sending Max to town for Charlotte."

Hank nodded in pain.

The next few hours were a blur for Lizzy. She was able to position the wagon close enough to load Hank into the back, but she decided to leave him in the wagon until she had more help to move the big man.

Help came sooner than she expected. Max had ridden Hank's horse into town. On the way, he caught up with the Tomlinsons. Jerry returned with Max while John raced into Shady Bluffs to get the doctor.

Together, Jerry and Lizzy were able to move Hank off the wagon and onto the long kitchen table. Lizzy knew from experience that Charlotte would not want to work on a soft bed. She brewed a pot of willow bark tea to help with the pain until her sister arrived with stronger medicine.

Charlotte arrived, accompanied by Luke and John. She examined Hank's left leg. "It's a compound fracture, and the thigh bone has broken through the skin," she told Lizzy and Luke. "I'll need to reset the bone, stabilize the leg, and then splint it. Luke and Jerry, I'm going to need both of you to hold Hank while I move the broken bone into place."

She measured out a spoonful of laudanum for her patient. "This will help with the pain."

He started to protest, but she overruled him. "No, don't be a hero. Take the laudanum. I'm going to reset the bone, and it will hurt like the dickens."

"John and Max, please unsaddle the horses and give them some feed in the barn," Lizzy instructed, hoping to put some distance between the medical procedure and the boys.

The four adults understood their roles: Luke and Jerry would immobilize the patient, Charlotte would reset the bone, and Lizzy would assist. It was done more quickly than Lizzy could have imagined. Hank had groaned, but the laudanum had helped dull the pain.

Next, Charlotte went to work cleaning and splinting the fracture. She bandaged it in clean, cotton cloth from Lizzy's supply of quilting material. By the time Charlotte completed her work, Hank had fallen into a fitful sleep.

Jerry and John set out once again for town. Luke, Charlotte, and Lizzy gathered in Lizzy's half of the double-wide house. The sisters relaxed as best they could with cups of tea. Luke requested something stronger and was sipping a tumbler of Missouri bourbon whiskey.

"Who's watching the children?" Lizzy asked her sister.

"Isabell is staying with the kids. She's a godsend," Charlotte answered.

"How long should I keep Hank here?" Lizzy said.

"As long as you can...but if you can convince him to stay off the leg for at least a week, that will give the bones time to mend. It's not enough, of course." Charlotte opened her hands in a gesture of futility and shrugged. "The laudanum will help. Change the bandages daily — more if you see bleeding. Then it's just up to Hank's constitution to do the rest."

Luke and Charlotte stayed at the farmhouse overnight but left in the morning. "We have to rescue Isabell," Luke told Lizzy. "She's not used to our wild bunch."

Hank surprised Lizzy by being an obedient patient and agreeing to stay at the farm for a week.

It was a week that changed Lizzy's relationship with Hank. She sat by his bed as much as she could. They talked about their lives before Shady Bluffs. Lizzy was astounded to learn that Hank had been married to a woman in New York during the war. It made her see him in a different light.

Lizzy told Hank stories about Quantrill's Raiders at the farm in Missouri.She swelled with pride when Hank said he admired her bravery.

Toward the end of the week, Hank insisted that Lizzy drive them out to the windmill.

"I want to make sure that all this pain was worth it," he said.

Pain coursed through Lizzy as she blamed herself for the accident.

He must have noticed the hurt show on her face because Hank said, "What I meant was I wanted to check my work to make sure the windmill is operating correctly."

With Max's help, Lizzy helped Hank into the buckboard wagon.

"It's a sight better to ride on the front bench than in the back," Hank said, remembering the ride from the accident to Lizzy's house.

Max rode in the back of the wagon, with Scout running alongside.

"We'll need to fix that," he said when they arrived at the work site and saw the water spilling onto the ground. Although the windmill was turning and pumping water, Lizzy still needed a tank to catch the water.

"I've already talked with Luke about finishing the holding tank. After that, we'll run pipes of some sort into the fields. It will make a world of difference for the crops."

Lizzy squeezed Hank's hand. "And I have you to thank for all of this, Hank. Thank you from the bottom of my heart."

"Well, we're partners in this endeavor, aren't we?" he responded.

After that, he declared the Savings and Loan would close if he wasn't there to manage affairs, and he should get back to work.

"I'm lucky I have a desk job," Hank said. "I'll stick pretty close to home until this bum leg is better. Now, don't you worry about me."

News of the Day

The Oskaloosa Herald, Oskaloosa, Iowa, July 31, 1873

Advertisement: Dexter Windmill

Best, simplest and most Durable Windmill in the World. All under cover; protected from the weather; stands on a solid foundation; takes the wind from every quarter without facing around; self-regulating; will last as long as two or three of any other kind. Mills built of the best material and in the most durable manner, on short notice. No pay is required until satisfaction is given.

A.H. Southwick, Patentee

Chapter 6 – Late Summer 1872
Railroad Survey

The new windmill was a game changer for crops in the west section. Instead of finishing the holding tank, Lizzy and Jerry simply dug channels from the water pond to the nearby fields. As the windmill pumped water, the channels carried the water to the crops, giving them the moisture they needed to grow despite the worsening drought.

The success of the windmill in the west pasture made Lizzy even more determined to install the second and third Eclipse windmills. She decided the south section, bordering Lizzy's ranch, would be the location of her next windmill. Lizzy wondered if Nellie might consider teaming up on this windmill so that the Jameson horses could benefit from the water, too.

While there were some mounds and small hills on the Dakota prairie, for the most part, it was flat — flat as far as the eye could see. From horseback, Lizzy could see a group of men working on the south field.

She trotted up to the group, surprised to see Adam Danbury directing a team of seven or eight men.

"Mr. Danbury, I see you're back," Lizzy said. "I don't recall receiving notification, much less a request to be on my property. Do you make a habit of trespassing?"

"My apologies, Miss Ward," Adam said. "According to these monumentations," he indicated the posts and piles of rock that marked the edge of Lizzy's land, "we're on the other side of your land."

"Which happens to belong to Nellie Jameson," Lizzy replied. "Do you have her permission to survey here?"

Adam sighed and slapped the rolled paper on his thigh. "My plat map is apparently outdated." He turned to a young man holding a length of chain. "Anderson, did you purchase the latest plat map in Yankton as I ordered?"

"The claims office was closed, sir. I found that there map in the wagon, and reckoned it would suffice," Anderson said, pointing to the rolled map that Adam was holding.

Adam shook his head as he walked over to where Lizzy sat on her horse. In a low voice, he said, "It's hard to find good help out here. Once again, I find myself apologizing to you."

Lizzy noticed that Adam was not dressed in his frock coat, vest, and top hat. Instead, he wore dark brown work pants with suspenders, a light brown shirt, and, of course, a tie. He had replaced the top hat with a more practical felt hat.

"If I may, could I explain what we're attempting to do here, Miss Ward?"

Lizzy nodded, dismounted from her horse, and tied the reins to one of the poles that marked the boundary of her land.

Adam cleared his throat and began to describe the surveying process.

"In our first encounter, you found me using my transit. The transit measures horizontal and vertical angles to determine relative points on a piece of land." He walked to an instrument on a tripod. "You'll need to squint a little to see through the eyepiece," he instructed her.

Lizzy attempted to look through the eyepiece, but she was too short. Hastily, Adam adjusted the tripod and stepped away so Lizzy could try again.

"The transit is usually the first step in my process. Now, I've brought the surveying crew to provide more exact measurements. Anderson is the chainman. He is in charge of the Gunter's chain."

They watched as Anderson and two other men stretched out the links of the metal chain.

"The Gunter chain is a sixty-six-foot chain made of one hundred links," Adam explained. "It's used to measure distances between two points."

"So you're surveying the land one foot at a time," Lizzy said.

"It must be accurate in order to lay track," Adam confirmed. "I'll draw up the survey map and then present it to railroad management along with my recommendations."

"What happened to the survey map you drew by Medicine Creek? The one you showed me in my kitchen?"

"That route is still under consideration, especially because of the water source. But it may not be the only option," Adam said. "Laying track here might be a more economical route. Unfortunately, I'm not sure we'll have the water we need to power the steam engine."

"I see," Lizzy said. She recalled Hank's suggestion that Frontier Railroad might build a windmill that would water her farm *and* provide water for the steam engines. "You know, I have something you might want to see. Can you ride with me?"

"I would be delighted," Adam said. He returned in a few minutes on the palomino. "Please lead the way. What brought you out to this part of your land? You're not farming it. I assume you use it for grazing?"

"Yes, it's too rough to plow — too many rocks, even for Dakota Territory," Lizzy said. "I'll move the cattle down here in a week or so. But I was out here to check on another project and to do some scouting."

As Lizzy said that, the windmill came into view. She pointed to the thirty-foot structure and said, "That's what I came to inspect."

"Wooo-weee," Adam said. "That's a beauty. I haven't seen a windmill in these parts until now."

"It's the first of its kind out here," Lizzy admitted. "I read about farmers back East using them to pump water. And now, with the new patents, there are companies that actually manufacture windmill kits. I just purchased lumber for the legs and braces."

Adam spurred his horse into a trot to reach the windmill. He jumped from the palomino and studied the tall framework. Then he strode around the structure, stopping at the wellhead that pumped water into the holding pond.

"Brilliant," Adam exclaimed.

"It's doing what a windmill is supposed to do," Lizzy said. "My crops were dying in the drought. I had to do something."

"The simplicity of a windmill makes so much sense out here on the prairie. Why didn't I think of it before," Adam said to Lizzy and to himself.

Lizzy furrowed her brows. "I'm not following you."

"At my last assignment in northern Minnesota, there was so much water that I had to plan routes *around* the rivers and lakes. I never had to worry about water stops for the trains. It's just the opposite out here. But this," he pointed to the windmill, "this could be the answer."

"That land you're surveying today is close to where I'm putting up my next windmill," Lizzy said. "Perhaps we could come to an agreement." She flashed a dimpled smile at Adam.

"Lizzy Ward, I believe you're offering me a deal."

"Oh no, I said 'perhaps we could come to an agreement,' Mr. Danbury. There would need to be some considerations from both parties. And we should bring Nellie into the conversation as well."

"Of course, it is all dependent on the viability of the route," Adam agreed.

"Of course," Lizzy repeated.

Adam looked up at the weathervane again before turning back to Lizzy. "Would you mind if I climbed up there and looked around?"

Lizzy had a flashback to Hank's fall from the tower. "It's very high. It's not safe."

"I'll take care. I've climbed towers before," he assured her.

"Very well," she said.

She couldn't watch as Adam ascended the tower. Instead, she wandered into the nearby field, intent on inspecting her wheat crop. Once Lizzy entered the wheat field, she forgot about the man climbing her windmill.

Lizzy was in paradise as she walked through the field of waving grain. The wheat was nearly heading, and the water had arrived just in time to help the plants reach maturity. She pulled up a couple of sample plants and inspected the wheat for signs of disease and pests.

She was so absorbed in inspecting the wheat that Lizzy didn't hear Adam call out to her.

"Lizzy!" Adam shouted from the top of the tower.

Finally, he got her attention, and Lizzy turned to see Adam on the platform next to the weathervane.

He shouted down to her again. "I can see the Missouri River from here!"

She nodded and waved at him. *Sometimes men were such...such boys*, she thought.

"Can you please come down now?" she asked. She made her way out of the wheat field and back to the windmill.

"On my way," he said.

When Adam was about six feet from the ground, he jumped off the foot peg ladder and hurried over to Lizzy.

"That was amazing! I bet I could see ten miles up there. You should see it!"

"Not today, thank you," Lizzy said. She could still see Hank plunging to the ground from the high tower. Lizzy wasn't afraid of heights, but she wasn't sure she ever wanted to go to the top of the windmill.

"I have calls to make on neighbors. I should be going," she said.

"And I should be getting back to my crew," Adam said. He took Lizzy's hand and looked into her eyes. "Thank you for a very pleasant afternoon, Lizzy. I do so enjoy being in your company. Perhaps we could..."

Lizzy pulled away her hand before he could kiss it. She recognized a rake and a womanizer when she saw one, and Adam Danbury had all the signs.

"Yes, it was a pleasant afternoon, Adam," Lizzy said, her tone turning to all business. "I'll stop at Nellie's on the way home and mention our discussion."

Adam's smile slipped for just a second before recovering. "Thank you, Lizzy. I'll eagerly await the outcome of that conversation."

The two rode toward the surveying crew. Instead of the methodical surveying and measuring that the crew had been doing when Adam and Lizzy left the railroad camp, the base was in chaos.

One of the men had just fired a shotgun into a clump of bushes. Another man, Lizzy recognized him as the chainman Anderson, was rolling on the ground, clutching his right leg.

"What in blue blazes..." Adam shouted at the crew.

"It's Anderson, sir," one of the men said. "He's been bitten."

"That's what this commotion is about," Adam said incredulously.

"It was a skunk, Mr. Danbury."

That got Lizzy's attention. "There was a skunk here in the daytime? Where is it now?"

"I shot it," said another man on the crew. "Or at least I shot at it. Not sure if I hit it. It's over yonder in those bushes."

"Someone needs to capture that animal," Lizzy commanded. "Be careful if it's still alive. It's not just about getting sprayed. We'll need to watch the skunk."

She jumped down from her horse and hurried over to where Anderson was lying. "Can I see the bite?" she asked.

Anderson pointed to his right calf. "The critter sprang up and bit me right there," he said.

"Adam, do you have a knife? I need a knife," Lizzy insisted.

"Are you gonna cut my leg off?" Anderson asked in horror.

"No, I'm going to slice open your pant leg so I can get a better look," she answered very matter-of-factly.

Lizzy saw there was blood on the pant leg. When she got the trouser leg opened, she saw the telltale puncture wounds on Anderson's calf. There was some bleeding, but not enough to cleanse the wound.

"Someone, please get me some alcohol…whiskey…or such to clean the bite," Lizzy said. "Do you have a medical kit?"

"Here you go, ma'am," said one of the crewmen. He handed Lizzy a bottle of cheap whiskey.

Another man brought a box of medical supplies: gauze rolls for bandages, needles and thread, scissors, tweezers, and various medicines such as laudanum and other tinctures.

Lizzy did what she could to tend the wound. The flesh around the bite marks was already starting to redden and swell.

"We should get him inside," Lizzy said. "Has anyone bagged that skunk?"

"It's caged in the back of the wagon," Adam told her. He bent down to speak in low tones to Lizzy. "You want to see if it's rabid, don't you?"

Lizzy nodded. "Let's get Mr. Anderson to my home."

Adam drove the chuck wagon with Bill Anderson on a bedroll in the back. Another member of the crew drove the wagon with the caged skunk. Lizzy led the procession back to her homestead.

Max and Scout ran out of the barn to greet Lizzy. When he saw the two wagons, he was as curious as any young boy might be.

"What's going on?" he asked Lizzy. "Who are these men?"

"Mr. Anderson, in the back of that wagon, was bitten by a skunk. The skunk is in a cage in the other wagon," Lizzy explained.

Max looked alarmed. "A skunk? In the daytime?" Max knew that when nocturnal animals like skunks and raccoons appeared during the day, there was a good chance the animals were sick or diseased. Lizzy had taught him to avoid these animals at all costs.

Scout was growling at the skunk in the second wagon.

"Take Scout into the barn and tie him up," Lizzy said. "We don't need to antagonize the skunk more than he already is."

Max and Scout disappeared into the barn. Lizzy instructed Adam and the other driver to carry Anderson into the house.

Once inside, Lizzy made a comfortable bed for Anderson. She could tell he was already running a fever, so she brewed a pot of willow bark tea to help reduce it.

"Are you hungry, Mr. Anderson?" she asked her patient.

He shook his head. "Just want to sleep."

"That's fine," Lizzy said. She went into the main room to talk with Adam.

"I'd feel better if the town doctor saw Mr. Anderson. Could you ask your crewman to fetch Doctor Jameson in Shady Bluffs?"

"Al, take the wagon into town and bring back the doc," Adam told his employee.

"Yes, sir," the man replied.

In the late afternoon, Gregory Collins was locking up the newspaper office just as Doctor Jameson was heading out of the doctor's office. Gregory was about to greet the doctor when a man he didn't recognize pulled a wagon up in front of them.

"Excuse me, ma'am," the man said to Doctor Jameson. "I need a doctor right quick."

Doctor Jameson turned and assessed the man. "You're not bleeding. Are you in pain?"

"No, ma'am. I need a doctor for a crewmate on the Frontier Railroad. He got bit by a skunk."

Doctor Jameson nodded. "First of all, I'm the doctor. Folks around here call me Doctor Charlie. Let me get my bag. Where is the patient now?"

The man looked confused at seeing a woman doctor but answered, "Bill and Mr. Danbury are in a soddy ten miles east of town. The homesteader's name is Lizzy something."

"That would be Lizzy Ward's farm. I know the place," Doctor Jameson said. "Please wait in your wagon while I saddle my horse."

While the man waited for Doctor Jameson, Gregory reflected on the man mentioning Frontier Railroad. Gregory realized the rumors he'd heard about the railroad planning a route through Dakota Territory were true. This could be his first big story. He decided to follow the wagon to see where the story might lead him.

News of the Day

Nashville Union and American, Nashville, Tennessee, July 5, 1874

Headline: Hydrophobia

There is no other disease to which man is liable, about which less is known than hydrophobia by the medical profession. So far as statistics have been collected on the subject, they go to prove that not over one person in twenty bitten by a rabid dog or cat ever has the disease at all. Nothing like this remarkable immunity is witnessed when one is bitten by a poisonous snake. ...The logical inference from the facts known seems to be that both dogs and persons may die of rabies, and either never develop the virus or it soon loses its power as a fatal and obscure poison.

Chapter 7 – Late Summer 1872
Dakota Dispatch

Gregory Collins was excited to have a big story drop in his lap. He had covered railroad stories when he was at the *St. Paul Dispatch*. Railroads were big business, and they could make or break a town. If Frontier Railroad was surveying routes near Shady Bluffs, this was front-page news for the *Dakota Dispatch*. He might even get a byline in the St. Paul, the Omaha, or even the Chicago newspaper!

As he followed the railroad wagon and Doctor Jameson, Gregory studied the terrain. This was the first time that he had a chance to see the western prairie up close. He was a Minnesota boy and was used to the rolling hills, the ravines, and the trees around the Mississippi River valley. The Dakota prairie was flat, and there was virtually no place to hide. If Doctor Jameson or the wagon driver turned around, they would, without a doubt, spot him, so he tried to follow as far behind as possible. He was glad for the long summer day so he could see the wagon and rider in the distance. The wagon and rider kicked up dust in their hurry to reach the homestead, making it even easier to track them.

Up ahead, Charlotte quizzed Al Benning about the incident.

"When did this happen?" she asked the wagon driver.

"It was after lunch," Benning said. "Maybe early afternoon. Mr. Danbury and the landowner had ridden off. Me and the boys were working the chains."

"Working the chains," Charlotte said. "What does that mean?"

"Mr. Danbury, he gave us a plat map to work from. We're doing a survey in case Frontier wants to lay track this way. The chain is used to measure distances." Benning thought he might be saying too much, so he finished with, "You know, ma'am, maybe you should talk with Mr. Danbury about it."

Charlotte had all the information she needed at this point. The man had been bitten several hours ago. She had seen several cases of rabies since coming to Shady Bluffs. Most victims lived a week or less after being bitten. She had seen the symptoms: frothing at the mouth, confusion, irritation, and other signs that rabies had taken hold. She also knew that often rabies victims were shunned, even though human-to-human transmission was nearly unheard of.

Soon, Lizzy's side-by-side soddy came into view. There was another Frontier wagon in front of the house.

As soon as Charlotte dismounted, Lizzy appeared at the doorway. "Thank goodness you're here," Lizzy said. "I've done all I can."

"I seem to be making a lot of house calls out here," Charlotte replied. "We need to get together for something more pleasant next time. Where is the patient?"

Lizzy showed Charlotte into the darkened room where Bill Anderson was sleeping fitfully. "I cleaned the wound — it was definitely an animal bite. He was in pain, so I gave him some willow bark tea to ease the pain and help him sleep."

Charlotte nodded. She placed a gentle hand on Bill Anderson's arm. "Mr. Anderson, I'm Doctor Jameson."

Anderson woke with a start.

"Mr. Anderson," Charlotte repeated. "I'm Doctor Jameson from Shady Bluffs. Your employer, Mr. Danbury, asked me to look in on you. May I see the injury?"

Anderson nodded.

Very gently and slowly, Charlotte unwrapped the wound and saw that it was an angry red. "Miss Ward did a good job of cleaning and bandaging the bite. Is your leg aching?"

"Yes, ma'am," Anderson said.

Charlotte nodded and applied a layer of honey as an antiseptic to the wound. Then she re-wrapped the bandage. "We'll re-dress the wound tomorrow. I'm going to give you something stronger for the pain."

Anderson nodded again. "Thank you, doctor," he said after Charlotte administered a spoonful of laudanum.

"You just rest now, Mr. Anderson."

"Doctor," Anderson said, "am I going to get the hydrophobia?"

"It's too soon to tell, Mr. Anderson," Charlotte replied. "We'll keep watch and take care of you. You should rest now."

Bill Anderson laid back on the bed and soon drifted off to sleep.

Charlotte found Lizzy and Adam Danbury on the other side of the house. Adam was pacing the floor while Lizzy made dinner.

"The driver, Mr. Benning, said you have the animal that bit Mr. Anderson," Charlotte said. "I'd like to see it."

"It's in a cage behind the smokehouse," Lizzy said. "Adam, can you accompany her?"

Adam nodded to Lizzy. He was relieved to have something to do besides pace.

"Lizzy said that the two of you came to the Territory during the war," Adam said as they made their way to the smokehouse.

"That's right," Charlotte answered. "I was a medic in the Union Army. After I left the Army, I came back to our farm in Missouri. It was Lizzy's idea to leave Missouri and stake claims for land in Dakota Territory."

Charlotte paused momentarily, reflecting on the three-month journey from St. Joseph to Yankton nearly a decade ago.

"It was one of my sister's better ideas, and she's had a lot of good ideas, in my opinion."

"Yes, I saw one of them earlier today," Adam said. "Her windmill."

"Lizzy is not afraid to try things," Charlotte confirmed. "That's what brought us here."

They stood before the metal cage that held the skunk. "It's lucky my men are not good shots, or we would be looking at a dead skunk," Adam said.

The skunk growled at Charlotte and Adam and attempted to charge through the cage.

"Mmmm." Charlotte studied the animal. Then she shook her head. "The critter is already showing rabies symptoms: foaming at the mouth, aggressive behavior, loss of coordination."

Charlotte stood up and backed away from the cage. "We can keep the animal alive a while longer if you wish to confirm the diagnosis, but what we really need to do is take care of Mr. Anderson. There's a good chance that he's been infected. We'll need to treat him and keep him comfortable. Let's talk with Lizzy about next steps."

After conferring with Lizzy, the sisters agreed that keeping Mr. Anderson at Lizzy's homestead was the best course of action. Adam protested that Lizzy should not be burdened with his problem and that Anderson could be transported back to the survey crew's work site.

"This is really the best place for him, Adam," Lizzy said. "He'll be more comfortable here and will receive better care."

Charlotte agreed with her sister. "If you're worried about the burden, as you say, perhaps you could arrange for someone from your crew — a familiar face — to stay with him."

"A capital idea, Doctor Jameson," Adam exclaimed. "And I will be that familiar face."

"Mr. Anderson *is* your responsibility. I think that's a sound idea, Mr. Danbury," said Charlotte.

"I'll send Benning back to the work site with the chuck wagon," Adam decided. Moments later, he returned and announced, "Miss Ward, you have a visitor."

Charlotte, Lizzy, and Adam went out to the porch as Nellie tied her buckskin quarter horse to the railing.

"Nellie, it's good to see you," Charlotte said.

Nellie gave Charlotte and Lizzy quick hugs.

"Hi, Charlie," Nellie said. "Are you making a house call? Who's sick?"

"It's one of the railroad survey crew members. He was bitten by a skunk," Charlotte explained.

"Those darn skunks," Nellie exclaimed. "I've been shooting them every chance I get. I don't want my animals coming down with rabies!"

"Nellie Jameson, have you met Mr. Danbury? He's with Frontier Railroad," Charlotte said as an introduction.

"Actually, we met a few weeks ago when he was surveying Lizzy's land by the creek," Nellie said. "I heard a couple of gunshots earlier today and rode out to investigate. I met some of his crew. They were surveying *my* land this time. Mr. Danbury had already left with Lizzy."

At that point, another rider trotted down the lane. Charlotte recognized the horse and rider but stayed silent about the visitor's identity.

"I'm going to check on the patient," Charlotte said.

From the front porch, Lizzy asked the new visitor, "Can I help you, sir?"

Gregory dismounted and tied his horse to the railing. "Hello, ma'am. Actually, I'm here to talk with a representative from the Frontier Railroad." He pointed to the wagon with the railroad's name on the side.

"That would be me," Adam said, extending his hand to shake Gregory's hand. "I'm Adam Danbury, Chief Survey Engineer for Frontier Railroad. And you are?"

"Gregory Collins, sir. I'm Editor of the *Dakota Dispatch* in Shady Bluffs. I'd like to talk with you about Frontier's plans," Gregory explained. "I saw your wagon in town, and I'm hoping there's a story here."

"Of course, Mr. Collins," Adam said. "Let's sit over here." He indicated two chairs on the far side of the porch. "You realize, of course, that the nature of my crew's work is confidential, but I'll try to answer your questions as best I can."

Gregory flipped out his reporter's notebook as he settled into a chair on the porch. Nellie wanted to hover and hear what the men were discussing but took the hint. She followed Lizzy into the house, and Charlotte began giving medical directions to Lizzy.

"Keep him comfortable and quiet. I'll stop out again day after tomorrow. If things progress faster, send Mr. Danbury into town for me," Charlotte said.

Lizzy winced. "So there's no hope?"

"There's always hope," Charlotte said, "but I'm nearly certain that skunk was infected. There's a good chance that he passed the rabies on to Mr. Anderson."

Lizzy understood that life on the frontier was tough. She had seen too many homesteaders battle against the weather and the land. But sometimes, the struggles were just too overwhelming. She sent up a prayer of thanksgiving that her family was safe and sound.

The three women walked out to Charlotte's horse.

"And how is Hank doing?" Lizzy asked.

"Oh, he's getting around better than I expected," Charlotte said. "He's still using a crutch, but I'm guessing he'll swap that for a cane soon. I'm not sure if he'll ever walk without a limp, but he's walking, and that's the goal."

"I feel responsible for his fall from my windmill," Lizzy said.

Charlotte grasped Lizzy's hands. "No, you're not responsible. Hank told me that you tried to discourage him from climbing that tower. It's all on him."

Charlotte sighed. "It's going to be dark soon, so I'm heading back to town. Like I said, if anything changes, send Mr. Danbury into town for me. Take care, Lizzy. We've got to stop meeting like this." Charlotte mounted her horse and rode down the lane to Shady Bluffs.

Lizzy turned to Nellie, "Would you like to stay for supper?"

"Did I smell roast chicken?" Nellie asked.

"If you mean 'prairie chicken,' you're right. If you'll let Max and our guests know that dinner is ready, I'll set the table."

Adam and Gregory had concluded their discussion by the time Nellie invited them to supper. "You can both wash up at the well," she told the men.

Lizzy, who admitted that she wasn't as good a cook as Charlotte, set an impressive table with roast prairie chicken, potatoes, garden vegetables, bread and butter, and fresh milk. For dessert, she served bread pudding with raisins.

"That was the best meal I've had in years," Adam said as he pushed back from the table. "You've done enough today, Lizzy. I'll wash the dishes, if you'll allow me."

Lizzy laughed. "I like a man who works for his meal. You'll get no argument from me." She turned to her son. "Max, it's time to milk the cows, and then you can read for a while before going to bed."

Finding they had no chores, Lizzy, Nellie, and Gregory returned to the front porch chairs.

"Miss Ward, I couldn't help but overhear you mention that you have a windmill. I didn't realize farmers were using windmills out here," Gregory said.

"Oh, Lizzy's a trailblazer," Nellie said. "Her windmill is the first in the Territory."

"Would you mind telling me about it?" Gregory asked. "I'd like to write a story for the *Dispatch*."

"What would you like to know, Mr. Collins?" Lizzy said.

"Just the basics of journalism: the who, what, when, where, why, and how," he answered.

Lizzy thought for a moment. "It started with an article in the *American Farmer* magazine. Hank Johnson did some research and recommended I put up Eclipse windmills. You'd have to get the specifics from him.

"Hank agreed to give me a loan to fund the project. He said it was to show other farmers the benefits of windmills. We ordered three kits, and I hired Jerry and John Tomlinson — you know them from Betsy's Place," she explained to the newcomer.

"That's the 'who' and the 'what,'" Lizzy said. "The 'when' and 'where' happened a few weeks back on the west section of my farm. You'll see it when you're riding back to town. The 'why' is easy; we're in a harvest-killing drought. My crops and my livestock need water to survive. What else did you ask?"

"How," Gregory supplied. "How did you do it?"

"It was a team effort. Hank, Jerry, John, Max, and I dug the well. Then the Tomlinson's built the tower while Hank — he was an engineer in the war — assembled the windmill motor. I just fed them all," she said with a laugh.

Gregory was hurriedly scribbling in his reporter's notebook. When he finished, he looked up and asked, "And the windmill is working?"

"Oh, yes it is," Lizzy said triumphantly. "The only … the only thing I regret is that when Hank climbed the tower to check the motor, he fell off and broke a leg. It was horrible!"

"This is a great story for the *Dispatch*, Miss Ward. Can I get some background about you and your son for the story?"

Lizzy complied, telling Gregory how she and Charlotte had left Missouri during the war and staked claims in Dakota Territory. She explained that she had adopted Max after the buffalo stampede killed his parents. And she told Gregory how important she thought it was for neighbors to help neighbors.

"That's one of the reasons that I'd like to partner with Nellie on the second windmill," Lizzy said.

At that point, Max returned from his chores in the barn. Lizzy followed him inside to tuck him in and hear his prayers. When she returned to the front porch a few minutes later, she heard Gregory and Nellie talking about Adam.

"Mr. Danbury said he is surveying on your land," Gregory said to Nellie.

Nellie cocked her head and said with some irritation, "Apparently so. This is the second time he has trespassed on someone's land."

"The second time?" Gregory asked.

"The first time Lizzy and I met Mr. Danbury, he was surveying by Medicine Creek, on Lizzy's land."

"Miss Jameson, I would appreciate the opportunity to see the land that railroad crew is surveying. Would that be possible?"

"Of course, Mr. Collins," Nellie replied.

"Would tomorrow be too soon?" he asked. "I mean, if you're not otherwise occupied, of course."

"I'll have my chores done by noon. I can meet you here after lunch, and we can ride to my place together. It'll be easier to find," Nellie suggested.

"Thank you, Miss Jameson," he said.

"Everyone calls me Nellie."

"If we're on a first-name basis, please call me Gregory."

Lizzy saw Nellie blush at the exchange. She had never seen the young woman blush at a comment from a young man. *If I'm not mistaken, this could be the start of a budding romance,* Lizzy thought. *Are those sparks that I'm seeing?*

She cleared her throat to declare her presence.

Gregory's eyes widened to see her there. "Thank you for the homecooked meal, Miss Ward," he said. "I must be going." He turned to Nellie and said, "I'll see you tomorrow."

"I should be going, too," Nellie said.

Right as they were about to leave, Adam returned to the porch.

"Miss Jameson, there are some things I'd like to discuss with you," Danbury said.

"It's getting late, Mr. Danbury," Nellie said. "But not to worry, I'll be back here tomorrow. Mr. Collins, er, Gregory, asked to see my horse ranch. We're going to meet here tomorrow afternoon since he already knows his way this far. Whatever you need to discuss with me, can it wait until tomorrow?"

"Of course, Miss Jameson," Adam said. "Of course."

"Thank you for the home-cooked meal, Miss Ward," Gregory said.

Turning to Adam, he said, "And thank you, Mr. Danbury, for the information about Frontier Railroad," Gregory said. "I know my readers will be interested in this new development."

Nellie and Gregory rode their separate ways, and Lizzy and Adam relaxed on the front porch.

"This is a busy place," Adam said. "And I must also thank you for opening your home to my crewman and to me."

"Doctor's orders," Lizzy said with a smile. "But truly, Max and I have plenty of room for visitors. And I'd feel much better with Mr. Anderson resting in a bed instead of a cot in a wagon."

They spent the remainder of the evening becoming better acquainted. Lizzy told Adam about growing up on a farm and how the war had impacted the farm and their life in Missouri.

"Have you ever heard about William Quantrill?" Lizzy asked her guest.

"By reputation only. But I have a feeling I'm about to learn more," Adam replied.

"Well, Quantrill's Raiders paid a visit to my farm in Missouri," Lizzy said with a twinkle in her eye. She told Adam about the skirmish between Quantrill's men and a gang of Jayhawkers, how she had hidden in a closet during the gun battle, and the terrible aftermath of that firefight.

"And you were alone on the farm," Adam said in disbelief.

"Oh, yes. Char was still in the Army and Max, our brother, had already passed away. It was just me on the farm. After that gunfight, I found a nearby cave to escape to when I saw riders approaching the farm. I kept a supply of food, water, lamps, furniture, and books in the cave for those times. That's where Char found me when she came home from the war."

"You've lived an exciting life," Adam said with admiration. "Quantrill's Raiders, a journey to Dakota Territory, staking a homestead claim, and now you're a successful landowner. What's next for Lizzy Ward?"

Lizzy sighed in contentment. "Hmmm, what's next? Well, I want to raise Max to be a good man. I want to see my family, friends, and neighbors prosper, and I want Shady Bluffs to be a place where people can live and work and raise their families in peace."

"That's a tall order," Adam said, "but something tells me that you can accomplish it."

"I'm afraid I've been doing all the talking, Adam," Lizzy said. "Tell me about yourself. What brings you out to the wild and wooly frontier?"

"Well," Adam began. "I've always been fascinated by transportation — especially locomotives. I grew up on Lake Erie, Cleveland, Ohio, to be exact. That's the birthplace of the Ohio and Erie Canal."

His story started picking up steam, just like his beloved locomotives. "I worked on the B&O, that's the Baltimore and Ohio Railroad, during the war. That's where I learned surveying. The railroads played a major role in the Union's success, you know. The B&O was a lifeline for the Union Army. After the war, I joined the Northern Pacific Railway and worked in Minnesota for a time. When Frontier Railroad offered me the job as Chief Survey Engineer, it was too good an offer to pass up. And now I'm in Dakota Territory, surveying and mapping possible routes across what you call the 'wild and wooly' frontier."

Lizzy nodded. His "life story" seemed more like an employment resume than a personal history. She decided to steer the discussion in that direction.

"Do you still have family in Ohio?" Lizzy asked.

Adam paused, then said, "My father died before the war. My mother lives with her sister in Akron."

Lizzy wanted to ask about sweethearts but thought that might be too personal. Instead, she said, "The railroad industry is certainly going to modernize our nation. It sounds as if you've hitched your wagon to a star, Adam."

Lizzy took a deep breath and looked into the starry sky. "Speaking of stars, look! There's a falling star. Quick, make a wish."

Lizzy and Adam each made silent, secret wishes as the meteor fell to earth.

She decided that enough personal details had been shared for one evening. "I'm going to check on our patient," she said. "I've left a blanket and pillow for you on the cot near Mr. Anderson's bed."

Adam followed her into the soddy. They found Bill Anderson sleeping uneasily.

"Let me know if you need anything," Lizzy said. "Good night, Adam."

"Good night, Lizzy."

News of the Day

Dakota Dispatch, **Shady Bluffs, Dakota Territory, August 20, 1872**

Headline: First Windmill Erected in Dakota Territory

Although windmills are a common sight on streams and rivers in Eastern states, the tall structures have not appeared in Dakota Territory until now. Miss Elizabeth Ward recently had an Eclipse windmill erected on the western fields of her farm. Miss Ward said the decision to build the windmill was prompted by the severe drought that is impacting crops and livestock this summer.

"We're in a harvest-killing drought," Miss Ward said. "My crops and my livestock need water to survive. I hope other farmers and ranchers will follow my lead."

This is the first of three windmills that Miss Ward will be installing, thanks to a loan from Shady Bluffs Savings and Loan.

Miss Ward and her sister moved to Dakota Territory in 1863. She and her adopted son, Max, farm midway between Shady Bluffs and Yankton, the Territorial capital. Max, now age seven, was one of the few survivors from the buffalo stampede that killed his parents in April 1865.

Chapter 8 – Late Summer 1872
The Patient

Bill Anderson had a restless night, which meant that Adam did not get much sleep. It gave Adam time to reflect on his conversation with Lizzy.

He admired Lizzy Ward. No, he was intrigued by Lizzy Ward. He'd never known a woman with so much grit and determination. Of course, Lizzy's sister was made of the same stuff. Adam thought about Charlotte joining the Army as a man in order to retrieve a wayward brother!

But it was Lizzy who managed a farm alone during the war, faced Bushwhackers and Jayhawkers, and decided the Ward sisters should leave the family farm and start new lives on the frontier. Now, Lizzy was one of the most successful farmers and ranchers on the prairie. She was leading the way with innovative farming practices, such as her windmills.

Lizzy was a woman of action, Adam thought. He couldn't imagine any of the women he'd known would have had the gumption to adopt an orphaned infant. Adam had almost told Lizzy about Margaret. Why didn't he?

Then Anderson groaned in pain, and Adam's attention turned to the man on the bed in the far corner.

"How's our patient doing?" Lizzy asked as she entered the room. "I'm guessing you can use this," she said, handing Adam a steaming cup of coffee.

"You're a mind-reader," Adam replied. Then, in a lower tone, he said, "Bill had a rough night. His fever is worse and he's complaining about pain in his leg."

"Charlotte said to expect that. The best thing we can do is try to keep him comfortable. I've made bacon and eggs for breakfast. Can you leave Bill for a few minutes?" Lizzy asked.

Max was already waiting at the table when Lizzy and Adam sat down. Lizzy turned to her son, "Please give thanks, Max."

"Lord, thank you for the bounty on our table and on our land," Max prayed. "In your name we pray. Amen."

Lizzy nodded in approval. "Amen," she said.

After breakfast, Adam insisted on clearing the table and doing the dishes. Max and Lizzy left the soddy to do chores: milk the cows, feed the chickens and pigs, and water the large garden.

As Lizzy carried a bucket of water to the garden, she decided there should be a windmill by the house. *No more pumping water by hand for this family,* she said to herself.

Nellie showed up at Lizzy's house just before lunch, but she didn't arrive empty-handed. She held up two plump grouse she'd shot on the ride over. "I brought dinner."

"Max's favorite meal," Lizzy said. "Max, Aunt Nellie has a couple of grouse to skin. Can you please help her?"

Nellie handed the birds to Max. "Thanks, Maxie." He headed back to the barn to skin and gut the birds.

Nellie plopped into one of the wooden rocking chairs on the porch and fanned herself. "It's going to be a hot one today," she said to Lizzy.

"Hot and dry," Lizzy agreed as she joined Nellie in the other chair.

As if on cue, Adam carried out a tray of cold tea in tall glasses. "This might help," he said, offering cool glasses of tea to the women.

"How's the man with the skunk bite?" Nellie asked.

Lizzy shook her head.

"He had a bad night," Adam said. "But he's sleeping now."

Adam pulled up a stool and joined the women on the porch. "Nellie, I have a proposition for you."

"Actually, *we* have a proposition for you, Nellie," Lizzy clarified.

Nellie tilted her head. "I'm listening."

Lizzy started the conversation. "The other day when I found the survey crew on the boundary between my farm and your claim, I was looking for a likely spot for my next windmill."

"Why put it on the edge of your farm?" Nellie asked.

"That land is better suited for grazing," Lizzy said. She nodded to Adam to jump in.

"If a windmill could pump water for Lizzy's livestock and yours, it's a win-win," Adam said. "Doesn't it make sense to share the water source?"

"It does, but I don't have the money to chip in for the windmill," Nellie said cautiously.

"I have two Eclipse windmill kits in the barn, just waiting to be put up," Lizzy said. "After Hank's accident, I figured I would need to wait until next year to find someone to build the motors."

Nellie looked puzzled. "And you've found someone?" she asked Lizzy.

Lizzy nodded at Adam. "Adam and I talked about this yesterday. But let him explain."

"Assuming that Frontier lays track in that area, a windmill and water tank would be needed where we were surveying," Adam said. "Steam engines can go one hundred to one hundred fifty miles between water stops. We'd be pushing it if we didn't have a stop there."

"So the windmill would belong to the railroad company," Nellie cut in.

"No, that's the beauty of this idea," Adam said. "It will be on your land and Lizzy's land. My crew can build the tower in a couple of days. With my engineering background, I can assemble the motor. I'll also supply the lumber with the assumption that we *might* be laying track through the area. Consider it an act of goodwill.

"If, or when, Frontier Railroad decides it wants the route on your land, this would go a long way to convincing you to allow us to lay track," Adam concluded.

Nellie nodded. "I like the idea of a 'win-win.' But," she frowned, "it seems too good to be true."

"That's what I said," Lizzy admitted. "But Adam assures me that the railroads do business like this all the time. If the railroad doesn't choose our land, we still have a windmill and stock tank for our livestock."

"Most of the land that the railroad companies get is through land grants by the U.S. government," Adam explained. "These are twenty- to fifty-mile sections of public land for every mile of track that's laid. The railroads sell parcels of land to pay for the construction of the track. But sometimes, we find routes that aren't on public land. Then we need to make deals."

"So what happens then?" Nellie asked.

Adam winced at this question for a second but quickly put a smile back on. "That depends. Sometimes we are able to purchase the land. Other times, the government allows the railroads to acquire the land through a process called eminent domain. Even then, the landowners receive fair compensation for the land."

Nellie frowned.

Adam continued, "I'm not saying we'll lay track on your land, Nellie. That's still to be determined. But I'm willing to put my crew to work for a couple of days to build the windmill, regardless of whether the tracks get laid on your property line. What do you think?"

"Can I sleep on it?" Nellie asked. "I like the idea of having a stock tank, but I'm pretty new at this whole landowner thing. I'll give you an answer in a day or two."

"Fair enough," Adam said.

The conversation moved on to other topics. Lizzy, Nellie, and Adam talked about everything except the railroad, from the weather to the new foals in Nellie's herd.

It was just after noon when Nellie saw Gregory Collins trot up to the farmhouse.

Today, Gregory looked more like a cowboy than a newspaperman. With his dark brown, broad-brimmed western hat, blue work shirt with the sleeves rolled up, leather vest, and black work trousers, Gregory would have fit in on any cattle ranch.

Nellie took a second look at Gregory and said, "I almost didn't recognize you. You look like a trailhand."

Gregory chuckled. "Before I was a newspaper reporter, writing about the goings on in politics, railroads, and the Indian uprising, I did my share of herding cattle, Miss Jameson…uh, Nellie. I grew up on a farm in Minnesota. It's not exactly Texas, but my pa ran beef cattle. Now, are you ready to show me your ranch?"

"I sure am," Nellie replied.

The lady rancher and the newspaperman-cowboy said their goodbyes to Lizzy and Adam and headed south to Nellie's claim.

The ride to Nellie's place was windy and hot. She was quiet on the ride; she was considering Adam's offer. Turning in her saddle, she said to Gregory, "Back at Lizzy's, you said you wrote stories about the railroads."

"That's right. The Northern Pacific laid a lot of track in Minnesota. Why do you ask?"

"Mr. Danbury offered to build Lizzy's next windmill on the border between her farm and my ranch. I can't for the life of me figure out why he wants to do that. He seems like a nice man, but 'just to be nice' is not enough to commit a railroad work crew to building a windmill. What do you think?"

"I think the railroads always have an angle. They're spending millions of dollars laying track from the East Coast to the West Coast. But they're set to make millions *and millions of dollars* after the track is laid. You're right to be cautious. Tell me about the offer."

Nellie explained that the border between Lizzy's farm and her ranch was one of the possible routes for Frontier Railroad. The windmill would be a water stop for the steam engines.

"It sounds logical," Gregory said. "But the railroads are getting huge grants of land from the government as incentives for laying track."

"Mr. Danbury said this is only a possible option. Personally, I think he's sweet on Lizzy, and this is another way to spend time with her."

"You may be on to something."

Nellie reined up her quarter horse on a slight rise. Gregory halted his horse and followed Nellie's gaze to the tidy ranch in the distance.

"I staked my claim two years ago, but there's still a lot of work to do," Nellie said.

Gregory studied the homestead. A small, wooden house with a peaked roof sat a short distance from a large barn. There was a fenced corral behind the barn.

"Very nice," he said. "Most of the homes out here are soddies or dugouts. But you've got a timber-built house."

"I've got a sister-in-law to thank for that," Nellie said. "Charlie hated the creepy-crawlers that come with a soddy. She convinced Luke to use some of the lumber from the barn for a small — a very small — house. So I have a wooden house." She shrugged.

"Lizzy is a little envious, I think," Nellie added. "She's been wishing for a proper house for a couple of years, but there's always something that the farm needs: more cattle, a new plow, and now windmills."

Nellie clicked her tongue, and the buckskin mare trotted toward the homestead.

"Wait," Gregory said. "Before we continue, can you give me an idea of boundaries for your claim?"

Nellie circled her horse back to stand by Gregory's mount. She pointed at a ridge to the north. "Lizzy's land is just past that ridge. That's where the survey crew was when Mr. Anderson got bit by the skunk."

"So we've been on your ranch for a while," Gregory confirmed.

"Uh huh," Nellie said. "Now, see those piles of rocks over there? That's the eastern edge of my claim."

"Those are called monumentations, right?" Gregory asked.

Nellie nodded. "You can't see the southern boundary from here, but we can ride there. I'd like to water the horses first, though." She clicked her tongue again and rode toward the ranch house.

"I believe you can see Omaha from here," he said with a laugh.

"On a clear day, I bet you can," Nellie said.

At Nellie's house, they watered their horses. "Want to see the barn?" she asked Gregory. "The barn is the most important building on the ranch. It's where the work is done."

Gregory followed her through the double barn doors. He took a deep breath and inhaled the earthy smells of the barn: the sweet scent of leather, the sharp smell of iron and rust, and the smell of grain and hay.

"It needs to be mucked out," Nellie said defensively.

"No, the smells in this barn — the leather, the hay, the horses — they bring me back to when I was a boy. Yeah, there's the smell of manure, but my dad always said manure smells like money."

Nellie started laughing.

"That's funny?" Gregory asked.

"That's what my pa said, too. 'Manure smells like money.'" They both laughed.

"Let's go see my beauties," Nellie said. At the far end of the barn, she opened the double doors to reveal a large, fenced corral. Inside were fifteen horses.

"You've got a nice-looking string of horses, Nellie," Gregory said. "

She shrugged, but inside, she was bursting with pride. "It's a start."

She held out a piece of apple, and an enormous stallion trotted over. "This is Thunder," Nellie said to Gregory. "He's the start of my bloodline."

Gregory admired the bay. "He is a beauty. Thunder is going to make a name for the Jameson Ranch."

"That's the plan," she replied. "Let's get something cool to drink. We can watch the horses from the back porch."

Nellie headed to the house, and Gregory followed.

The tiny house took the efficient use of space to a new level. Nellie's bed was behind a curtain in an alcove. There were drawers for storage underneath it. Beside the alcove, there was a built-in table with two chairs. Next to the table was a dry sink, dishes, and linens. On the opposite side of the room, a cookstove stood next to shelving that held dry goods and cooking supplies.

"I don't spend a lot of time in here," Nellie said sheepishly. She picked two tall glasses and a pitcher from the cupboard and went out to the well. Again, Gregory trailed after her.

"We have good water out here," she said. She drew the bucket from the well. Gregory held the glasses while Nellie filled the pitcher.

Together, they walked around to the back of the tiny house where Nellie had placed a long bench.

"At night, I watch the sun go down from here," she said as she sat down on the rough-hewn log bench. "I can see everything I love from right here."

"Tell me," Gregory murmured.

"The horses, the prairie, the sun, and the stars," she said. "In the summer, the fireflies dance for me. It's heavenly."

"Do you ever miss Missouri?" Gregory asked.

"I miss ma and pa and the family back in Missouri, but the rest of my family — Luke, Charlie, Lizzy, and the kids — they're all here."

"It sounds like you have a good life, Nellie Jameson," Gregory said.

She sighed in agreement.

Without exchanging another word, Gregory reached for Nellie's hand. She smiled.

News of the Day

Dakota Dispatch, **Shady Bluffs, Dakota Territory, August 27, 1872**

Headline: Frontier Railroad Surveying Land Around Shady Bluffs

Frontier Railroad Company crews have been spotted surveying land for possible routes through Dakota Territory. Mr. Adam Danbury, Chief Survey Engineer for Frontier Railroad, confirmed that the railroad is exploring several possible routes.

"Nothing is certain or approved at this point," Mr. Danbury said. "It is my responsibility to survey all potential routes for the railroad and then to make a recommendation based on land formations, elevations, water sources, and other variables. The Frontier Railroad Board of Directors will make the final decision regarding track routes."

Frontier Railroad's survey crew is currently evaluating a potential route bordering Miss Elizabeth Ward's farm and Miss Nellie Jameson's ranch. Mr. Danbury explained that most land is acquired through a "land grants" system, where the federal government provides tracts of public land along the proposed railroad route for each mile of track constructed. Sometimes, however, a more efficient route may be selected based on a lower cost per mile of track laid.

"Everything is still speculative," Mr. Danbury emphasized. He said the land in question would need a water station so the steam locomotive could replenish its water supply. Frontier Railroad is currently considering constructing a windmill on the tract of land.

Chapter 9 – Late Summer 1872
Dinner in Town

Adam and Lizzy took turns watching over Bill Anderson. His condition continued to worsen. He was unconscious more than he was conscious, which made it difficult to administer medications or even to feed him.

As promised, Charlotte made a house call on the third day. When Anderson was awake, he was agitated. His symptoms had progressed rapidly. Charlotte prescribed a stronger dose of laudanum to lessen the agitation.

"I'm sorry. I wish there was more that I could do for Mr. Anderson," Charlotte said on the second visit.

"It's only been five days since he was bitten," Lizzy said. "Should I worry that he could transfer the disease to us?"

"No, that's pretty rare. Rabies spreads through saliva, usually from biting. It's extremely rare to transfer from person to person," Charlotte said. "But by keeping him sedated, we're reducing his agitation. I think that's the best course of action for now."

Two days later, Bill Anderson fell into a coma.

"He's gone, Lizzy," Adam told Lizzy the next morning. "I went to give him a dose of laudanum during the night, but he was gone."

"Oh. That was such a horrible way to die. "I hope he's at peace now."

Adam nodded. He appeared lost in his thoughts.

"We should take care of the body," Lizzy said. She stripped the bed linens, gathered the pillows, and prepared to burn everything that had come in contact with Anderson. She found an old but serviceable quilt and instructed Adam to wrap Anderson in the blanket.

"We'll bury him near the apple orchard," she said.

Adam dug a grave and said a few words over it. After it was all done, he said to Lizzy, "There's still a good part of the day left. You graciously opened your home to Anderson and me for nearly a week. While it's not nearly enough, I'd like to thank you for your hospitality. Would you and Max be my guests at Betsy's Place in town tonight?"

Lizzy thought it over for only a moment. "That's a wonderful offer, Adam. Max and I would love to be your guests for dinner."

She sent Max off to the creek with a bar of soap, a brush, and a towel to scrape off some of that "boy dirt." While he was cleaning up, Lizzy took a sponge bath at the house and selected her best summer-weight dress for the occasion.

When it appeared that he and Anderson would be staying for several days, Adam requested that his trunk and clothing be delivered to Lizzy's home. He took this opportunity to clean up, brush off his frock coat, and become the dandy whom Lizzy had first met.

After a cold lunch of sandwiches and fruit, the three set out for Shady Bluffs. Adam drove the company wagon and trailed his horse behind. Lizzy and Max took their buckboard, leaving Scout behind with orders to "watch the farm" while they were absent.

The prairie grasses were a rippling wave of gold, which was not unusual for this late in the summer. But the travelers also saw several "dust devils" on the dry-as-tinder plains. In the heat of the day, these small, whirling winds picked up dust, grasses, and leaves and swirled across the wide-open prairies. Lizzy kept a tight hold of the reins so the horses would not spook.

Along the way, Max peppered Adam with questions about the railroads back East.

"It's the way of the future, my boy," Adam told Max. "It was the railroads that won the war for the Union. Locomotives transported supplies and equipment for the Northern Armies. Now, they're carrying homesteaders west, and cattle and crops east. Steam engines are faster and more reliable than horse and wagons for transportation."

"Is that why they're called 'iron horses, Mr. Danbury?" Max asked.

"It is indeed," Adam replied.

It was mid-afternoon when the travelers arrived in the small prairie town.

"I need to pick up a few things at the mercantile," Lizzy said. "Max, you can come with me, and we'll do some back-to-school shopping…"

The pained look on Max's face told his mother all she needed to know about this plan.

"…or you can find your cousins and spend the afternoon getting into mischief."

"It's been a while since I've seen Will," Max told his mother.

"Mischief it is," Lizzy said with a laugh. She turned to Adam, "And what sorts of mischief are you planning to get into, Adam?"

"Now that you ask, I need to send several telegrams to the home office."

"All right, let's split up and meet at Betsy's Place at six o'clock," Lizzy suggested.

Isabell Vaughn smiled widely when Lizzy entered Vaughn's Mercantile.

"Lizzy Ward, as I live and breathe! How have you been?" Isabell asked.

"Spring and summer on the farm are busy times, Isabell," Lizzy replied. "But school is starting soon, and Max has outgrown every stitch of clothing! I'll need several lengths of serviceable fabric for britches and shirts. I'd like to place an order for a new winter coat for Max, too."

As Isabell measured out fabric for Lizzy, the shopkeeper looked up and said, "How's that new windmill working? Hank was certainly proud that he had a hand in that project."

"Hank nearly broke his back working on that project," Lizzy said. "He gave me quite the fright." Then Lizzy's tone softened. "But I really appreciated Hank's encouragement and help with the windmill. I don't think I would have followed through with it if it hadn't been for him. There are two more windmill kits ready and waiting in my barn."

"When are you going to put those windmills up?" Isabell asked.

"I'd like to get them up before next spring. It's so dry out there; I don't think the farm will make it if we have another dry year like this one. The crops in the west section are looking very good thanks to the water from the windmill."

The women discussed the news around town, and then the conversation turned to Gregory Collins.

"It's good to finally have a newspaper in town," Isabell said. "And Mr. Collins has turned the heads of several unattached, young women in town."

"Oh?" Lizzy responded. "He paid a call on Nellie last week. He said he wanted to 'see the frontier' for himself."

Isabell shrugged. "All I know is that the mamas of those young women are even more interested in Mr. Collins than their daughters are."

Both women laughed.

After Lizzy completed her purchases, she walked to the bank to pay a visit to Hank.

Hank Johnson was alone in the office and smiled broadly when he saw Lizzy. Grabbing his cane, he stood up and welcomed Lizzy.

"What brings you to town?" Hank asked.

"You heard about the patient with rabies, I assume," Lizzy said.

"Oh, yes. It was in the paper." Hank waved a copy of the *Dakota Dispatch* to emphasize his comment.

"The poor man died in the night," Lizzy said. "He's buried in the apple orchard. As a thank you for taking in Mr. Anderson during his…his illness, Mr. Danbury offered to take Max and me to dinner. I also had some shopping and errands to do, including checking on you.

She looked him over. "I see you've traded your crutches for a cane. How is your leg?"

"Much better, thank you," Hank replied. "I expect it will always ache when there's a change in the weather. To tell you the truth, I'm not sure if, in the future, I'll admit to falling off a windmill. I might just call it a 'war injury.'" Hank laughed.

"You certainly gave me a scare, Hank Johnson," Lizzy said.

"I'm sorry about that. I'm glad Jerry could help dig the trenches for the water. Say, when are you going to put up the other two windmills?"

"Mr. Danbury has offered to use his surveying crew to build a windmill on the border between my land and Nellie's land. I think we looked at the location as a likely place to water cattle," Lizzy said.

Hank nodded. "And the railroad is going to build the windmill?" he asked. "Why?"

"Adam…Mr. Danbury said it is an act of 'good faith' in case the railroad decides that location would be a good spot for the tracks."

Hank looked dubious, but he said, "I hope that works out for you and for Nellie."

"Nellie is still thinking over the offer," Lizzy said.

At that moment, Adam Danbury entered the bank. He extended his hand to Hank. "Hello again, Mr. Johnson."

Hank nodded at the finely dressed man. "Nice to see you again, too, Mr. Danbury."

Adam turned to Lizzy. "Are you ready for dinner, Lizzy? Max is already at Betsy's Place waiting for us."

"I'm looking forward to a meal that I didn't have to cook," Lizzy said.

"Enjoy your dinner," Hank said as the couple left the bank.

Adam took Lizzy's hand and placed it in the crook of his arm as they strolled down the wooden boardwalk to Betsy's Place.

Inside the diner, Max was munching on a biscuit. He looked at his mother a bit sheepishly. "I was hungry, Ma. Mrs. Tomlinson said I could have a biscuit while I waited."

Adam pulled out a chair for Lizzy to sit down. She smiled at her son and said, "That's fine, Max. I'm sure you were close to starvation." Lizzy couldn't imagine her life without this bundle of boyish energy.

Betsy Tomlinson approached the table and welcomed her guests. "Hello, Lizzy. It's so nice to see you. How's the windmill working?"

"It's working well, thanks to your husband and son," Lizzy answered. "That windmill is certainly the talk of the town."

"It's something new, and that always gets attention," Betsy said. She went to describe the diner's specials for the evening.

Lizzy, Max, and Adam each selected different entrees so they could share and taste all of Betsy's offerings. They finished the meal with generous portions of apple pie topped with whipped cream.

"Ma," Max said as he finished the last crumbs of apple pie, "Will asked if I'd stay the night. Can I?"

"I had a feeling that was going to happen. That's why I packed overnight bags for both of us," Lizzy said. "I'll stay at the hotel, and you may stay overnight with your cousin — as long as Aunt Charlotte approves."

"She already knows, ma," Max assured his mother.

"Then off with you. Be on your best behavior." Lizzy squeezed Max's arm, knowing that a hug — or heaven forbid, a kiss — would mortify the boy.

"That just leaves the two of us," Adam said. "Would you care to go for a stroll, Miss Ward?" Adam said with all the formality he could muster.

"That sounds lovely, Mr. Danbury," Lizzy replied.

The summer evening was still warm, however, a light breeze made the walk very enjoyable. The town ended at the boardwalk, but Lizzy and Adam continued their stroll.

"People have a lot of admiration for you, Lizzy," Adam said. "Several people today mentioned that you aren't afraid to try something new — like your windmill. And the fact that the windmill is going to help your harvest makes people want to follow your lead."

"I didn't put up the windmill to prove a point," Lizzy said. "I just knew I had to get water to those fields somehow. It's like every other decision I've made, from leaving Missouri to adopting Max. It was the right thing to do."

"What's next for Lizzy Ward?"

Lizzy considered the question. "Well, once the three windmills are up and producing for the farm, I'm going to do something I've wanted to do for a long time."

"Do tell."

"I'm going to build a new house. A real house like the one we had in Missouri," Lizzy said. "The sod house that Charlotte and I built back in '63 has served us well. But I want a timber-built home, one that doesn't have bugs crawling out of the walls and ceiling. And I want a real, wooden floor. Something that echoes when I walk on it. That's a lot, I know. But that's my dream."

Adam nodded and said, "It's what you deserve, Lizzy."

They continued walking in silence. They listened to the coyotes calling and the hoots of the night birds.

Adam broke the silence. "It's really beautiful out here. Thank you for showing me the frontier through your eyes, Lizzy."

He turned and, taking her into his arms, Adam kissed Lizzy for the first time. Then he pulled back. "My apologies, Lizzy. I didn't mean to be so forward."

"Truth be told, it's been a long time since I've been kissed. I forgot what I've been missing," Lizzy said. "Kiss me again."

And he did.

This is what I've been missing, Lizzy thought as Adam's lips trailed from her mouth to her neck and back again. Adam's attention made Lizzy feel desirable.

She tingled as Adam's hands traced a path from Lizzy's shoulders down to her firm bottom. It was a good feeling to know that someone, especially an attractive man like Adam, had romantic thoughts about her. Adam's kisses trailed from Lizzy's lips to her neck and back again to her lips, while his hands explored the curves of her waist and hips.

Then he broke away. "Forgive me. I'm forgetting myself. I'm a gentleman…" Adam's words trailed off just as his lips and hands had trailed her body.

"Thank you," Lizzy said. "Thank you for the attention, and thank you for your restraint. Perhaps we should return to town."

Adam escorted Lizzy to the one hotel in Shady Bluffs, where they had both reserved rooms for the night. They parted in the lobby. She could feel Adam's hot gaze on her as she ascended the stairway. Lizzy wondered what the night could have offered if they had acted on their impulses.

Lizzy drifted off to sleep alone in her bed, dreaming of curling into the warm embrace of a man who desired her. In her dreams, though, that man was Hank.

News of the Day

Dakota Dispatch, Shady Bluffs, Dakota Territory, August 27, 1872

Headline: Railroad Worker Dies from Rabies

A rabid skunk attacked a survey crewman from Frontier Railroad Company last Thursday out by Nellie Jameson's claim. The railroad worker, Bill Anderson, was immediately transported to the home of Miss Elizabeth Ward, whose land bordered the incident.

Doctor Charlotte Jameson made a house call to Miss Ward's home to treat the victim. Mr. Anderson remained in Miss Ward's home throughout his illness. Mr. Anderson died from hydrophobia two days ago.

Mr. Adam Danbury, Chief Survey Engineer for Frontier Railroad, assured the Dispatch that the rabid animal was killed and disposed of so that no additional animals or humans would be infected.

Chapter 10 – Late Summer 1872
Second Windmill

When Lizzy and Adam entered the diner the next morning, she noticed Hank Johnson having his usual breakfast of bacon, eggs, toast, and coffee at the corner table. She gave him a friendly wave as Adam pulled out a chair for Lizzy to sit.

Lizzy noticed that Hank scowled at Adam and wondered if the two men had clashed about something. Fleetingly she thought it could be Adam's attentions toward her, but discounted that idea immediately. They were simply friends.

Besides, Lizzy thought, *I'm free to encourage the affections of another man.*

"Can I...er, may I join you," Lizzy heard someone say.

Lizzy looked up from her menu to see Nellie standing by the table. "Of course, Nellie."

Adam started to rise to pull out a chair for Nellie, but the young woman had already seated herself in the other empty chair at the table.

"What brings you to town so early?" Lizzy asked.

"I'm starting farrier lessons today," Nellie replied. "I already know how to care for horses' hooves and legs. Heck, I've been tending to horses as long as I can remember. It's the blacksmithing piece of the work that Luke is going to teach me."

"A woman blacksmith," Adam said. "That's an unusual occupation for a woman."

"Not out in these parts, Mr. Danbury," Nellie said. "If a woman sets her mind to it, then she can do the job. Just look at Charlie. She wanted to be a doctor. There aren't too many women doctors here or back East, but Charlie was determined."

"That's true," Lizzy said. "Char always wanted to be a doctor. She just needed the training. And, thanks to her time in the Union Army, she developed the skills and knowledge she needed to be our town doctor. People rely on and trust Char."

Lizzy took Nellie's hand. "Follow your dream, my girl. You'll be a marvelous farrier, and I'll be your first customer."

"Thank you for the encouragement." Nellie squeezed Lizzy's hand.

While Nellie was eating, Adam took the opportunity to pitch the windmill proposal one more time.

"Like I said before, this is a win-win," Adam said. "Actually, it's a win-win-win."

He ticked off the three partners in the project: "Your horses will have water. Lizzy's crops and cattle will have water, and our steam engines will have a watering spot."

Nellie nodded. "I've thought it over, Mr. Danbury. As long as we have it in writing from you and Frontier Railroad that the windmill and the water it pumps will belong to Lizzy and me, I'm in."

"Splendid!" Adam clapped his hands. "It's a deal, ladies." He shook hands with Nellie and Lizzy. "I'll pick up the lumber this morning and bring it to the work site. Ladies, you will have a working windmill by next week!"

"And the paperwork?" Nellie asked.

"I will write up a contract tonight for all parties to sign," Adam promised.

Lizzy beamed. "We're bringing water to the prairie!"

Hank got up from his breakfast and stopped at their table. "Good morning, ladies." He tipped his hat to Lizzy and Nellie. "Good morning to you, sir," he said to Adam. "I couldn't help but hear the news. I'm pleased that you're proceeding with the windmills, Lizzy. You're going to make the frontier bloom!"

"I like the sound of that, Hank," Lizzy said. Her dimples accentuated her smile.

"How long will you be in town?" Hank asked her.

"Max and I are returning to the farm this morning. Why?"

"I have some business in the country later today and would like to stop by," Hank said.

"You're always welcome at the farm, Hank."

"I'm grateful. Well, I'd best be on my way to the bank. Have a good day. The big man smiled at the three diners and left the café.

"I should be going too," Nellie said. She reached into a pocket for money to pay for the meal, but Adam stopped her. "This is my treat, Nellie."

"Thank you kindly, Mr. Danbury," Nellie said. She collected her riding gloves and excused herself from the table.

"It's just us again," Adam said to Lizzy.

"Thank you for dinner last night, and for breakfast today," Lizzy said to Adam. "Now, I should fetch Max. Or rather, I should rescue my sister from two boisterous young boys." She laughed.

"I'll keep you informed regarding the progress on the windmill," Adam promised.

They rose from the table. Just like the previous night, Adam tucked Lizzy's hand into the crook of his arm. They walked to the livery where their horses and wagons had been stabled for the night.

"Despite the tragic circumstances, I thoroughly enjoyed my time in your home," Adam said.

"It was the least I could do. I wish Mr. Anderson had not died, but he is at rest now."

He took Lizzy's hand and, raising it to his lips, kissed her hand in the most gallant manner Lizzy could imagine. Adam hitched the horses to both his wagon and Lizzy's wagon, then headed to the lumber yard.

Lizzy decided to stop in the blacksmith's shop to give Nellie a word of encouragement and to greet her brother-in-law. When Lizzy entered the shop, Luke was demonstrating how to custom-size the horseshoe.

"You've got to heat the shoe until it's red hot, Nell," Luke instructed his sister. "Once it's red, pull it out of the fire. Pound it on the anvil until it's the shape you need for the hoof. Let it cool just a bit — you'll know after some practice. Then, press the shoe against the hoof to make sure the shape is perfect."

He sized the shoe on the horse they were working on. "That's about right." He handed the horseshoe to Nellie. "Now grind the shoe smooth to get rid of the rough edges."

While Nellie worked on the horseshoe, Luke continued the lesson. "After that, you'll nail the shoe in place and bend over the nails so they don't poke out. And finally…"

"And then I'll sand and plane the hoof to make sure it's a smooth fit," Nellie said.

"You've got it. Now you just need to practice, practice, practice."

"You're just looking for free labor," Nellie responded.

"Hey, I should be charging you for the lessons," Luke teased back.

Although she concentrated on the process, Nellie said, "With all sincerity, I appreciate you teaching me the finer points of blacksmithing."

"It's more like the basics," Luke said, "but you're a fast learner."

Lizzy laughed at the banter between the brother and sister. "Oh, how I miss having a brother to tease," Lizzy said, making her presence known. "Nellie, you're going to be a fine farrier."

"I would agree with that," Luke admitted. "She knows horses better than anyone in these parts."

"She does, indeed," Lizzy agreed. "Luke, I'm headed back to the farm after I pick up Max at your house. I hope he behaved."

"You know kids, Lizzy," Luke said. "They always behave better for others than for their own parents. Max was the perfect guest. He even offered to wash dishes! You've trained him well."

"That's a relief!" Lizzy smiled at the compliment, then she turned to Nellie.

"Thank you again for agreeing to partner on the well and windmill," Lizzy said to Nellie.

"If you think it's a good idea, I'm all for it," Nellie said.

"If anyone cares, I think the windmills are a good idea, too," Luke said.

Lizzy laughed. "It's unanimous then. And Nellie, let me know when you're ready to shoe some horses and mules on the Ward farm."

Nellie blew a coppery curl out of her face. "Thanks. I'm not ready yet, but when I am, you'll be the first to know."

On the ride to the farm, Lizzy reviewed the events of the past few days and looked forward to having the second windmill up and pumping.

She thought about Adam Danbury. He was an intriguing man. He was certainly a fine dresser, maybe a bit too fine for her taste, but she knew she was used to the rough cowboys and farmers on the frontier. Adam proved his dedication to his crew when he stayed by Bill Anderson's bedside throughout the ordeal. There was more to Adam Danbury than his frock coat and top hat. She wondered if the fancy dress was simply to fit the part he played as a railroad man.

Their dinner last night had been lovely. And the walk under the stars, well, that was the most romantic thing Lizzy had done in years. She was glad he had kissed her. And, if Lizzy admitted in her heart of hearts, she longed for more than a kiss. She remembered how it felt to have his hands trail down the curve of her back…

The memory made Lizzy blush. She put her hand up to her face to cover the color on her fair cheeks.

"What's wrong, Ma?" Max asked.

"It's the heat, Max," Lizzy replied. "It's just the heat."

Before they knew it, they reached Medicine Creek, which was now only a trickle.

"Do you think Mr. Crawford dammed the creek again?" Max said.

"No, it's the drought, Sweets. We need a good, hard rain."

Max nodded in agreement and looked at the wispy clouds. "Not today, though."

"Max, after we get our chores done, let's have a picnic. How does that sound?"

"Sounds great, ma!"

Lizzy knew the incentive would spur the boy to complete his tasks more quickly. Besides, she hadn't spent much time with her son while Bill Anderson was languishing in their home.

Lizzy and Max fed the chickens and pigs, collected eggs, and watered the kitchen garden. While Lizzy packed a picnic lunch, Max hitched the wagon.

"Where should we go?" Lizzy asked her son.

"Let's go visit our windmill in the west section," he suggested.

As Lizzy and Max rode west, they spotted Hank Johnson riding east toward the Ward Farm.

"Lizzy! Max!" Hank shouted.

Lizzy waved to the banker.

"Where you two headed?" he asked when he reached them.

"We're having lunch at the windmill," Max replied. "Ma, can Mr. Johnson join us?"

"Of course," Lizzy said. She patted her saddle bags. "There's plenty for three here. But if you'd rather not go to the windmill, we can find another picnic spot."

"The site of my fall from grace? Or maybe my graceless fall? I'm not holding a grudge against the tower," Hank said with a laugh. "In fact, I haven't seen the windmill in action, and I'd like to watch the blades turning. Lead on, Max!"

With Max holding the reins, they quickly reached the windmill.

"Look at her spin," Max said. "She's a wonder, isn't she?"

Max and Hank let the horses drink their fill from the water pond while Lizzy spread a quilt and unpacked the picnic fixings. They enjoyed sandwiches, fruit breads, and icy cold water pumped from the windmill.

After lunch, Max wandered off to watch the antics of a colony of prairie dogs.

"This is the life," Hank said. He stretched his long legs out.

Lizzy eyed Hank's injured leg. "I have to ask, how is your leg feeling these days?"

"It gets better every day," he replied.

"I still feel guilty about your accident," Lizzy said.

"I was the darn fool who got knocked off the platform, Lizzy. I was lucky it was just my leg." He looked up at the spinning blades of the windmill. "But that windmill is a thing of beauty, isn't she?"

"She is indeed! But why are we referring to the windmill as a 'she'?" Lizzy followed Hank's gaze.

"The windmill is a 'she' because she's gonna make the prairie bloom — just like you do," Hank told Lizzy. "I read a poem about windmills a while back."

"I love poetry," Lizzy said to encourage him.

"It goes something like this:

Windmills teach us about life.

They teach us to be reliable and steady.

They teach us that the gentlest breeze can produce the greatest results.

They teach us to stand tall against the sky."

"That's beautiful," Lizzy said. "And *she* is going to save my harvest this fall, thanks to you."

"So, Adam Danbury is going to build your second windmill," Hank said.

"Actually, the railroad is building it. But yes, Adam made the offer," Lizzy confirmed.

"Hmmm," Hank said noncommittally. "And the third windmill…where's that going to be?"

"Selfishly, I've decided it will be in the farmyard, next to the house," Lizzy said. "I'm tired of hand-pumping water for laundry, baths, and watering the animals and the garden."

"That's not selfish, Liz," Hank responded. "It's good sense. I can help with that one, if you like. I may not be able to climb the tower, but I'll help on the ground, and I'll assemble the pump motor."

"Hank, you've already done so much," Lizzy protested.

"Nope, I promised to help with your windmills. And I aim to keep that promise."

Then, he rose to his feet and extended a hand to Lizzy. "Can I entice you into a walk, Miss Ward?"

Lizzy took his hand — it enveloped her own — and allowed Hank to pull her to her feet. "I'd be delighted, Mr. Johnson."

Hand in hand, they ambled through the prairie grass, stopping from time to time so that Lizzy could gather a bright bouquet of yellow sunflowers.

"This has been the perfect day, Hank. I'm glad you could join us." Lizzy thought back to that morning at Betsy's. "You said you had business out here. Who were you stopping to see?"

"You, Lizzy. I wanted to see you," Hank said.

To her surprise, Hank bent down and kissed Lizzy. His hand moved to the small of her back, pulling her into an embrace. Lizzy shifted her weight and leaned into the kiss. Her arms went around Hank's neck as she deepened the kiss.

Waves of heat coursed through Lizzy's body. Her heart pounded and her legs went weak. Thankfully, Hank's strong embrace held her upright. This is what she had been waiting her entire life for — a kiss that was long and full of promise.

Hank's kiss was different from the flirtation that Adam had offered. There was passion and promise in the way Hank held her against his body. Her heart soared with his embrace. This kiss made Lizzy feel desired and loved.

Too soon, it seemed, they pulled apart.

"Hank, I had no idea you felt that way," Lizzy said breathlessly.

He stared into her eyes. "I thought I should declare myself."

And about time, Lizzy thought.

"Umm, you were okay with the kiss?" he asked.

"I kissed you back, didn't I?"

"That you did, Lizzy. In fact, just to make sure…" He moved in and kissed her again. This time it was gentler, slower, and left a promise of more to come. "Yep, it was just as good the second time."

Lizzy laughed now. "Hank Johnson, you never cease to surprise me." Tenderly, she caressed his cheek.

Then they heard a boy's laughter and saw Max staring at them.

"Kissing!" Max's tone conveyed the disgust that only a seven-year-old boy can display.

Lizzy and Hank smiled at each other and then at Max.

"I reckon it's time to head home," Hank said. "I'll ride with you to the house. Max, you get the horses while I help your mother pack up the picnic fixings."

They chatted about inconsequential things on the ride to the farmhouse. Upon reaching the farmyard, Hank said, "Lizzy, you said you want the third windmill in the yard?"

Lizzy nodded and pointed to the well. "No sense in digging another well. The third tower and pump can go here."

"Yep," Hank said. "That'll make this one a lot easier, too. Jerry and John Tomlinson can build the tower. I'll build the motor. You're going to have the most modern farmstead in the Territory!"

Lizzy tilted her head, thinking about that comment. "I believe that's a compliment. I'll take it."

"It is indeed," Hank replied.

"Would you like to stay for supper?" Lizzy asked him.

"I'd never turn down your home cooking. Put me to work so I can earn my keep."

Nellie was shutting down the forge and putting away hammers, tongs, and punches used to shape the horseshoes when Gregory entered Luke's blacksmith shop.

"I heard you were working for your brother," Gregory said.

Luke laughed. "This is more of a teacher-student thing than an employer-employee situation, Greg. But, I've got to admit that for her first day at the forge, Nellie did darn good."

"Nellie, are you staying in town tonight," Gregory asked. "I'd be happy to treat you to dinner to celebrate your first day."

"I'd love to," Nellie said, "but I need to get back to the ranch. I was going to pick up supper at Betsy's and bring it home. You're welcome to join me."

"Tell you what, I'll pick up dinner and ride to the ranch with you," he offered.

"I can't refuse that invitation," Nellie replied.

"I'll meet you back here in ten minutes with Betsy's dinner special," Gregory said.

During this exchange, Luke was sorting through supplies in a dark corner of the shop, but he recognized the electricity between Nellie and Gregory.

After Gregory left the shop, Luke laughed. "Seems to me like sparks were flying. And not from making horse hooves. Do I need to ask that young man if his intentions are honorable, Nellie Ann Jameson?"

Nellie gave her brother a shove. "If you do, I'll tell ma — no, I'll tell Charlotte — about that time you and Florence Applegate got caught…"

"Okay, okay," Luke said in fake surrender. "Just behave yourselves, you hear?"

Nellie pushed a hank of hair off her forehead. "Ma taught me to act like a lady, even if I only do so when it suits me. But all joking aside, thank you again for the blacksmithing lesson today. I'll be back next week."

"Before you go, let's load up the farrier anvil that pa gave me when I left Missouri. It's a lot lighter than the one here, and you can use it to practice. We'll figure out a forge the next time I'm at your ranch."

"You mean it?!" Nellie said with excitement. "Thank you!"

Together, they strapped the smaller anvil to the saddle of Nellie's horse. Nellie hugged her brother before she mounted. Gregory was waiting for her outside the blacksmith shop.

The ride back to Nellie's ranch took forever … and went by in a flash. They talked about their childhoods, their families "back home," and why they came to Dakota Territory.

"My brother Roger and I both served in the 2nd Minnesota Sharpshooters under Colonel Berdan," Gregory said. "Roger joined first, and then I followed him. After the war, Rog came back to the farm. My father still farms, but his health is failing, so Rog does most of the work.

"During the war, I got to know a couple of newspaper reporters. That's what started me down this career path. I like telling stories about people and why they do the things they do.

"Take Adam Danbury," Gregory continued. "He's a curious fellow, isn't he? I haven't figured out his angle yet, but the railroads made a lot of shady deals in Minnesota. Jay Cooke and the Northern Pacific were infamous for graft and speculation from the management right down to the surveyors. They stopped laying track for a while. I reported on some of those deals."

Gregory shook his head. "Then again, maybe Danbury is a stand-up guy. I just need to do some digging."

"He said he's going to build a windmill for Lizzy and me," Nellie said. "But I insisted he put the agreement on paper."

"Get it in writing," Gregory counseled.

The late summer sun was hanging low on the horizon when Nellie and Gregory reached the ranch. She dismounted and tossed the reins to Gregory.

"If you'll take care of the horses, I'll freshen up. Blacksmithing is sooty work," Nellie said.

News of the Nation

The St. Paul Dispatch, September 2, 1872

The Chicago Tribune, **September 20, 1872**

The Boston Herald, **September 27, 1872**

Headline: As Reported by *Dakota Dispatch*, Dakota Territory

Although windmills are a common sight on streams and rivers in eastern states, the tall structures have not appeared in Dakota Territory until now. Miss Elizabeth Ward recently had an Eclipse windmill erected on the western fields of her farm. Miss Ward said the decision to build the windmill was prompted by the severe drought that is impacting crops and livestock this summer. Miss Ward and her adopted son, Max, farm midway west of Yankton, the Territorial capital. Max, age seven, survived a buffalo stampede that killed his parents in April 1865.

Chapter 11 – Late Autumn 1872
Prairie Madness

Lizzy surveyed the harvested wheat field. The shocks of grain weren't as full as in past years, but at least she had a respectable yield. The drought had stunted the growth of wheat and corn on neighboring farms, but Lizzy's windmill had made the difference between a decent harvest and a poor harvest — or no harvest at all.

Using her horse-drawn reaper, Lizzy cut the wheat stalks while Max and John Tomlinson followed behind, tying the stalks into bundles. Then, they stacked the stalks into standing shocks to dry. Lizzy would take the grain to the mill to be ground into flour when the grain was dry enough.

The corn harvest would wait until after the first frost.

After they finished tying the last shock of wheat, Lizzy and the boys walked back to the homestead.

Over a hearty meal of cold chicken, biscuits, garden vegetables, and chocolate cake, Lizzy said, "John, you were a big help with the harvest. Here's what I owe you for your work." She handed the teen a handful of coins for his labor on the farm. "Can I count on you for the corn harvest after the frost?"

"Well, ma'am," John replied. "Ma says I need to keep up with my schoolwork. I'm not sure I'll have time."

"Schooling is important," Lizzy said. "Max will be attending school this year too. He's staying with the Jamesons during the week. It's going to be a year of changes for us, isn't it, Max?"

"Yes, Ma," Max replied. He poured honey on another biscuit.

"I'd best be going, ma'am," John said. "Thank you again for the work."

Lizzy and Max followed John out to the farmyard. Lizzy could see the dust devils swirling in the distance as John mounted his pony.

She called to John, "Pull up your neckerchief so you don't breathe in the dirt."

He nodded and trotted west toward town.

"The dust storms are increasing in strength and regularity," Lizzy told her son. "Harvesting the wheat and corn from the dry fields will just make it worse."

She pointed to the dirty brown clouds and shook her head. "That's a bad sign, Maxie. Help me plug the windows to keep out the dirt."

Together, Lizzy and Max dampened old rags and stuffed them into the crevices between the windows and the window frames of the sod house. The house was airtight except for the windows and door, and years of whitewashing the interior walls had created a hard surface that kept out most of the bugs.

"One day, Max…one day, I'm going to have a timber-built house like we had in Missouri," Lizzy said. The dust storm reached the house, making Lizzy and Max thankful that their daily chores were done.

Every night, the wind screamed across the prairie, leaving behind piles of dirt that, except for the dirty color, looked more like snowdrifts after a blizzard. Even though they had plugged all the cracks and crannies around the windows, there was still a fine layer of dust coating everything in the house.

On the morning of the first day of school, Lizzy ran a finger over the film of dust covering the kitchen table and shuttered in disgust. "Dirt everywhere," she said. Then she remembered all the challenges she had faced, squared her shoulders, and began wiping down the table, the counter, and the cookware.

"Max, make sure you pack extra underwear along with two clean shirts," she instructed. "After breakfast, we'll ride into town and leave your belongings with Aunt Charlotte. Then it's on to school for you."

Until now, Lizzy had homeschooled her son. Like Lizzy, Max had a love of books. She'd seen to that by reading to her son every night before bed and on long winter days. But Lizzy knew that school was more than reading, writing, and arithmetic; it was a place where children learned how to play and work with others, to make friends, and to appreciate their neighbors. That was something that, as a single mother, Lizzy couldn't provide for her only son. She was thankful that Charlotte and Luke had offered to board Max so he wouldn't have to make the long ride into town and back every day.

"You'll like school, Max," Lizzy said as they rode into Shady Bluffs. "Miss Girton is a very good teacher. And you'll be back home after school on Friday..." her voice trailed off. Sending her child to school for the first time was an emotional occasion.

"Don't worry about me, Ma," Max said. "I already know some of the boys. Cousin Will and John Tomlinson will be there, and it will be an adventure — just like the new Jules Verne book we've been reading."

Lizzy sniffed and wiped a tear from her eye. "I think I'll miss you more than you'll miss me. But it will be an adventure, Max! A good adventure."

When they reached Charlotte's house in town, Lizzy and Max dismounted. "Let me kiss you here so I don't embarrass you." She hugged Max and kissed him on the forehead. "Now you mind your aunt and uncle."

"I will, Ma," Max promised.

Will Jameson emerged from the house with Charlotte and Luke right behind him.

"I can't believe our boys are old enough for school," Charlotte said. Then she turned to Max and William. "Better run on to the schoolhouse now, boys. The bell will be ringing shortly."

Luke, Charlotte, and Lizzy watched as their sons raced off to the one-room schoolhouse.

"There goes trouble," Luke said with a laugh. "I remember my first day of school."

Charlotte shuddered. "Please don't tell me about it. Lizzy, I've got coffee on the stove. Come in and have a cup."

"We'll need fresh cream for that," Lizzy said. She handed a pail of cream to her sister.

Charlotte wiped a layer of dust from the kitchen table, just as Lizzy had done in her own kitchen that morning.

"I can't remember when it's been so dusty and dirty," Charlotte said.

"It's worse in the country," Lizzy replied. "The dust storms are longer and stronger every day."

"Hmmm," said Charlotte. "I'm hearing stories about prairie fever. The wind and the isolation are causing some people — especially women — to go mad."

"That happened in Missouri, too." Lizzy recalled the stories of neighbors who went insane. "We just didn't hear so much about it because we had the war to worry about. But there were women left alone on the farm who were afflicted."

Luke changed the subject. "How's your harvest?"

"It's better than most out here," she answered. "I have the windmill and Hank Johnson to thank for that."

"I heard that Elias Crawford didn't get more than a couple bushels of wheat off his fields this fall." Luke shook his head with pity. "It's going to be a tough winter."

"I'm sorry to hear that," Lizzy said. "Even though Elias and I have had our differences, he's still a neighbor. I'll stop there on my way home."

151

Lizzy stood up. "It's time for you 'town people' to get to work, I imagine. I'll make a couple of calls and then head home. Thank you again for boarding Max during the week. It's a relief that he's not riding back and forth every day."

"It's what families do, sis," Charlotte said. She hugged Lizzy and waved goodbye.

Luke grabbed his hat from the rack by the door and kissed his wife goodbye. "Wanna bet her first 'call' is on Hank?" he said.

"I hope so," Charlotte said. "Hank's had his eye on Lizzy for years. I can't understand why those two don't realize that they're made for each other."

"He's been spending considerable time out at the farm," Luke said. "Of course, I've heard talk of that railroad man — Danbury, I think — flitting around your sister too."

"Yes, she's mentioned Adam Danbury. Apparently, he offered to build a windmill on the boundary between Nellie's ranch and Lizzy's farm."

"Nellie told me about that," Luke said. "Danbury said the railroad might 'need' a water stop thereabouts. I think it's an excuse to cozy up to your sister. 'Course, I could be wrong."

Hank Johnson was talking with a farmer when Lizzy entered.

"I'm terribly sorry, Ted, but you don't have enough collateral for another loan," Hank was saying to his customer. Ted Nesbitt sat in the chair across from Hank's desk and nervously rolled his felt work hat in his hands. His dusty overalls covered long johns with holes at both elbows.

It was apparent to Lizzy that the bank loan was Nesbitt's last hope. She cleared her throat to get the men's attention.

"I hate to interrupt, but I'll be hiring someone to help with the corn harvest," she said.

Both men turned to look at Lizzy. She was wearing a freshly starched shirtwaist dress. She untied and removed her sunbonnet as she smiled at the two men.

"I'm not lookin' fer a handout, Miss Ward," Nesbitt said. "Besides, the corn won't be ready for harvest until after the frost. That's a few weeks off. I was hoping to get a loan today."

"I'm not offering a handout, Mr. Nesbitt. I'll pay a fair wage for a fair day's work. If you can start now, I'll pay you to build a windmill tower in my farmyard."

"I'm decent with a hammer and saw," Nesbitt replied. "You've got a deal, Miss Ward."

"Wonderful. I'll see you tomorrow morning." She held out her hand for Ted to shake. Surprised at the manly gesture, Ted rose from the chair and shook Lizzy's hand.

"Yes, ma'am," he said. "Tomorrow morning, ma'am."

"Call me Lizzy," she said.

He nodded. "I reckon we're done here, Mr. Johnson." He put on his work hat and left the bank.

"That was mighty kind of you, Lizzy," Hank said.

"His wife passed away last spring, birthing their eighth child," Lizzy said. "He has a lot of mouths to feed. But it's not charity, Hank. I've been meaning to look for a hired hand. Nellie was a big help when she lived on the farm, but now she's got her own claim to work. And my half-section is more than one person can manage during harvest.

"That windmill was a blessing. My wheat harvest was one of the best I've had. I'll be able to repay part of my loan for the windmill once the miller pays me for the flour. I can afford to help one of my neighbors, and he'll be helping me."

"You're a smart businesswoman, Lizzy," Hank said. "A smart businesswoman with heart."

"Out here on the frontier, we all have to pull together," she replied. "The neighbor I help today could be the neighbor who helps me tomorrow."

"You're right about that. So, what brings you to Shady Bluffs?"

"It's the first day of school for Max. He'll be staying in town with Char and Luke."

"He's growing up fast," Hank commented.

"Soon, he'll be taller than I am. Of course, that's not saying much," Lizzy laughed. "I actually stopped by to invite you for dinner on Friday night if you're available."

"My social calendar is pretty open," Hank said. "I'd enjoy a homecooked meal. Thank you kindly. What can I bring?"

"You know me so well," Lizzy said with a sparkle in her eyes. "I'm hoping you can bring my schoolboy home. It will save me a trip to town. And, over dinner, we can talk about the new windmills I want to build."

"I'd be delighted on all accounts," he said with a smile. "And Lizzy, thank you for helping out the Nesbitts. I would have made the loan if I could have, but…"

"This works out better for all of us," she assured him. "I'll see you on Friday evening." She gave his hand an affectionate squeeze.

Lizzy stopped in the mercantile and purchased coffee, sugar, and a lilac-scented soap that Isabell had just received. Her next stop was the lumber yard to order the wood needed to build the third windmill.

Her last visit was to Luke's blacksmith shop. She found her brother-in-law working the bellows and hammering horseshoes on his anvil.

When Luke looked up from his work, Lizzy said, "I was hoping that Nellie might be here today."

"Not today," he replied. "Maybe tomorrow, though. Is there something I can tell her?"

"No, I might ride over to see her later this week. I'm wondering how the railroad crew is coming on the new windmill."

Lizzy mounted her horse and began the trip back to her farm. Then she remembered Elias Crawford.

Instead of riding directly east, she took the northeast trail to Crawford's farm.

When she arrived, she wondered what disaster had struck the homestead. The door to the tar shack was hanging off its hinges. The family's milk cow was roaming in a nearby field, along with several pigs. It appeared that neither the cow nor the pigs had been fed recently.

Tentatively, Lizzy got off her horse and tied it to a post by the house. She knocked on the busted door and called inside. "Elias, it's Lizzy Ward. Elias, are you in there?"

Then she heard the wailing. A woman inside was wailing and screaming. "Make it stop. Make it stop."

Lizzy stepped into the dark, dirty shack and saw a woman tied to the leg of the bed. She wore a torn, ragged night dress over her skeletal frame. The woman was crouching on the dirt floor next to the bed, which had a filthy mattress.

Recognizing the woman, Lizzy said in a soothing voice, "Florence...Florence...it's Lizzy Ward."

The woman wailed again. "Make it stop. Make it stop."

"Make what stop, Florence?" Lizzy asked. Lizzy had met her neighbor last spring at a church social. Even then, Florence Crawford was mostly silent, letting her unpleasant husband speak for her.

A figure darkened the door.

"What's the likes of you doin' here?" Elias Crawford growled.

Lizzy wasn't one to let Crawford intimidate her. "I was paying a neighborly call, Elias. I knocked on the door and heard Flo…Florence…inside. She sounded like she was in pain, so I came in to help."

"She's ailin' alright," he said. "But it's in her head. She's gone stir crazy, she has."

"What happened?" Lizzy asked.

"Don't know," he said. "A while back she started screaming about the wind. Claimed it was talking to her. Then she started wandering — day and night. I had to tie her to the bed when I left to do chores." He indicated the rope that tied his wife to the bed. "It's fer her own good."

"She needs help."

"Don't you go preachin' to me, Miss High-and-Mighty. We Crawfords take care of our own. You can be on your way. Be gone with ye."

Lizzy knew better than to argue with Elias Crawford. She took a different tact.

"Maybe Florence would appreciate some female company from time to time," Lizzy said. "I could stop by with coffee and biscuits." She turned to Florence. "Would you like me to come by for a visit, Flo?"

That seemed to settle the distraught woman. She looked at Lizzy, smiled, and nodded. Then, a beetle ran across her foot, and she started screaming again.

"It might soothe her some, Elias," Lizzy said. "And you'd be able to work in peace, knowing that someone was watching over her for a spell."

"Hmmm," Crawford muttered. "Mebbe."

He considered the offer momentarily. "Coffee, you say? Yeah, I could do with some coffee. Ain't had any real coffee in months. Yeah, you bring coffee and biscuits."

"I'll be back tomorrow," Lizzy said.

The visit had shaken Lizzy, but she wasn't about to let Elias Crawford see her distress. Instead, Lizzy started thinking about ways she could help her crazed neighbor. She'd heard stories about homesteaders — especially women — suffering from prairie madness or prairie fever caused by the continual winds, the isolation, or a combination of factors.

Oftentimes, these poor souls were shuttled off to insane asylums. Other times, the victims starved to death or wandered off into the vast prairies, never to be seen again.

News of the Day

The St. Paul Daily Globe, **St. Paul, Minnesota, April 12, 1879**

Headline: "Minnesota News"

Nineteen insane patients at St. Peter, belonging to Dakota, have recently been removed to the insane asylum at Yankton.

Chapter 12 – Autumn 1872
Letter from Home

The spectacle of Florence Crawford tied to a bed frame haunted Lizzy as she rode away from the Crawford farm. In her mind, she turned over options for helping her neighbor. Before she did anything, however, Lizzy decided she would discuss Florence's plight with Charlotte.

I need something — or someone — to cheer me up after that! Lizzy thought. She knew chores were waiting for her at the farm, but, shaking her head, she urged her mare down a path that led to Nellie's ranch.

Before she could cross the boundary between her farm and Nellie's claim, Lizzy saw the railroad crew working hard at building the new windmill. Nellie was on horseback, overseeing the operation.

Lizzy trotted up to Nellie.

"They're making good progress," Nellie reported. "The well has been dug, and the men are assembling the tower."

"This one looks taller than the one in my west section," Lizzy observed.

"Mr. Danbury — Adam — said your other windmill is on a rise, giving it a natural advantage. This windmill," Nellie gestured to the spot the new tower would stand, "is sitting on flatter-than-flat prairie. Adam said the taller tower would help it catch more wind."

"Makes sense," Lizzy agreed. She looked around for Adam among the working crew but didn't see him. "Where is Adam?"

"He was here, but then he received a telegram and took off in a hurry. I didn't even know the telegraph office would deliver telegrams!"

"It must have been important," Lizzy said.

"Must have been," Nellie replied.

Then, with a mischievous glint, Nellie said, "So you were hoping to see Adam? I'm pretty sure he's sweet on you too. Asks all sorts of questions about you."

"You make it sound like we're sweethearts — which we're not," Lizzy said. "Other than…"

"You kissed him, didn't you, Lizzy Ward!"

"More like he kissed me," Lizzy admitted. "But…I've discovered I like being kissed. It's nice."

"It is, isn't it?" Nellie said before she could stop herself. A bright red blush bloomed on her freckled face.

Lizzy scrutinized Nellie. "I believe there's a story there…a news story, if I'm not mistaken. I've seen how our town newspaperman looks at you. Am I right?"

If it were possible, Nellie's face blushed an even deeper red.

"I thought so," Lizzy said. "You've always been one to run headlong into any situation. For once, take a step back and just enjoy the courtship. You were awfully young when your parents sent you up to Dakota. I assume this is your first beau."

"I was only fifteen, and all the eligible beaus had gone to war," Nellie said. "So yes, Gregory is my first beau. But please don't say anything to Char or Luke. If Luke finds out, he'll be asking Gregory if his intentions are *honorable*."

"All right, I'll keep the news to myself — for now. But if you need any sisterly advice, you know you can always come to me."

"I'm not sure if you're the right person to ask," Nellie teased Lizzy. "Hank Johnson has been dancing around you for years, and you don't seem to take notice. Now this fancy-dressed railroad man shows up and you're ready for romance?"

"I always thought of Hank as a friend." Lizzy took a deep breath. "But recently something changed. I'm not sure what…"

"I can tell you in two words: Adam Danbury," Nellie said. "Lizzy, you've got two men who want to court you!"

"I'm an old maid — with a seven-year-old son, to boot! Most men would be running the other way."

"I think you're underestimating yourself. Char told me more than once that you were known as 'the pretty Ward girl' back in Missouri. You're still a looker."

"Enough! Now you're making *me* blush," Lizzy said. She felt the heat on her cheeks. "I actually rode down here to get cheered up. It's been quite a day."

"What's wrong?" Nellie inquired.

Lizzy described the scene she'd found at the Crawford farm. Nellie agreed that Charlotte should be alerted to Florence Crawford's condition.

"And it's not just the Crawfords who are hurting. The drought has ruined the harvest for so many of the farmers around here. I'll do what I can to help, but I'm afraid there will be homesteaders pulling up stakes and leaving."

She didn't share Ted Nesbitt's problems with Nellie, feeling it was more gossip than necessary.

"On top of all that, Max started school!" Lizzy continued. "He was so excited! But I'm going to miss him. He's staying with Char and Luke during the week."

A rider appeared on the horizon to the west. Lizzy didn't recognize the form in the distance, but it appeared Nellie did. Nellie began smoothing her unruly copper curls and bit her lips to redden them.

Lizzy caught Nellie's primping and raised an eyebrow. "That must be Gregory Collins. I imagine he's out here following a news story."

"Hello, ladies," Gregory called out. "I came to see how the Territory's second windmill is proceeding."

He jumped down from his horse and strode over to where the surveying crew — now a construction crew — was building the tall, latticed windmill tower.

"Who's the foreman here?" Gregory asked no one in particular. "Is Mr. Danbury around?"

"Mr. Danbury was called into town on business," said one of the men. "That means I'm in charge. We're following the sketch Mr. Danbury gave us. We're almost done with the main tower struts. Once we get the platform built, we're done here. Mr. Danbury is gonna assemble the gear shaft and the blades."

Somewhat disappointed that there wasn't more drama here, Gregory returned to where Nellie and Lizzy sat on their horses.

"It's not real exciting, Gregory," said Nellie. "Not like when Hank Johnson fell off the platform and broke his leg."

"Thank goodness," Lizzy exclaimed. "If that happened again, I'd say these windmills were cursed!"

She watched the lovesick looks that Nellie and Gregory exchanged and decided now was a good time to leave.

"I've been gone from the farm since sunup," Lizzy said. "There's a hired man coming tomorrow to start on the third windmill. I'd best be on my way."

She clicked her tongue to let her horse know it was time to go.

After she made some distance, she glanced back and saw Nellie and Gregory riding south to Nellie's ranch. Lizzy smiled to herself, happy for her friend.

If Adam Danbury had known that Lizzy would ride out to the construction site, he might have delayed his trip into town. But the Frontier Railroad home office telegram wasn't news that Adam had expected or hoped for.

Frontier Railroad's management was considering an offer to move the new line north to a town called Garfield, named for the Civil War general. Driven by politics and an incentive from local businessmen, Frontier Railroad instructed Danbury to take the crew north to begin surveying the new potential route.

Route changes weren't unusual, and Danbury was used to bidding wars between towns. A railroad line could mean the difference between a town flourishing or failing. Railroads were the country's lifeblood, transporting goods across wide stretches of the nation. The railroads also brought people west — people to populate the wide-open frontier. People who would purchase plots of land from the railroads and enrich railroad shareholders.

This wasn't the first time Danbury had abandoned one prospective route for another location based on which town would offer the most incentives to the railroad. Still, he'd gotten to know the folks in Shady Bluffs and hated to burn those bridges.

He arrived in town and went directly to the telegraph office. After sending a reply that he understood the instructions, he picked up his mail at the post office. There was another letter from home.

Adam opened the letter after he found a corner table at Betsy's Place.

September 20, 1872

My dearest Adam,

I had hoped that you would take time away from work for a visit home, but I understand the responsibilities of your job. Your Aunt Suzanne is doing poorly. Although your mother and I continue to nurse her, I fear the consumption will take her before winter is over. If that happens, I would like to invite your mother to come live with you, with your permission, of course.

But if, with God's help, Aunt Suzanne does rally and her health improves, I would like to travel to Dakota Territory in the Spring. I long to see this beautiful country that you always write home about. And perhaps it is time for us to set up housekeeping closer to your work.

Until then, please know that I live to receive your letters.

Your loving wife,

Margaret

Adam had just finished reading the letter and returned it to the envelope when Besty Tomlinson approached his table.

"News from home, Mr. Danbury?" Betsy asked.

"Uh, yes," he replied. "My aunt is ill."

He wasn't ready to discuss his marital status with anyone in Shady Bluffs.

"I'm sorry to hear that, sir. What would you be having for dinner tonight?" Our specials tonight are lamb chops and beef stew with biscuits."

As he ate the lamb chop dinner, Adam also chewed on his next steps. Tomorrow, he would have the crew finish up the windmill tower. They would pack up and move to the new survey site as soon as possible. He wouldn't have time to install the gear motor and the blades, and that would require a visit to Lizzy's farm.

Adam struggled with the fact that he was married but had still romantically pursued Lizzy. They had not consummated the relationship, but a dalliance was a dalliance. The letter seemed to burn a hole in his breast pocket.

The railroad's instructions were paramount. As for Margaret, spring was a long way off. Margaret might change her mind about coming west.

That night, Adam wrote back to his wife.

October 7, 1872

Dear Margaret,

I am sorry to learn of Aunt Suzanne's poor health. She is indeed fortunate to have you and my mother caring for her. Do not abandon her at this point. Although I long to see you, I know that your presence is a comfort to both my aunt and my mother.

My assignments in Dakota Territory continue to change. I am about to leave Shady Bluffs and will forward a new mailing address when I relocate. I fear I could not

offer a reliable home for you out here on the wild frontier.
The situation may improve with my next promotion.
Please be patient with me, I beg of you.

Give my love to Mother and Aunt Suzanne. As for
you, I keep you in my heart always.

Your loving husband,

Adam

Adam hoped his letter would dissuade Margaret from traveling to Dakota Territory. He liked to keep his personal life and his work separate. Having his wife live one thousand miles away was part of that plan.

Adam saddled his horse the next morning and returned to the work site. He intended the surveying crew to be on their way to Garfield by midday. He would stop at Lizzy's farm after that and make his excuses.

Danbury was pleased to see the crew had finished digging the well. The windmill tower was nearly complete. But he would not be able to install the pump motor as he'd promised. He hated to think that Hank Johnson might benefit from this lack of follow-through.

He instructed the crew to clean up the work site as much as possible, then pack up and head to Garfield, about forty miles north. They would camp outside town until he arrived.

On his way to Lizzy's farm, Adam considered what he would tell the feisty, blonde homesteader. He found her in the farmyard, working alongside a thin, rangy man in patched overalls. Lizzy looked up as Adam rode into the yard.

"Good morning," she said cheerily. "I didn't expect to see you today."

Adam jumped off the palomino. "I have some news. Could we…could we speak in private?"

"Come inside and have a cup of coffee," Lizzy suggested.

They walked together to the soddy. "What's going on out there?" Adam asked, referring to the hired man.

"That's Ted Nesbitt," Lizzy answered. "He's going to build the windmill for the farmyard. Then, when the corn's ready, he's going to help with the harvest."

"Hmmm," Adam responded.

"There are a lot of families who didn't have a decent harvest this year. Times are hard. He needs work, and I need someone to help around the farm," Lizzy said.

Adam took in this information and realized he couldn't tell Lizzy the railroad might be moving away from Shady Bluffs. That would be one more blow to the frontier town when drought and dust storms had already ravaged the pioneers.

"He lives near here?" Adam asked.

"His claim is directly east of here. His wife passed away a few months back, leaving him with eight children."

"He's lucky to have a neighbor like you, Lizzy."

"I'm the lucky one, Adam," she said. "I've had good fortune since coming to Dakota Territory. I have my health, my family, and friends, and this year I had a good harvest. I've seen what the frontier can do to folks. If we don't help our neighbors…"

His hand caressed Lizzy's face. "You're as beautiful as you are compassionate. I'm going to miss you."

Lizzy frowned. "Miss me? Where are you going?"

"The survey crew is moving on. We've completed our work here — more than completed it, by the way. Your windmill tower is ready to erect. But I'm afraid I won't be able to assemble and install the pump motor for you."

"Thank you! Digging the well and building the tower was more than enough help. But tell me more about your new survey work."

"Remember I told you that railroads often survey a number of potential routes? The home office wants us to check out an option north of here." He tried to keep information about the new survey as vague as possible.

"Yes, yes, I recall that. I'm sure you won't find anything as attractive as the route through Shady Bluffs," Lizzy said.

"You're right, I'm sure. But the railroads are competing for every mile of track between Chicago and San Francisco. This is an exciting time for the industry. It's my job to make sure Frontier is winning the war for miles of track laid."

He picked up his work hat — not the fancy top hat — and stood up, ready to leave. "There's just one more thing, Lizzy."

He pulled Lizzy to her feet and took her face in his hands. "I'll miss you, Lizzy Ward. I'll miss how your dimples frame your smile. I'll miss your bewitching green eyes. I'll miss the sound of your laugh. And I'll miss your kisses."

Then Adam bent down and covered Lizzy's mouth with his. As his hands moved down Lizzy's neck and back, he pulled her closer.

As he rode out of the farmyard, Lizzy couldn't help but compare Adam's kiss to Hank's kiss. Just as the men looked and dressed differently, Lizzy wasn't surprised to realize they kissed differently, too. Adam's kisses were…Lizzy searched for the right word…more theatrical, more planned.

Then she thought of Hank's kisses. Passionate was the word to describe those kisses, she decided.

News of the Day

Marshall County Republican, **Plymouth, Indiana, September 12, 1872**

News Summary: The West

Track-laying has been commenced on the Dakota Southern railroad, between Sioux City and Yankton, and will be pushed forward at the rate of a mile a day.

Dakota Dispatch, **Shady Bluffs, Dakota Territory, September 22, 1872**

Headline: Frontier Railroad Completes Survey Work

After a summer of surveying potential routes for Frontier Railroad's entry into Dakota Territory, the survey crew has moved on to a new location, according to Mr. Adam Danbury, Chief Survey Engineer. Mr. Danbury said he is preparing his recommendations for the line through Shady Bluffs. The town council expects the railroad to significantly boost Shady Bluff's economy with an influx of new homesteaders and a steady source of manufactured goods, supplies, and mail. Farmers and ranchers in the region will be able to send cattle and crops more easily and efficiently. The Railroad is now laying track in southern Minnesota.

Chapter 13 – Late Autumn 1872
Third Windmill

Lizzy was one of the few farmers in Shady Bluffs who harvested enough corn to sell to the mill for grinding in the fall of 1872. Most of her neighbors had kept what little corn yield they had harvested to feed their livestock through the winter.

When she stopped at the Savings and Loan to deposit her payment from the mill, Lizzy found Hank reading the weekly edition of the *Dakota Dispatch*.

"I find it curious that we haven't seen hide nor hair of the railroad men since the crew moved on," he said. "I heard they're surveying up by Garfield." He paused and looked up from the newspaper. "Not to pry, Lizzy, but have you heard from Danbury?"

"I assume they've been busy surveying," Lizzy said. "And, no, I haven't heard from Adam since they left."

"Did they get that windmill working on your southern boundary?"

As much as Lizzy hated to admit it, she said, "The tower is ready to erect, but it's still on the ground."

"And the pump motor?" Hank asked.

Lizzy shook her head.

The banker folded the newspaper and slapped it on his desk. "Dang it, Lizzy. We need to get that windmill up and running. Is Nesbitt still working for you?"

"He is. He's a hard worker, but he's not good with machinery."

"All right, then," Hank said. "I'm closing the Savings and Loan for a day or two and coming back to the farm with you. Between Nesbitt and me, we can erect the tower in the south field. How about the windmill in the farmyard?"

Lizzy bit her lip. "Ted finished construction on the tower, but it's on the ground too."

"That's not like you to put off finishing a project, Lizzy. What's going on?" This time, Hank's tone was less strident.

"Well, we had the corn to harvest, and I've been spending some time at Crawfords' farm," she explained.

"Elias Crawford? What in the blue blazes — pardon my language, but why are you visiting Elias Crawford?"

"Not Elias. It's his wife, Florence," Lizzy explained. "She's in a bad way. I've been bringing meals up to them. He has her tied to a bed frame, Hank. *A bed frame.*"

"What?"

Lizzy continued, "Florence isn't eating or speaking. Mostly, she just moans and rocks from side to side. Sometimes she screams. It's awful, Hank. I asked Char to make a house call, and she said Florence has prairie madness. Char said she's been reading that the never-ending winds and dust storms are driving folks mad."

Hank was stunned. "I've heard of prairie madness but thought it was an exaggeration or an excuse to put family members in asylums." He contemplated the news about Florence. "Can I come with you when you visit them again?" he asked.

Lizzy nodded. "Elias might take better to having a man stop by. He doesn't like me much. But then, I don't think he likes women in general."

"I'll pack some work clothes and saddle my horse. Do you have other business in town?"

"I had lunch with Max at school, and I've done my shopping. I'm ready when you are."

As they rode east to Lizzy's farm, they passed a stranger riding into Shady Bluffs. He tipped his black bowler hat to them.

"Shady Bluffs is getting busier every day," Hank commented after they'd passed the rider.

Ted Nesbitt was coming out of the barn when Lizzy and Hank arrived at the farm.

"Afternoon, Miss," Ted addressed Lizzy. "I've fed the hogs and chickens. The cattle are in the south pasture, but we might want to bring 'em closer to the barn. Feels like the weather is gonna turn."

"Thank you, Ted," Lizzy said. "I think you're right about the weather. We'll bring in the herd tomorrow."

She gestured to Hank. "Mr. Johnson is going to help assemble the windmill motors and install them."

"Howdy, Mr. Johnson. That day at your office turned out to be a lucky break for me and my young'uns. A steady job is a sight better than a loan."

"I'm glad it worked out for you, Nesbitt," Hank said. "I'll start assembling the pump motors tonight so we can work on the windmills tomorrow."

Nesbitt nodded and then smiled at Lizzy. "I'll finish up here, ma'am, and head for home. It'll be dark soon."

While Ted finished his work and Hank unsaddled the horses, Lizzy packed a basket with a meat pie and a dozen eggs for Ted's family. When Ted went to the soddy to let Lizzy know he was leaving, she handed him the basket

"I wish I had a boss who made supper for me," Hank said in jest after Nesbitt had gone.

"I'd say that you do since you're here to finish my windmills," Lizzy replied. "Now wash up. There's a meat pie waiting for us on the table."

Afterward, Lizzy cleared the table so Hank could spread out the motor parts for assembly. While he worked at the table, Lizzy sat with her cat, Butter, in her lap and read a book.

"What are you reading?" he asked Lizzy.

"This is *Little Women* by Louisa May Alcott," Lizzy answered. "But that's enough for one night." She tucked a ribbon into the book, closed it, and put it beside the reading lamp on the table. "Up you go, Butter," she said as the cat hopped off her lap. "Time to hunt."

She let out the yellow cat, then stood behind Hank with her hand on his shoulder. She watched as he assembled the gear shafts.

"I had no idea there were so many tiny parts," Lizzy said.

"The instructions help, but it's easier since this is the second one I've built. I'll be able to assemble the third one in my sleep." He laughed.

"Speaking of sleep," Lizzy said, "I've made up the guest room on Char's side of the house for you. I'm turning in for the night."

"You're right. That's enough for one night." Hank rose from the kitchen table and turned to Lizzy. "Would I be too forward to ask for a goodnight kiss?"

She smiled; her hazel eyes met Hank's brown eyes. Then she closed her eyes and wrapped her arms around Hank's broad shoulders, showing him the kiss was welcome.

Hank bent down and enfolded the petite woman in his arms.

It was more than a goodnight kiss. It was a kiss that promised more. His hands moved down Lizzy's back and rested on her full hips.

He pulled her closer and whispered, "I want you, Lizzy Ward. I think I've wanted you since the day I first saw you. The day of the buffalo stampede."

"Mmmm," Lizzy murmured. "You made an impression on me that day too."

He pulled back from the embrace as if he were looking at her for the first time. "Lizzy Ward, I'd like to court you proper-like."

Lizzy gave a small laugh. "Hank, I'm a little old for courting. I have a son, for heaven's sake."

"You deserve to be courted, and that's what I'm gonna do, complete with flowers and sweets and buggy rides in the country," he asserted. "And now, like a proper gentleman, I'm going off to bed — alone."

She stood on tiptoes, pulled his head down level with hers, and kissed him one more time. "All right, then. Goodnight, Hank Johnson."

Life is curious, Lizzy thought as she prepared for bed. *Sometimes, Prince Charming isn't the one riding in on a white horse. Sometimes, the hero has been there all along, supporting and helping in small ways that make a big difference.*

She shook her head to physically clear Adam Danbury out of her thoughts. Oh, it was flattering to have a sophisticated man like Adam show an interest in her, but Lizzy's initial impression that he was a rake and a womanizer still lingered. Then her thoughts turned to the man sleeping on the other side of the house, and she smiled.

Hank was working on the windmill for the farmyard the following morning when he thought back to spending time with Lizzy the night before. *It was a domestic scene that I could get used to,* Hank thought.

When he declared his feelings the day of the picnic by the windmill, he had no idea if Lizzy returned his sentiments. They had been friends for so long that he wasn't sure they could move beyond that. Lizzy's kiss said otherwise.

Then last night, when he announced that he wanted to court her with flowers and buggy rides, he knew it was the right thing to do. The War had upended everyone's lives. Young people didn't have time for courtships. Couples rushed into marriages and then men rushed off to fight. Some people never even had a chance to know love. This was a second chance for Hank, and he intended to make the most of it.

He was still thinking about their kiss when Ted arrived for work.

"Lizzy's in the barn, Nesbitt," Hank told the hired man. "Our job today is to get this thing in working order. The motor is ready to install. First, let's get the tower in place."

The two men used a system of ropes, pulleys, and actual horsepower to position the structure over the top of the existing well.

"Lizzy's not gonna like this, but I need to climb the tower to attach the blades and the gearbox. Last time I did this, things didn't go well," Hank said. "Tell you what, Nesbitt. You climb up there, and I'll send up the blades and pump motor with ropes. Together, we can attach the blades and the gearbox."

Hank tossed Nesbitt an improvised safety harness. "Put this on and clip it to the rope. We're not taking chances this time."

With safety harnesses in place, Ted scaled the tower. Once at the top, he lowered a rope to the ground so Hank could wrap it around the windmill blades. One by one, Nesbitt pulled the blades to the tower platform.

"And now the gearbox," Hank said. He put the assembled motor in a burlap bag and sent that up to Ted by way of the pulley mechanism.

Then, Hank started climbing the tower.

"You're not going up on that tower, Hank Johnson. Not after breaking a leg last time," Lizzy ordered as she emerged from the barn.

"You know, you have a bossy streak about you, Lizzy," Hank said. "Don't worry. We're playing it safe this time." He motioned to the safety harness he was wearing.

"All right, but I'm going to be the ground crew," Lizzy compromised.

Together, the three-person team completed the farmyard windmill before sunset.

"We've set it up with a stock tank for now," Hank explained when the water started pumping into the storage tank.

Lizzy dipped a pitcher into the water tank. "No more hand-pumping water! This is such a luxury! Thank you, gentlemen."

She watched as the stock tank filled up. "Does it just keep pumping, or does it turn off?" she asked Hank.

The banker-turned-engineer pointed to a balance bar mounted on the windmill tower. "That's connected to a floating valve inside the tank. As the water reaches a certain level, it pulls the balance bar down. Then, the vane and the blades turn sideways to the wind, and the windmill stops."

"Ingenious," Lizzy said as she took in this mechanical marvel in her farmyard. "I should have asked when we put up the first windmill, but then you fell and, well, I didn't have time for questions."

Hank just smiled. "We'll do it all again tomorrow in the south pasture. Thanks for all your help today, Nesbitt."

"My pleasure, Mr. Johnson."

"Hank. Call me Hank."

"Sure thing, Hank," Ted said. "See you tomorrow."

That evening, Hank worked on the third windmill gearbox while Lizzy wiped down the accumulated dust and dirt in the soddy.

"The winds are really whipping up tonight," Lizzy commented.

"Sounds like someone screaming out there," Hank said. "I never noticed that in town." He stretched his arms to loosen the muscles in his neck and back.

"It's worse out here," Lizzy agreed. She finished cleaning and went to stand behind Hank at the kitchen table. She began massaging his shoulders.

"That feels...you have magic hands, Lizzy. A man could get used to this," Hank said, leaning into the massage.

"I appreciate your help with the windmills, Hank," Lizzy replied. "It's the least I can do."

Hank turned and pulled Lizzy into his lap. "Well, maybe a kiss would help, too," he suggested.

They nuzzled and kissed for a time until Lizzy finally stood up. Taking Hank's face in her hands, she said, "As much as I enjoy this 'courting,' it's time for me to turn in...alone. Goodnight, Hank." She gave Hank a final kiss and disappeared into her room.

The next day was a repeat of the previous day — this time on the border that separated Nelly's ranch and Lizzy's farm. The railroad crew had built a solid tower, and the new well was deep enough to produce water for both sections of land. The survey crew had also built a good-sized water tank that would serve the railroad's needs when the steam locomotives stopped to refill.

Hank and Ted dug supporting holes for the windmill tower, then used ropes, pulleys, and a team of horses to erect the thirty-foot tower. Once it was secure, both men climbed the structure and attached the blades and gearbox. As soon as Hank connected the pipes from the well to the water tank, the blades began turning, and the windmill began pumping water.

And, as men do, Hank and Ted stood back and admired their work.

"That's a good day's work, Ted," Hank said. "Let's get back to the farm and let Lizzy know she has three working windmills."

Lizzy wanted to celebrate. "Ted, I know you need to return home, so I've packed a feast for you to share with your family. There's a baked ham in the basket, along with potatoes, biscuits and gravy, and for dessert, I made a chocolate cake!"

"Th-thank you, ma'am," Ted said, seemingly overwhelmed.

"I would have invited them all over here, but it gets dark early these days. You'd best be on your way. Oh, and take tomorrow off. You probably have chores at your place that need your attention."

"Thank you, ma'am," Ted repeated. He remounted his horse and rode home with Lizzy's picnic basket tied to the back of his saddle.

"That's one happy man," Hank said as Ted disappeared down the road.

"He — and you — deserve it," Lizzy said. "There's a special dinner waiting for us inside."

They, too, enjoyed baked ham with all the fixings.

"Hank, I can't thank you enough for getting the windmills up and running."

"I told you I would support you throughout the project. 'Course, I didn't factor in the broken leg. Just needed a little time to heal." His brown eyes twinkled.

"But that's not the real reason I offered to help with the windmills."

He held her hands. "I want to be part of your dream to tame the frontier. To grow and expand this farm of yours. To build a legacy for years to come. People in these parts look up to you. The saying 'love thy neighbor' isn't just words to you."

"I think you're exaggerating."

"No, I'm not. Ted Nesbitt is supporting his family, not through a loan or charity, but through meaningful work — work that he enjoys. You've been tending to Florence Crawford even though Elias is a mean son-of-a...gun. He's never had a kind word to say about any of his neighbors, but that didn't matter to you. And when Nellie Jameson needed a home, you opened yours to her."

"Nellie is family," Lizzy protested.

"You would have done it for anyone. Heck, you adopted an orphaned baby without a second thought. That's just who you are. Lizzy, I love you for it.

"There, I've said it," Hank declared with triumph in his voice.

"Well, that's quite a speech," Lizzy responded. She put her hands to her flushed cheeks. "I don't know quite what to say."

Hank got to his feet and pulled Lizzy from her kitchen chair. He whispered in her ear, "You don't need to say anything. I just wanted you to know how I feel."

He kissed her soundly, then said, "But this banker is plum tuckered out after two days of hard labor. I'm calling it a night and turning in…unless you'd like to join me."

Lizzy reluctantly shook her head, turned, and retreated into her own sleeping quarters.

The windstorms howled for a second night. The sod house stood secure, but the windows rattled throughout the night.

In the morning, Lizzy wiped away a thick layer of dirt and dust from the counters, the table, and the stove before she began cooking breakfast.

"Coffee's ready," she said to Hank when he emerged from the far bedroom. Lizzy wiped out a coffee mug and poured a steaming cup of coffee for Hank. "Cream and sugar are on the table."

"I've gotta admit, I'm a little sore and stiff today," Hank said. "I'm looking forward to getting back to the bank and sitting at my desk for a spell."

"Could we check on Florence Crawford before you leave? You mentioned that Elias might take more kindly to your suggestions," Lizzy reminded him.

Hank nodded but concentrated on mopping up the last eggs with his bread.

"Mighty good breakfast, Lizzy," he said when he finished his meal. "Let's go call on the neighbors."

When Hank and Lizzy rode into the Crawfords' farmyard, they could see smoke rising from the chimney.

"That's a good sign. Somebody's home," Hank said. He dismounted and knocked on the door.

"Howdy," Hank called out. "Elias...Elias Crawford...are you home?"

Elias came barreling out of a shed that might have served as a barn. He leveled his shotgun at Hank and Lizzy.

"What do you want?" he yelled at them.

"Just making a neighborly call, Elias," Hank said. "Lizzy here said that your wife is doing poorly. I wondered if there was anything I could do for you."

"Ain't none of your business, banker. If Flo would stop that infernal yowling, we'd be just fine," Elias retorted.

"I brought some fresh eggs, a loaf of bread, and some side pork, Elias," Lizzy said. "I'll just leave it on the table inside."

Elias nodded in acceptance.

In the shanty, Lizzy found that Florence was still tied to the bed frame, but now she had a blanket wrapped around her to ward off the cold winds that blew through the shanty. Lizzy could see that Florence was still rail thin, but there was a bit of color to the woman's face. *Perhaps Flo is eating better,* Lizzy thought with hope.

Lizzy returned to her horse and nodded to Hank.

"Offer still stands, Crawford," Hank said. "Let me know if you're needing firewood for the winter."

"Humph," Elias said. "We can take care of our own."

Lizzy and Hank rode away from the Crawford farm. "How long do you reckon they can make it there?" Hank asked Lizzy.

"He's got a few pigs and a milk cow. Didn't have much of a harvest this fall. Your guess is as good as mine," Lizzy said.

"It's a sad story, one that I'm seeing way too often these days," Hank said. "I wish I could do more."

When they were out of sight of the farm, Hank dismounted and extended a hand for Lizzy to get off her horse.

"I need to get back to town, but I couldn't do it without one more kiss from my gal," Hank said. He pulled Lizzy into his arms and gave her a goodbye kiss that she would remember for many days to come.

Lizzy watched Hank ride toward Shady Bluffs, and then she turned her horse to ride back to her house.

A visitor was waiting for Hank when he opened the door to the Savings and Loan. Hank recognized the man as the rider who had asked about Gregory Collins when he and Lizzy rode out of town two days ago. The man was wearing a black bowler hat and a conservative, three-piece suit.

"Good day, sir. I'm Hank Johnson, manager of the Savings and Loan." Hank shook the man's hand. "What brings you to Shady Bluffs?"

"Mr. Johnson, I'm with the Pinkerton Agency."
He handed Hank an embossed card with the name "Josiah
Chatton, Detective." Below his name was printed
"Pinkerton National Detective Agency" and the motto
"WE NEVER SLEEP."

"I'm here about a missing person," Josiah
Chatton said.

News of the Day

The Weekly Miner, **Butte, Montana Territory, June 24, 1879**

Headline: Offering a Reward

Last Thursday officer Beck, Mr. J.B. Williams of the Pinkerton Agency and several other gentlemen formed a party visiting Mr. and Mrs. Thos. Godfrey, the parents of the child lost a week ago last Sunday....Finding it impossible to get any clue to the lead to the unraveling of the mystery connected with the disappearance of the little waif, the visiting gentlemen returned to town. One of their number, Mr. Robert McMinn, a well-to-do citizen of Butte, then had posters published and distributed offering a reward of two hundred and fifty dollars for such information as would lead to the recovery of the child, dead or alive.

Chapter 14 – December 1872
Pinkerton Agent

The Pinkerton detective's words got Hank's attention.

"A missing person, Mr. Chatton? How can I help?" We haven't had any strangers passing through lately — except for you."

"This event happened some time ago. The Pinkerton Agency has been retained to look for a missing child."

"Well, that's even more curious," Hank said. "There have been stories about tribes adopting children and raising them, but I haven't heard of any such incidents around Shady Bluffs. Maybe you should search further west."

"We believe the incident occurred *in* Shady Bluffs," the detective insisted.

Hank shook his head. "What makes you think that?"

Chatton pulled out a copy of the *Chicago Tribune*. He opened the newspaper to the story Gregory Collins had written about Lizzy's windmill. Hank scanned the story until he found this sentence: *Max, now age seven, was one of the few survivors from the buffalo stampede that killed his parents in April 1865.*

Hank was a good poker player, and now his poker face served him well. "I'm not following you, Mr...er, Detective Chatton."

"It seems fairly clear to me, Mr. Johnson. I interviewed Mr. Collins yesterday, and he confirmed that he wrote the article. He also confirmed that Miss Elizabeth Ward adopted an orphaned baby approximately seven years ago. That matches the period of time when my client's family — a son, his wife, and an infant — disappeared. My client has not heard from their family members since the spring of 1865."

"That doesn't prove anything," Hank replied. "Lots of people come west for all sorts of reasons, and sometimes it's to escape their families."

"That could be the case. That's what I'm here to investigate. Mr. Collins said you were present the day of the stampede."

"Yes, yes I was," Hank said.

"Can you describe the scene?"

"Bushwhackers — actually, former Confederate soldiers — stampeded the buffalo. The renegades funneled the herd right into town, down Main Street. I wasn't there when they found the baby."

Hank intended to keep Lizzy's name out of the story as long as possible.

"Lots of people were injured that day," he continued. "Some died that day. Others died in the days after the stampede." He looked directly into the Pinkerton man's eyes. "I saw a lot of carnage during the war, but I've never seen anything the likes of that stampede. Buildings were smashed. People were pinned under debris. We were fortunate that Doc Jameson was here."

Chatton made notes in a pocket-sized book while Hank continued to speak.

"When the baby was rescued, he was underneath the mother's body. She had shielded the baby. The baby's father wasn't far away. He'd been trampled. It was a bad day." Hank shook his head at the memory. "Ben Wilson, the sheriff, tried to identify the bodies, but the couple's wagon and belongings were smashed beyond recognition. There was nothing left to trace them, so notices were sent to Yankton and Sioux City. Have you talked with Sheriff Wilson?"

"I met with him immediately after confirming the veracity of the newspaper story," Chatton said.

"Then you probably have more information than I do," Hank said.

"I intend to speak with Miss Ward, the woman who adopted the orphaned baby," Chatton said.

"Hmm…and how will you prove — or disprove — that Miss Ward's son is the relative of your client?"

"My task is to ascertain the possibility, regardless of how remote that possibility may be, that young Max Ward is the grandson of my client. If my investigation concludes that he could indeed be their long-lost grandson, they will follow through."

"And what would that include?"

"Any number of actions, Mr. Johnson. I hesitate to expound on the options open to the family."

"I see," Hank said. He knew from experience that no good could come from it when men spoke in pretentious language as Mr. Chatton was using.

"If you do not have any other questions for me, I have work to do," Hank said, indicating that the interview was over.

"One more question," Chatton said.

Hank looked up and waited for Chatton's question.

"Can you direct me to Miss Ward's farm?"

"No," Hank answered. "You're a detective. Figure it out."

Hank watched as Josiah Chatton exited the bank. He pondered his next steps, then decided a conversation with Luke was in order. Turning the "Open" sign to "Closed," Hank locked the front door and headed to the blacksmith's shop.

Luke was watching Nellie shape and pound a horseshoe when Hank walked in. She pumped the bellows to make the fire hotter, then stuck the horseshoe in the flames to soften the metal.

"Nice job," Luke said. "You'd make a decent blacksmith, and you're already a better farrier than I am."

Nellie beamed.

Luke looked up when Hank made his presence known. "Morning, Hank. Help yourself to a cup of coffee." Luke motioned to the always-ready pot of coffee on the stove. "You've been out of town a couple of days. Bank business?"

"Yes and no," Hank answered. "I was helping Lizzy get those last two windmills up and running. Since the bank loaned her part of the money to purchase the equipment, it was bank business, but I also wanted to help her out. The railroad crew up and left before the tower and gearbox were in place."

He turned to Nellie and said, "The windmill on your north section is now working."

Nellie nodded. "I rode by the site this morning. The water tank is nearly full. Thank you."

"My pleasure. I just hope more farmers and ranchers follow Lizzy's lead. That was one of the reasons the bank loaned her the money. It's smart business."

"I'm hoping so, Mr. Johnson," Nellie said. She pulled off the heavy leather gloves and apron and hung them on a hook. "That does it for me today. I've got a couple of stops to make in town, then I'll be back for my horse."

Nellie tucked her tumble of hair into the hood of her coat. She pulled on thick, woolen mittens and waved goodbye to the two men.

"By 'couple of stops to make,' Nellie means she's going to visit Greg Collins," Luke snorted. "Ah, young love. Speaking of romance, Johnson, when are you going to declare for my sister-in-law?"

"Working on it, Jameson," Hank replied. "But that's not what brings me here. I just had a conversation with that Pinkerton man. Have you talked with him?"

"Oh, yeah," Luke said. "He's gonna be trouble. He paid Charlie and me a visit last night after supper. He's making the rounds."

"Do you think there's any chance that Lizzy's boy is the missing grandson? Hiring a Pinkerton agent takes money. They won't stop until they get what they want."

"My thoughts exactly," Luke said.

"Still, I don't know how they can *prove* that Max is the missing boy after all these years," Hank said. "Chatton said the family would be taking action. I suppose that means legal action."

"That's how those people work," Luke agreed.

"Did Chatton see Max when he was at your house?"

"No, the boys were doing schoolwork. Besides, I'm not certain that Chatton knows that Max is in town. He didn't mention anything."

"He's a detective. He'll find out sooner or later," Hank said. "I'm thinking I should let Lizzy know about this. I don't want her to be ambushed by this guy."

"Good idea," Luke agreed.

"I'll ride out today," Hank decided.

"Weather is gonna turn, Hank. If you're lucky, the weather will blow in before the Pinkerton man can leave town." Luke said.

Nellie went straight to the newspaper office after leaving the blacksmith shop. Gregory Collins was at his desk in the front office, rapidly writing his next front-page story.

He looked up when Nellie entered.

"Am I interrupting?" Nellie asked him.

"A welcome interruption," Gregory replied. "The newspapers back East are filled with stories about corruption and graft. They're calling it the 'Credit Mobilier Scandal.'"

"Credit Mobilier..." Nellie repeated the unfamiliar phrase.

"Credit Mobilier is a construction company that's working with the Union Pacific Railroad. Apparently, the two companies were overcharging the government for construction of the eastern portion of the transcontinental railroad. It seems that Credit Mobilier's stockholders also owned stock in the railroad."

"How convenient," Nellie observed.

"And illegal," Gregory said. "The stockholders were pocketing millions of dollars in overcharges.

"The thing is, Nellie, there were similar instances of graft when the Northern Pacific was laying track in Minnesota. I uncovered instances of fraudulent purchasing and shoddy construction. That was one of my first big stories for the *St. Paul Dispatch*. Railroad expansion appears to be built on graft and corruption."

"But that was the Northern Pacific in Minnesota and the Union Pacific out East," Nellie said. "Do you think Frontier Railroad is corrupt too?"

"All I know is that it seems odd that they literally pulled up stakes in Shady Bluffs this fall, and we haven't heard from them since. Danbury said he would be making recommendations to the board a couple of months ago."

"How can you find out what's going on?" Nellie asked. "It's not like the board of directors will do an interview with you, even if you could go to the home office."

"No, but maybe someone in Garfield knows what's going on," Gregory mused. "I think I'll make a trip to our neighboring town to the north. Frontier Railroad will be under pressure from shareholders to turn a profit quickly now that Dakota Southern Railway has just about completed the line from Sioux City to Yankton.

"But first, there's something that might interest you in the press room," he said. He rose from his desk chair and, taking Nellie's hand, led her into the adjourning room behind the front office.

Under the bright lights of the Gutenberg printing press, Gregory removed Nellie's hood and ran his fingers through her hair. "I've wanted to do that since you entered the office," he said. "It's hard to keep my mind on work when you're around, Nellie. All I can think about is kissing you and…" He covered Nellie's mouth with his own and demonstrated what he was thinking.

"You are delicious, Nellie Jameson," he whispered as he nuzzled her ear.

"I had no idea that journalism was so exciting," Nellie said in jest.

"It has its moments, Miss Jameson," Gregory said, picking up on Nellie's banter.

"As much as I'd like to stay and continue our conversation, I need to get back to the ranch. Luke thinks there's a storm brewing."

Gregory cradled Nellie's face in his hands and kissed her. "Be safe, Nellie."

"Gregory, what if someone saw us kissing in your front office! It's scandalous," Nellie exclaimed.

"Nellie, it would hardly be a scandal — everyone knows we're courting."

"Really?"

"Yes, really," Gregory confirmed.

"Even my brother?"

"Especially your brother," Gregory replied. "I'll stop by when I return from Garfield."

As it happened, Nellie was riding out of town when Hank set out for Lizzy's farm.

"Would you mind some company for part of the way?" he asked Nellie. "I'm headed to Lizzy's farm."

"Your company is always welcome," she said. "But I thought you just returned this morning?"

"I've got some news that can't wait."

"Oh?"

"It's confidential. Lizzy can tell you if she wishes," Hank answered.

"Fair enough," Nellie said.

They discussed Gregory's suspicions regarding the Frontier Railroad, the Credit Mobilier scandal, and the ongoing drought.

"It was a dry summer and fall…and we've seen barely a trace of snow so far," Nellie said. "The coming year will be worse if we don't get some snow this winter and some good rains in the spring."

"I've already heard talk about several homesteaders abandoning their claims and moving west," Hank said.

The two riders parted after crossing Medicine Creek, the western border to Lizzy's lands.

Nellie waved goodbye and said, "Give Lizzy my love. Tell her I'll stop by later this week."

He was at Lizzy's farm by early afternoon.

Lizzy greeted him in the farmyard. "Did you lose your way? You just left a few hours ago." Then she saw the concerned look on his face. "What's happened? Did something happen to Max? Is he alright?"

"Max is safe and sound, but I *am* here about him." Hank dismounted and tied up the horse at the hitching rail by Lizzy's porch.

"Come on in. That's a cold ride from town," she said.

Lizzy dried her hands on a towel, then sat across from Hank at the table. She waited for Hank to speak.

"There's a man in town — a Pinkerton detective — asking around about a family that died during the stampede. Questions about Max, in particular."

Lizzy shook her head in disbelief.

"It seems that the story Gregory wrote about your windmill was picked up by papers back East. Someone made a connection between the time when you found Max and when their relatives disappeared on their way West. The Pinkerton man is trying to connect the dots.

"Lizzy, the timing is right, but I don't see how they can prove that Max is the missing baby they're looking for," Hank concluded.

"What do I do?"

"That's why I'm here. The detective, Josiah Chatton, is planning to come out here to talk with you. I didn't want you to be blindsided." He took Lizzy's trembling hands in his and rubbed them reassuringly. "Take a breath. We can handle this together."

They discussed the possibility that Max was the grandson someone out East was searching for. Hank related the other interviews that Chatton had conducted with Sheriff Wilson, Luke and Charlotte, and Gregory Collins.

"I think I was the last one on his list. From what I could gather, Chatton doesn't have any conclusive evidence. He's just poking around, but he might ask you some rough questions."

"Like what?"

"Did you find any photos or letters in Max's blankets? Was there a family name on anything you found?"

Lizzy shook her head. "You know the answers to those questions. You were there."

"Yes, but Chatton has to prove something to earn his fee. If he can't prove anything, he can at least cast a shadow of doubt on Max's identity."

"I don't want to lose him, Hank. He's my son. He's family," Lizzy said. A tear rolled down her cheek.

He wiped away her tear, then pulled out his handkerchief and handed it to her.

"I'll stick around until Chatton shows up. I won't let him question you alone."

As if on cue, there was a knock on the door. Lizzy opened the door to see a stranger wearing a dark bowler hat and a long duster coat.

He tipped his hat and said, "Ma'am, I'm looking for Miss Elizabeth Ward."

"And you are…" Lizzy replied.

"I am Josiah Chatton with the Pinkerton Agency." He handed Lizzy an embossed card identical to the one he'd given Hank.

Lizzy invited Chatton into the soddy. She couldn't tell if he was surprised to see Hank at the kitchen table. Chatton's face was expressionless.

"Have a seat, Mr. Chatton. Would you like a cup of coffee?"

"Yes, please. There's a chill in the air today." Chatton removed his hat, gloves, and duster. "I expect you know why I'm here."

"Why don't you tell me," Lizzy said calmly. Her tears were gone, and she was ready to defend her family.

Chatton relayed the background information and how his clients had read about an orphaned baby that matched the timeline of when their family members had headed West. Without divulging his client's name, Chatton implied that the family was wealthy and had the means to pursue this case.

"Mr. Chatton, thousands of people journey West every year, and hundreds of them are never heard from again," Lizzy said.

"You're correct, of course. But not every family had an infant son who would be seven years old now. That is what piqued my client's attention and why I'm here. I'd like to meet the boy."

"He's not here," Lizzy countered.

The detective tilted his head in question. "Where is he?"

Before Lizzy could respond, Hank said, "Lizzy's son is away at school."

"I can see we are at an impasse," the detective said. "I will prepare my report for our client. You may be assured you will be hearing from us again."

With that, Josiah Chatton donned his long coat and gathered his hat and gloves.

"Good day, Miss Ward and Mr. Johnson."

Lizzy did not see Chatton to the door. When the detective had departed, Lizzy slumped in her chair.

"Lizzy, you did well," Hank said. "You stood your ground. You were calm and collected. If Chatton returns, it won't be because you gave him reason to suspect Max is the missing boy."

The strain of the interview came crashing down on Lizzy, and she began to cry uncontrollably. Hank came around to her side of the table and rubbed her shoulders.

"I can't lose Max. What would I do? I always knew he belonged to another family, but with his parents gone, I thought I could be his family."

Hank helped Lizzy out of her chair and walked her to her favorite reading chair. "You sit and relax while I make you a cup of tea," he said.

Lizzy sipped a cup of chamomile tea while Hank cooked dinner for the couple. There was little conversation that evening, but there was not much need for talk. Hank's presence was all the comfort that Lizzy required.

News of the Day

The Chicago Tribune, **Chicago, Illinois, September 17, 1872**

Headline: The Credit Mobilier and Old Tammany

But the Credit Mobilier was formed on purpose to abstract from the Union Pacific Company, and divide among shareholders of the Credit Mobilier, the surplus funds that would otherwise have reduced the bonds loaned to the Union Pacific by the Government. …They contrived that the Credit Mobilier should milk the Union Pacific dry, draining it of half its proper capital, and dividing the same as profits of the Credit Mobilier. In this Pacific Railroad swindle, the Pacific Railroad takes the place of Garvey, who draws the money from the Treasury. The Credit Mobilier takes the place of the Tammany thieves, who divide it.

Chapter 15 – December 1872

Midnight Caller

Light snow had started falling when Lizzy and Hank retired to their separate sleeping quarters. Lizzy woke after midnight to the sounds of someone pounding on her front door. Pulling on her robe, she got to the door about the same time as Hank.

Much to her surprise, it was a frantic Elias Crawford.

"She's gone! Flo got loose, and she's gone," he screamed in a frenzy.

"Elias, come in and tell us what's happened," Lizzy said, trying to calm her hysterical neighbor. When she pulled Elias into the soddy, she saw that there was now a raging blizzard outside.

"When did you notice that your wife was gone?" Hank asked.

"Johnson? What are you doing here? Are you shacking up with 'Miss' Ward," Crawford taunted Hank.

"Crawford, I'm not putting up with insults. You came here for help. If you want our help, you'd best mind your manners," Hank said. "Now, when did Florence get out?"

Elias raked his hand through his snow-covered hair. "Must've been a few hours ago. The fire had gone out in the stove, and I went to feed it. That's when I saw her bed was empty. I went out looking for her, but the blowing snow has covered her footprints. I figured I'd start tracking her south — thought she might come this way since you've been kind to her, Miss Lizzy."

Lizzy handed Elias a cup of hot coffee. "Here, warm yourself."

Elias took a sip and then continued his story. "But when I went out into the storm, I realized there's no way Flo would know which direction to go. I kept going this way because I thought you could help me search for her."

"We'll do what we can," Hank said. "It's hard enough to search for someone on the prairie during the day — blizzard or no blizzard — but it's downright dangerous at night. It'll be light in a few hours. Hunker down here until morning. There's no sense in all three of us going out in the dark and getting lost in the blizzard."

It seemed like sunrise would never arrive. Elias Crawford spent the night pacing the floor. Lizzy baked biscuits and cooked sausage gravy. Hank took Crawford's horse to the barn and decided to feed and water all the animals to save time in the morning.

Eventually, there was a golden glow on the eastern horizon. The search party was ready to set out when there was sufficient daylight. The snowfall tapered off, and the winds subsided. Hank determined it was safe enough to set out as long as they kept each other within sight. Since Florence had fled on foot, they rode north toward Crawford's farm.

"We'll start searching as we ride to your farm, Crawford," Hank said. "Then, when we get to your place, we'll search in expanding circles around your house. Look for snow drifts that seem out of place. I hate to say it, but Florence might be in one of those drifts. Use your pole to 'test' the drift."

Each member of the team had a long pole to gently probe unusual snow drifts for the missing woman. Lizzy wasn't sure whether or not she wanted to find Florence in a snow drift.

The glare on the new-fallen snow was blinding. Lizzy wrapped a scarf around her head, covering her entire face except for a slit across her eyes. The men followed Lizzy's example. They rode three-across with ten to twenty feet of space between riders. It was slow-going through the new-fallen snow. The cold temperatures and the drought resulted in a thick blanket of light and powdery snow that was difficult to ride through. The snow drifted, creating an uncertain terrain for horses and riders, so they rode slowly, which gave them time to search for Florence.

When they reached Crawford's tar paper shanty, they still hadn't seen any evidence of the missing woman.

"Let's go in and warm up," Elias suggested.

Hank, Lizzy, and Elias tied their horse to the hitching rail and trudged into the tiny house through the knee-deep snow drifts. The cookstove still had fuel, so the house was tolerably warm.

Lizzy unwrapped her scarf. It was stiff because the snow that had melted from her breath had refrozen to create an icy shield. She draped it near the stove to thaw out. Removing her mittens, she placed the coffee pot on the stove and reheated the day-old brew.

Hank and Elias gratefully accepted hot coffee while they planned their next steps.

"We'll use the house as the center of the grid," Hank said, "and we'll ride in expanding circles. That way, we'll cover all the possible routes that Florence might have taken."

Elias was so cold that he shook as he brought the coffee mug to his mouth. "Good plan," he responded.

Hank took control of the search party. After he'd finished his coffee, he put his hat, mittens, and scarf back on. He had kept his coat on to save time and stay warmer in the shanty. Lizzy and Elias followed suit. Soon, the searchers were back on horseback. They started close to the house and rode circles around the farmyard. Just as they did earlier, they rode three abreast, enabling them to cover and search more land.

The winter sun was high in the sky, probably past noon when Hank spotted an irregular shape. Using his "testing stick," he probed the bump. It did not go very deep.

"I may have something here," Hank called out as he jumped off his horse.

This wasn't the first time they'd stopped their search to investigate. Lizzy and Elias waited until the obstacle had been identified.

Hank brushed the snow away and let out a groan.

"Elias, Lizzy... I've found her," he called out.

They rushed to the spot where Hank was. In his haste, Elias nearly fell off his horse. Lizzy dismounted and helped Elias wade through the snow drifts.

Hank continued to brush away the snow, uncovering a body curled into a fetal position. It was Florence. Her skin was pale blue-gray, as if all the blood had left her body. She was wearing only her thin nightgown and was barefoot.

"How did she get so far?" Elias asked no one in particular. "She's hundreds of yards from the house. How...why...," his voice trailed off. He started crying inconsolably.

"Let's get her home," Lizzy said softly.

Hank picked up Florence's frozen form and began walking back to the farmhouse. Elias led his horse and walked with Hank while Lizzy caught the reins of Hank's horse and rode back to the shanty.

Lizzy put more buffalo chips in the stove to warm the house. By the time Hank and Elias returned with Florence's body, Lizzy had fresh coffee brewing and had reheated the dinner from the night before. She spread a quilt on the floor and helped Elias wrap Florence in the blanket.

"What do I do now?" Elias asked. "I can't bury her. The ground is frozen."

"We'll put her in the barn until we can make a permanent resting place for her," Hank told Elias.

"But it's so cold in the barn," Elias sobbed.

Hank and Lizzy looked at each other and wondered how to handle this new dilemma. Lizzy put her arm around Elias. "She'll be alright for now, Elias," Lizzy comforted him.

Elias seemed to regain some composure. "Yes, that would be the best place for her," he agreed.

Gathering his dead wife into his arms, Elias Crawford carried Florence to the barn. He placed her in the back of his wagon.

"I'll build her a coffin this week. We'll say words over her this spring when the ground thaws," he said.

"Elias, would you like us to stay with you tonight?" Lizzy asked.

"Nah. Flo wasn't much company when she was alive. I reckon I won't feel too alone without her. You folks go home. And thank you kindly for coming out to help search for her. I don't know anyone else in the Territory who would've done that, Miss Lizzy," Elias said.

"We'd best head out directly. It'll be dark soon," Hank said. "I'll saddle the horses, Lizzy."

While Hank cared for the horses, Lizzy had a heart-to-heart talk with her neighbor. "Elias, we've had our differences in the past, but neighbors should take care of neighbors. I'm glad you felt you could come to me in a time of need. If there's anything else I can do to help you, please let me know."

"Thank you again," Elias said.

It was a frigid ride back to Lizzy's farm, but Lizzy and Hank made good time. They arrived at Lizzy's sod house just as the sun was setting in the winter sky. Ice crystals in the air colored the sunset shades of lavender, pink, and orange. The few trees that dotted the prairie were draped in snowy white capes.

She dismounted and pointed to the vivid sunset. "This is why I'm here. Mother Nature's paintings are breathtaking."

"That they are," Hank said. "But nothing takes my breath away like the sight of you, Lizzy Ward."

He stepped closer, put an arm around Lizzy's waist, and whispered, "The golden sheen of your hair, those dazzling green-gray eyes, and your rosy lips are what men dream of — what *I* dream of."

Lizzy turned her hazel eyes on the big man. "You're a sight to behold, too, Hank Johnson. And, truth be told, I've been thinking a lot about 'us' today."

"We should continue this conversation after I've seen to the horses," Hank suggested.

"Yes, we should."

When Hank returned from the barn, Lizzy had soup boiling and biscuits warming in the cookstove. He hung his long riding coat and hat on the pegs by the door and took a seat at the table.

"You were saying, Miss Ward," Hank said.

Lizzy took a deep breath and began.

"I'm not a young woman. I thought the time had passed for courting and romance. I was ready to settle into 'old maid status.' Yes, I have Max to watch over but he's growing up so fast, and," there was a hitch in her voice. "And now this business with the Pinkertons. But it was seeing Florence Crawford's frozen body that made me realize how lonely her death must have been. I don't want to die alone, Hank. I don't want to be alone anymore."

"Lizzy, I declared for you a while ago. I love you, and I want to share my life with you. Could you share your life with me?"

"Yes, Hank." A single tear ran down Lizzy's cheek.

"Why are you crying?"

"You really don't understand women, do you, Hank Johnson?" She swiped away the tear. "This is a tear of joy. Yes, I want to share my life with someone who loves me and who I love. I want to spend my life with you."

Hank stood up so fast that the kitchen chair tipped backward, but he didn't give it a second thought. He pulled Lizzy into his enormous arms and kissed her. She returned the kiss with an ardor that Hank had not expected but very much enjoyed.

"Am I being too wanton if I say that I'd like you to stay with me tonight?"

"No, ma'am. It's all I could hope for."

Lizzy laughed. "Ma'am?"

"Guess I'm a little tongue-tied," he replied, looking a bit sheepish. "It's been a while since I've been with a woman."

"Show me what you remember," Lizzy said, surprised at her own brazenness. She led Hank to her bedroom.

He watched as she unwound and unbraided her golden hair until it hung down her back. She unbuttoned her pale blue woolen dress and dropped it to the floor. At last, she stood before Hank in her chemise. He took a ragged breath.

Hank moved his mouth to cover Lizzy's. She returned the kiss with passion. His left hand held Lizzy securely while his right hand roamed Lizzy's lush curves, coming to rest on the swell of her breast.

Running his fingers through Lizzy's wavy blonde hair, he said, "You're the most beautiful woman I've ever laid eyes on. I thought I'd be romancing you with buggy rides and flowers. And here you are, standing in front of me as bold as can be."

"Oh, I still want those flowers and buggy rides," Lizzy said. "But I want this too."

She began unbuttoning Hank's shirt. Hank stood statue-still as she slowly undressed him. Finally, he took matters into his own hands and quickly finished stripping off his trousers.

Hank carried Lizzy to her bed. His lips traced kisses from Lizzy's mouth to her long neck and shoulders while his hands memorized the curves of her breasts and hips.

With a boldness she didn't realize she possessed, Lizzy explored Hank's body in response. Her hand traveled from the thick hair of his muscled chest to his flat abdomen and beyond. Hank moaned.

"Lizzy, are you sure?"

"I don't want to be an old maid forever."

That night, the winter winds howled, but Lizzy and Hank heard only the sweet murmurings of love.

News of the Day

Dakota Dispatch, Shady Bluffs, Dakota Territory, December 17, 1872

Headline: Dakota Southern Railway Nears Completion

It is reported that the Dakota Southern Railway is nearing completion. The railway was chartered by Yankton businessmen eager to improve commerce in the Territorial Capitol. The Dakota Southern Railway began construction just seven months ago and will connect Sioux City to Vermillion. Readers may recall that the Dakota Southern's precise route was controversial. The Yankton business community wanted to bypass Sioux City. Citizens in Clay and Union counties favored the southeastern route to Sioux City.

Chapter 16 – Late Winter 1873
Garfield Story

Gregory Collins' investigation into Frontier Railroad's behind-the-scenes maneuvering turned up a flood of information. His trip to Garfield resulted in a series of stories about a bidding war for Frontier's westward route.

Gregory suspected that the railroad was involved in some underhanded dealings, but he needed proof. Rather than present himself as a newspaper reporter from a rival town, he posed as Nick Jones, a land speculator.

When he arrived in Garfield, Gregory headed directly for the place where gossip and news thrive — the local watering hole. This watering hole was called the Dusty Trail Saloon.

Gregory — now Jones — stepped up to the saloon's polished bar and waved down the bartender.

"What can I get you?" the barkeeper asked.

"Something wet and cold," Gregory replied.

The bartender served a foam-topped draught beer. "First one's on the house."

"What are we celebrating?" Gregory asked.

"Word is out that there's a railroad comin' to town," the bartender said. "It's gonna put Garfield on the map."

"That so," Gregory said noncommittally. "I did some work with the Northern Pacific a while ago. Didn't know they were this far south."

"It's not the NP," the bartender said. "Those gents at the corner table are with Frontier Railroad." He pointed to a group of men playing poker on the far side of the saloon. Gregory saw that Adam Danbury was dealing the cards.

Danbury was easy to spot in his "dandy" apparel: a fancy gray frock coat over a silver-threaded brocade vest. The starched, white shirt was tied with a cravat that sported a large, pearl stick pin. The rest of the players were similarly attired. These were not the men who worked on the survey crew. These men were the decision-makers: the managers, owners, and shareholders in Frontier Railroad.

Gregory quickly turned away before Danbury spotted him.

"How long have they been here?" Gregory asked his new acquaintance.

From the talkative bartender, Gregory learned that the Frontier survey crew had arrived in town the previous fall. That meant the crew went directly from Shady Bluffs to Garfield. When Garfield's town fathers learned of the survey crew's presence, they began a campaign to convince Frontier Railroad management that Garfield would be a more profitable route for the company. Gregory needed to discover how much of that convincing was in the form of bribes and other fraudulent practices.

"And it's a done deal?" Gregory asked, probing for details.

"The mayor and his friends are celebrating, so I'd say it is," the bartender confirmed. "They're the ones who bought you this beer." Another patron signaled to the bartender, and the man moved down the length of the bar to take the order.

Gregory was familiar with the railroad industry's practice of pitting one town against another when a route hung in the balance. The railroads haggled for more land, the businessmen in small towns offered bribes, and the trading continued until a deal was struck.

But, Gregory thought, he hadn't heard of any deal-making in Shady Bluffs. That puzzled him. He needed to do some more digging.

Oftentimes, bartenders had their fingers on the pulse of a town. But next in line, Gregory considered, was the town newspaper.

The next morning, in the guise of Nick Jones, land speculator, Gregory visited the *Garfield Weekly Press*. He was pleased to see that the *Weekly Press* office was smaller than *Dakota Dispatch's* office. Also, he didn't hear the mechanical sounds of a printing press, so he wondered where the *Weekly Press* was printed.

Gregory found a portly man sitting at the solitary desk in the newspaper office. Gregory had decided that purchasing an ad in the paper might loosen the newspaper publisher's tongue. It would also allow Gregory to ask questions about the business community.

"Hello. Name's Nick Jones," Gregory said to the man at the desk.

"Howdy, Mr. Jones. I'm Murray Bales, editor and publisher of the *Garfield Weekly Press*. What can I do you for?" the jovial man replied. His office chair squeaked as he rose to greet Gregory.

"I need to place an announcement in your paper, Mr. Bales," Gregory said. "I heard there's a railroad coming through town. I'm a land developer."

"That's the rumor," Bales said.

"Railroads bring homesteaders, and homesteaders need land. That's where I come in," Gregory said. Gregory had watched as appraisers and land speculators in northern Minnesota made fortunes selling land to homesteaders when the Northern Pacific began laying track across the state. Gregory recalled that the speculators acquired the land legally or illegally and then sold it for huge profits.

But Gregory needed more information for his report. "So the mayor — I don't recall his name — is working with Danbury's group. Is that right?" Gregory thought dropping Danbury's name into the conversation made his story more believable.

"Yep. You're thinking of Mayor Robby Wiley," Bales supplied.

"I've been following Frontier's expansion for some time now," Gregory said. "Last I heard, Danbury's survey crew was down by Shady Bluffs. Why'd they move the route to Garfield?"

The newspaperman chuckled and rubbed his thumb and forefinger together in the international symbol for money. "Money talks and Garfield's businessmen spoke up."

Murray Bales paused a moment and then said, "Where did you say your tract of land is? Last I heard, Wiley and his group had acquired all the open land hereabouts."

Gregory knew his story could fall apart at any minute if he had to give Bales more details. "I'm afraid I am not at liberty to divulge those details at this time."

"Thought you wanted to place an advertisement. You'll need to provide particulars about location, acres, and such."

"My intent was to build anticipation, but I've decided to hold off for now. Have a good day, Mr. Bales." Having gathered more information for his story, Gregory left the newspaper office.

Now, he was ready to confront Adam Danbury.

Frontier Railroad had set up an office in a storefront several doors from the newspaper office. When he entered the railroad office, Gregory was taken aback by the lavish decor. Imported rugs covered the floor. Huge, ornate desks filled half of the room, with a luxurious velvet couch and matching settee in the waiting area. A crystal chandelier hung in the center of the room. Several private offices lined the back wall of the space.

A thin, young man in a brown tweed vest over a high-collared white shirt with a long, black necktie sat at the desk closest to the front door. The young man looked up when Gregory entered.

"Welcome to Frontier Railroad. May I inquire as to your business here?"

Gregory cleared his throat and said, "Yes. Tell Mr. Danbury that Mr. Collins is here to see him."

"Do you have an appointment?" the receptionist inquired.

"Give him my name. He will want to see me," Gregory said with authority.

The man scurried into one of the private offices. He returned in less than a minute and said, "Mr. Danbury will see you now."

Gregory followed the young man into the center office. Adam Danbury sat behind a dark mahogany desk. Except for a short stack of papers on the corner and a writing blotter, the desk was clear and gleamed from constant polishing. Danbury stood up and held out his hand when Gregory entered the office.

Addressing the office worker, Adam said, "Danny, please shut the door when you leave." When the solid door closed, Adam asked, "Gregory, what brings you to Garfield?"

"I think the better question is 'What brings Frontier Railroad to Garfield?'" Gregory replied.

"Have a seat," Adam said. "I'm a company man, Gregory. Just like you take orders from the *St. Paul*

Dispatch, I take direction from Frontier Railroad. When the shareholders in the home office told me to move my survey team to Garfield, I did so."

"There's more to it than that," Gregory said. "You gave the townspeople in Shady Bluffs the impression that the railroad was coming through our town."

"That *was* the original plan," Adam said. "But plans change. The businessmen of Garfield wanted the railroad more than the people of Shady Bluffs did."

"How do you even know that? No one in Shady Bluffs knows about the deal you've made up here," Gregory said angrily. "Don't get me wrong. I'm not trying to start a bidding war. Still, you understand the impact, the *economic impact,* that a railroad has on a small town. Why not give Shady Bluffs the opportunity to counter Garfield's offer?"

"It's that old game of 'who you know,'" Adam said. "Apparently, one of the shareholders was in the same army unit as Garfield's mayor. The deal was made before I got here."

Gregory's eyes narrowed. "I've seen enough of the way railroads do business to understand that deals can be made, and deals can be broken. Until the last spike gets pounded into the track, there's a chance that something will change. And even then, routes change when money changes hands."

Adam's poker face didn't hint at whether or not he agreed with Gregory.

Then Gregory Collins played his ace. "Does Lizzy know? Does Lizzy Ward know that you've moved the railroad? It will ruin Shady Bluffs. You owe her an explanation. She's the heart and soul of that town."

That statement stopped Adam Danbury cold. He shifted uncomfortably.

"Danbury, are you listening to me?" Gregory asked.

Danbury tapped his fountain pen on the desk blotter as he thought.

"You've brought up some excellent points, Collins. If Shady Bluffs wants to enter the game, I'll welcome them to the table. Thank you. It was good to see you."

Adam stood up from his desk and shook Gregory's hand. "You can see yourself out."

With that, Gregory Collins was dismissed. Dismissed from Adam Danbury's presence. Dismissed from the Frontier Railroad office.

Not having a plan after the meeting with Danbury, Gregory turned into the Dusty Trail Saloon.

I've ended up where I started, Gregory thought.

It wasn't that Gregory wanted a feud between Shady Bluffs and Garfield, but having a railroad was high stakes for any town. Gregory wanted to see Shady Bluffs prosper. In truth, he was a little surprised at how easily he had persuaded Danbury.

He snapped his fingers. *It was Lizzy,* he concluded. *When I brought up Lizzy Ward, Danbury's demeanor changed.* He nodded as he sipped his beer. *It was Lizzy Ward that turned the tide.*

As many reporters did, Gregory began composing his first news report in his head as he rode south from Garfield. As he imagined it, the story would enlighten readers about the railroad's survey work in Garfield after abandoning Shady Bluffs. Gregory would wait to see if Danbury actually showed up in Shady Bluffs before he wrote the next story in the series. Gregory was excited to see how this story would play out.

He toyed with the idea of stopping to see Nellie as he rode south. It had been a long winter with few chances to spend time together. So, instead of riding directly into town, Gregory took a trail leading him to Nellie's ranch.

Nellie's ranch soon came into view. Gregory saw Nellie working her stock in the corral. She was putting Thunder, Nellie's bay stallion, through his paces.

As he approached the corral, Gregory called out, "That's one impressive horse."

Nellie grinned when she saw Gregory. "Thunder is a natural, isn't he?" She trotted the stallion over to the corral fence. "What brings you out this way?"

"I'm returning from a business trip and thought I'd stop by on my way," he casually replied.

"My ranch isn't really 'on the way' from anywhere."

"You're going to make me say it, aren't you, Nellie Jameson?"

"I am, Gregory Collins."

"I've missed you, my red-haired vixen," he said with a smile. "It's been a loooong winter."

"It has indeed," Nellie agreed.

Quickly, they unsaddled and stabled their horses and disappeared into Nellie's house.

News of the Day

Dakota Dispatch, **Shady Bluffs, Dakota Territory, February 26, 1873**

Headline: Frontier Railroad Surveys Alternate Route Through Garfield

The absence of Frontier Railroad personnel in Shady Bluffs was not a coincidence. This reporter investigated the railroad's activities since leaving town. It was discovered that Frontier's survey crew was busy exploring an alternate route through Garfield, a town forty miles north of Shady Bluffs. It was also discovered that Garfield's town fathers enticed Frontier Railroad to change its route, thanks to financial incentives and personal connections. Shady Bluffs would be left high and dry in the race for railroad routes if not for the work of the Dispatch's intrepid reporter. Further discussions with Frontier Railroad's management may have resulted in an opportunity for Shady Bluffs to regain the upper hand in this negotiation.

Chapter 17 – Early Spring 1873
Second Chances

Ever since Gregory Collins had shown up in February, Adam Danbury kept thinking about Lizzy Ward and the chance of seeing her again. It wasn't difficult for Adam to convince his superiors that a bidding war between Garfield and Shady Bluffs would be profitable. Despite a wartime friendship that prompted the move to Garfield, the shareholders were always looking for ways to line their pockets. After exchanging several telegrams, Adam packed his bags and headed back to Shady Bluffs.

But Shady Bluffs did not roll out the red carpet for him or for Frontier Railroad this time. Gregory's series of articles about Frontier's under-the-table dealings created a firestorm in the small town. That firestorm resulted in Adam receiving the cold shoulder from businesses and town leaders.

When he checked into the town's only hotel, Adam's previous spacious suite was unavailable. Instead, Adam had to settle for a cramped room with two other boarders.

Adam took it in stride. He realized that he and Frontier Railroad had snubbed the people of Shady Bluffs. It was up to him to prove that Shady Bluffs *needed* Frontier Railroad's business.

His first stop was to meet with the town mayor, William Bartholomew, who owned and operated Bart's Mill, the only grain, or "grist" mill, in this part of Dakota Territory. People trusted William to give them a fair return for the corn or wheat they brought for grinding. That trust extended to electing him as the town mayor.

Bart's Mill, located south of town, had been built on the banks of the Mighty Mo — the Missouri River. The river's currents powered a huge water wheel on the outside of the building. That water wheel was connected to grinding stones inside the mill, which ground wheat and corn into flour.

Adam found William in the mill's basement, checking the drive shaft and gears that moved the grinding stones on the floor above. The noise in the mechanical room was deafening. When Adam finally got William's attention, the miller motioned that they should talk "upstairs."

William was a tall, slender man. He had wavy, salt-and-pepper hair and a bare stubble of a beard. A pair of gold, wire-rimmed glasses sat midway on his long, thin nose. He wore khaki-colored overalls over a button-up work shirt. There was a dusting of flour on the front of the overalls.

While it was somewhat quieter, the grinding stones and the moving gears beneath the floor were still noisy.

Adam introduced himself. "I'm pleased to finally meet you, Mr. Bartholomew. My name is Adam Danbury, and I'm with Frontier Railroad. Could I have a few minutes of your time?"

"I've heard your name, Danbury," William said. "I don't expect you're here to talk about the price of flour."

"No, sir. I'm here to speak with you in your capacity as mayor of Shady Bluffs."

"No one else wanted the job, so it fell to me," Bartholomew said. From his height advantage, Bartholomew looked down on the railroad man. "I thought Frontier Railroad was done with Shady Bluffs and never looking back. On to greener pastures, and by 'greener,' I'm referring to money."

Danbury gave an uncomfortable chuckle and said, "Never say 'never' in the railroad business. That's why I'm here. I'm hoping there's still a chance to route the tracks through Shady Bluffs."

"The land surveys around Garfield didn't pan out?" asked Bartholomew.

"Oh, the lay of the land is acceptable, but Frontier wants to make sure we're choosing the right route based on a number of factors," Adam explained.

"Such as…" Bartholomew followed up.

"To be frank, Mayor, we're looking for business advantages."

"And we're back to money." Bartholomew said it with more than a little sarcasm.

"Money is part of it," Adam admitted, "but there are other incentives that can come into play."

"Enlighten me."

"Building a railroad is a costly venture. The railroad companies offset those costs by selling tracts of land along the route," Adam said.

Bartholomew nodded. "This is a discussion that we need to have with the town council, Mr. Danbury."

"My thoughts exactly," Adam exclaimed.

"The next meeting is Tuesday night at seven," Bartholomew said. "We meet at the Savings and Loan."

"Thank you, Mr. Bartholomew," Adam said. "I look forward to it."

The men shook hands. Adam was pleased the meeting had gone as well as it did. He wasn't so sure about his next stop. He was bound for Lizzy's farm.

Spring was making its appearance on the prairie. Pasque flowers, the first flowers of the season, were blooming in patches along the trail. Lizzy was in her garden, hoeing furrows to plant vegetables. She bent down to test a clump of the newly turned earth, when she heard someone approach.

"You're in your garden, just as I imagined you," Adam said as he dismounted his horse. He held out a bouquet of pasque flowers.

"Adam, I'm surprised to see you," Lizzy said. She stood up, brushed the soil from her hands, and accepted the flowers. "And you're bearing gifts. Thank you. I'll put these in water."

She started walking toward the sod house and motioned Adam to join her. "What brings you to Shady Bluffs?"

"I see you put up the third windmill in the farmyard," he said.

"Yes, Hank and my hired man took care of it. They also finished the windmill that was supposed to be for the railroad's water stop," Lizzy said sharply.

She softened her tone. "I guess I should be thanking you and your crew for doing as much as you did. Hank and Ted had the windmill up in a day."

"I'm glad to hear that. I regret that we had to leave so abruptly, but we had orders from the home office," Adam explained.

And then a cloud came over Lizzy's face. "Orders, yes. I read about those orders in the *Dakota Dispatch*. Gregory Collins' stories made it very clear that Frontier had decided on another route. Frontier is leaving Shady Bluffs high and dry…just like most of the farmland around here."

Her hand made a sweeping gesture to indicate the tinder-dry prairies.

Adam put up his hand. "Whoa, Lizzy. That's why I'm back. When Collins visited me, he made a good case for taking a second look at Shady Bluffs. I talked with the shareholders, and here I am." He tipped his hat and bowed theatrically.

"I've already talked with Mayor Bartholomew," Adam continued. "He invited me to the next town council meeting. So, I'll be staying around for a while. I'd like to invite you to dinner tomorrow night at Betsy's Place. I was hoping we could pick up where we left off, if I might be so bold."

Lizzy chewed her lip as she considered the dinner invitation. There was Hank to consider. Her friendship with Hank had blossomed into a romance that she never could have hoped for.

"I must be honest with you, Adam. Hank Johnson has been courting me, and I don't want you to get the wrong impression. I'm not that kind of woman."

"It's just dinner between friends. And it's the end of the week. I thought you might be coming into town to fetch Max from school."

"I will be in town tomorrow," Lizzy conceded. "As long as you understand it's just a friendly dinner."

"Of course. Just a friendly dinner."

They agreed on a time to meet at Betsy's Place.

On the ride into town the next day, Lizzy thought back to her conversations with Adam. She had gotten to know Adam while Bill Anderson lay dying from rabies in her guest room. Lizzy remembered that summer evening they had strolled on the boardwalk after dinner at Betsy's Place. His attention had been flattering, but that was it.

She shook her head to shake away the memories. After all, it was just a dinner between friends. To cement that notion, Lizzy decided her first stop in town would be to see Hank.

She entered the Savings and Loan just as Hank spun the lock on the bank's vault.

"Hey, I was hoping I'd see you. After you pick up Max, would you like to join me for dinner?" Hank asked.

"I would, but I already have dinner plans," Lizzy said without elaborating. She decided telling Hank about dinner with Adam would just upset him. She didn't want that outcome.

"All right, next time then. I was thinking I'd come out to the farm tomorrow and take Max fishing. I'll stop at Betsy's and pick up fried chicken for a picnic. How does that sound?"

"That sounds wonderful," Lizzy said enthusiastically. "I know Max is itching to go fishing. Let's do it."

Lizzy's next stop was to see her sister. The bell on the door tinkled when she entered the doctor's office. Charlotte was finishing up with a patient in the exam room and called out, "I'll be right with you. Just have a seat."

Lizzy did as instructed, not wanting to interrupt the doctor's work.

At last, Charlotte and her patient emerged from the examination room. Charlotte told her patient, "Leave the bandage on until tomorrow, wash it with soap and water, and put a clean bandage on. Come back next week, and I'll see how the stitches look."

The boy pulled on his wide-brimmed felt hat and said, "Thanks, Doctor Charlie."

"Oh, and say hello to your folks for me."

"Sure thing, doc," the boy promised.

Lizzy watched the patient leave. "Was that really Betsy Tomlinson's younger son? He's grown so tall."

233

"I know. They grow up so fast! Just look at our boys, Will and Max. Pretty soon, Max will be taller than you. Of course, that's not saying much. You've always been," Charlotte paused to find the right word, "diminutive."

"Say it, I'm short. I know it. What I lack in height, I make up for in grit and sass."

Charlotte laughed and hugged Lizzy. "Don't I know it! It's good to see you. The school day is almost over, and the boys will be home soon. Come have a cup of tea while you wait."

"Tell me what's new," Charlotte said as the sisters walked into her home.

"I'm going to plow that field on the southwest side of your land this spring," Lizzy said.

"Of course, you would talk about farming," Charlotte said. "I want to know about *you*. How's the romance between you and Hank going?"

"Char," Lizzy scolded. "What are you implying?"

Charlotte laughed and. "You're blushing! You are blushing, Elizabeth Ruby Ward."

Lizzy's face turned a deep shade of pink. "You're impossible. It's like we're schoolgirls again."

"Love keeps us young, Lizzy. Seriously, it's about time that Hank declared for you. I won't press for details, but if you'd like to tell your older, married sister..."

"Ladies never tell," Lizzy said primly.

Then both sisters began laughing hysterically.

"I think we need some whiskey in that tea," Charlotte suggested.

"I'll drink to that," Lizzy said.

The sisters, who had always been the other's best friend, discussed the minute details of their lives, including Lizzy's love life.

"You were pretty frank with me when Luke and I started...," Charlotte's voice trailed off. She cleared her throat. "You were very clear about the possibility of becoming pregnant, if you recall."

"Yes, I remember that talk. It was actually one of our worst fights," Lizzy said. "Why are you bringing it up?"

"Not to be indelicate, but speaking as a doctor to her patient, if you need a prescription of Mother's Friend to keep you...regular...let me know. You would not be my only unmarried, or married patient for that matter, who uses a preventative."

"Thank you, Charlotte. I will consider it if the need arises."

The conversation moved on to town gossip. Isabell Vaughn had a gentleman friend, according to Charlotte.

"That's wonderful," Lizzy said. "Isabell deserves companionship."

"As do you, Lizzy," Char said. "Are you staying in town tonight to have dinner with Hank?"

Lizzy blushed again. "Actually, I'm having dinner with Adam Danbury."

"Really?!"

"This is just a friendly dinner, Char," Lizzy protested. "I told Adam that Hank was courting me."

"That just increases the competitive spirit in a man," Charlotte said jokingly. "The race is on!"

Lizzy laughed and shook her head. "It's just a dinner between friends."

Charlotte nodded. "Does Hank know?"

"No. I was going to mention it, but, well…. Oh, you know, Char."

"Indeed I do."

At that point, two boisterous seven-year-old schoolboys burst into Charlotte's kitchen.

"We're really hungry, ma," said Will.

"There's a plate of cookies on the counter," Charlotte said.

"And I brought fresh milk," Lizzy said. "Help yourself. But first, give your mothers hugs."

Char and Lizzy's conversation changed to family talk.

"Are you ready for school to be done for the year?" Charlotte asked.

"Yes, I miss having Max home. He's a big help."

"Have you heard anything more from the Pinkerton agent?"

"It's been on my mind, but, no, I haven't heard a thing. Maybe their investigation came to nought," Lizzy replied.

"Let's hope so," Charlotte said. "When are you meeting your *friend* for dinner?"

"Soon. I've got a couple of errands first. It was good to catch up with you, Char."

"And just remember, if you decide you need a prescription of any sort, you can come to me," Charlotte said.

The sisters hugged.

On her way out, Lizzy told Max she would return to collect him in two hours. He was to have his school clothes packed for the laundry and bring his books if he had schoolwork.

Lizzy made a quick stop at Vaughn's Mercantile. "How's business these days, Isabell?" Lizzy asked.

The shopkeeper grimaced. "I'm sure hoping we get some rain soon. The drought has everyone tightening their belt. And with the railroad being re-routed north, that going to hurt business too."

"I heard there's a town council meeting about that very thing next week," Lizzy said.

"So that's what it's about. I'll be there."

Lizzy pulled out the list from her handbag. The two women gathered Lizzy's groceries and supplies, carrying the purchases out to Lizzy's buckboard.

The post office was Lizzy's last stop before meeting Adam for dinner.

Shady Bluff's postmistress, Edith Somman, greeted Lizzy when she entered the small office.

"Good afternoon, Edith," Lizzy said. Please check to see if I have any mail."

The tiny woman — she was even shorter than Lizzy — turned to a wall of cubicles, searching for Lizzy's mailbox. As luck would have it, Lizzy Ward's mailbox was in the top row of cubicles. Edith wheeled a library ladder to the correct location, climbed up, and retrieved a handful of letters and a farming magazine addressed to Lizzy.

"Thank you," Lizzy said as she thumbed through the envelopes. There were two letters from friends in Missouri, a letter from Adam, and an official-looking envelope from Chicago.

Curious, Lizzy thought about the letter from Chicago. She was unfamiliar with the name and address.

She reached Betsy's Place and saw Adam waiting for her.

Adam rose from his seat and pulled out the chair for Lizzy.

"You look lovely today, Lizzy," Adam said. "How was your day?"

Lizzy was unaccustomed to such flattery, but she enjoyed receiving it.

"Thank you. I actually had a nice visit with my sister, did some shopping, and stopped at the post office. Say, I have a letter from you."

She pulled out the envelope with Adam's return address in Garfield.

Adam coughed in surprise. "Have you read it yet?" he asked.

"Not yet. Should I?"

From across the table, Adam took Lizzy's hands and looked into her eyes. "You were on my mind a lot when I was in Garfield. Instead of you reading it, why not let me read it to you? My words in my voice," Adam suggested.

"All right," Lizzy said as she handed the sealed envelope to Adam.

Before he could begin, Betsy Tomlinson stepped up to the table and greeted her customers. "Lizzy, Adam," Betsy said. "It's good to see you both here. Tonight's special is smoked ham from Lizzy's smokehouse, mashed potatoes, fresh spinach, and beets."

"Sounds delicious," Adam said. "I'll have the special." Lizzy nodded in agreement.

After Betsy had bustled away, Adam opened the letter he had sent to Lizzy. Clearing his throat theatrically, he began.

"My dearest Lizzy, it seems ages since we've been together. I was hoping to break away from my railroad duties to visit you this winter. Unfortunately, my work in Garfield is much more time-intensive than I had thought it would be.

Despite the tragic circumstances that led to Bill Anderson's death, I treasure our time together last summer. And although I could not finish your windmill, I am proud that my crew was able to dig the well and construct the tower. I hope you will think of me when you see that windmill in action.

Yours fondly, Adam."

He folded the letter, returned it to its envelope, and tucked it into his breast pocket.

"Lovely sentiments," Lizzy said. "And thank you again for your work on that windmill. It looks like this year will be as dry or drier than last year. Water from the windmills will make all the difference."

Lizzy continued talking about the state of farming, the drought, how her neighbors were doing, and what she would be planting this spring.

As Adam had framed, it was indeed just a friendly dinner. When they finished their meal, Adam helped Lizzy onto her buckboard and kissed her hand as a parting gesture.

Lizzy picked up Max, and they headed for the farm.

Lizzy was up early the next morning. She let her son sleep a while longer, knowing that her world would not slow down as soon as he was awake. She settled into her favorite reading chair with a cup of coffee and her letters from yesterday.

Curious about the letter from Chicago, Lizzy decided to read that first. It was from a law firm in Chicago.

March 30, 1873

Miss Elizabeth Ward,

This letter is to update you regarding the outcome of our investigation conducted by the well-respected Pinkerton Agency. The identity of our client's grandson points to the possibility that your son, Maxwell Ward, is that missing person. We will conduct additional inquiries into this issue and will be in touch.

Regards,

Sullivan, McIntosh & Baker Law Firm

Lizzy dropped the letter to the floor and began shaking.

News of the Day

The State Journal, Jefferson City, Missouri, August 14, 1874

Headline: State News

The corn crop in this part of the Southwest is suffering greatly from the protracted drought. In many localities the crop will be an entire failure, while in others it will be cut short fully one-half. – Neosho Times

The drought continues, the people are sore and much distressed, seeing that their labors are not likely to be remunerated with more than half crops. – Plattsburg Register

Complaints reach us from every direction that corn and vegetables have been destroyed by the drought, and that on this account, many fields will not be harvested. – Joplin Bulletin

Chapter 18 – Spring 1873

Dust Storm

Lizzy was in her reading chair, still as a statue. Max came in, followed by Hank.

Hank knelt on his good knee and looked directly into Lizzy's eyes. "Lizzy, what's wrong? What happened?"

Lizzy simply gestured to the letter at her feet.

Hank scanned the short missive from the law firm. He took a deep breath, then said, "Max, please make a cup of tea for your mother."

With Max in the kitchen, Hank took Lizzy's hands in his. "We will deal with this together." He squeezed Lizzy's hands in reassurance.

"The letter doesn't say they have *proof* of Max's heritage. It's all circumstantial. The timing, the lack of communication after the stampede. It's not cold, hard proof. They're saying that there is a possibility. But they can't prove it, Lizzy. No one can."

Lizzy focused on Hank's face. "He's not mine. They're going to take him."

"We looked for his kin after the stampede," Hank said. "There were posters and notices in the papers. No one responded."

"I'm going to lose him, Hank. He's my world," Lizzy's tears began to flow again.

Max returned with a cup of chamomile tea. "What's wrong, Ma?" Max asked, seeing her tears. "Did I do something? Why are you crying?"

"He should know, Elizabeth," Hank said.

Lizzy waved her hand. "I can't talk. You tell him."

"Max, you know how you came to be Lizzy's son? Your parents were killed in the buffalo stampede."

"Ma told me," Max said. "She found me after the stampede. My birth mother had covered me with her body, but she died."

"And you know that we did our darndest to find your kin back east."

The boy nodded his head. "No one claimed me. But Ma wanted me."

"That's right," Hank continued. "Well, it seems there are some people back East who think you might be their grandson."

"What does that mean, Mr. Johnson? Would they want me to leave home and live with them?"

"We don't know what their plans are," Hank said. "We need to wait and see. But we'll make it clear that you belong here with your mother."

Max's face crumpled. "I don't want a new family. I want to stay here with my family. I want to stay here."

The boy collapsed into Hank's arms and began crying. Hank hugged Max tightly and patted his back.

Lizzy slipped off her chair and kneeled on the floor with Hank and Max. She joined in the embrace.

"We know, Max. We know," Lizzy whispered. She rained kisses on his head, stroking the boy's hair as mothers do when trying to calm a frantic child.

After a time, the three pulled apart. Max wiped his face with his hands. Hank handed Lizzy a handkerchief for her tears.

"Let's put this behind us for the day," Hank suggested. "I have a picnic basket of Betsy's fried chicken for lunch and…"

"…and I baked a chocolate cake last night," Lizzy completed Hank's sentence.

Max's face brightened. "You mean we can still go fishing?"

"Those fish aren't going to catch themselves," Hank said. He rose from the floor and held out a hand to pull Lizzy to her feet.

They spent the day by the banks of Medicine Creek. Hank and Max filled their stringers with walleye, perch, and smallmouth bass. Lizzy watched the clouds drift across the bluer-than-blue spring sky. When she tired of watching the fishermen, she wandered through the fields of new spring grass and prairie flowers.

Lizzy gathered a bouquet of pasque flowers and thought about Adam's visit just two days ago. She realized he hadn't returned the letter he'd read to her at dinner.

How odd, she thought.

As they walked back to the sod house, Max and Hank talked about the ones that got away. Lizzy smiled at the banter. She loved her life. She would fight for her son. And Hank would be there to fight with her.

Max was exhausted from the activities of the day. He dropped into his bed shortly after supper. As Lizzy tucked him in, Max looked up at her with those deep green eyes of his. "I'll always be your son, Ma."

She kissed him on the forehead. "My mother used to tell me 'Worrying never did anyone any good. Ninety percent of what we worry about will never come to be, and we can't do anything about the other ten percent.' I'll always be your mother."

Lizzy joined Hank on the bench outside.

"I heard what you said to the boy, Lizzy. Your mother was right...no use worrying about things that won't happen. But *we will* fight for that other ten percent." He put his arm around Lizzy's shoulders, and she nestled into Hank's sheltering embrace.

Hank stayed the night, but given Max's presence in the house, he slept in the guest room.

Sunday morning dawned in a hazy whirlwind of dust.

Lizzy was stuffing rags into window frames when Hank entered the kitchen. "Help yourself to a cup of coffee," she said over her shoulder. "I've got my hands full trying to keep the dust out."

Hank poked his head outdoors and quickly retreated. "It's nasty out there," he exclaimed. "I might just have to hunker down until the wind subsides. Until then, I'll make myself useful by feeding the stock and milking the cows. But first, I'm having a slice of that chocolate cake."

Lizzy poured herself another cup of coffee, added cream, and joined Hank at the table.

"Thank you for staying last night. I was in a bad way," she said.

"Don't give it another thought. I'm just glad I was here for you."

Changing topics, Lizzy said, "I heard the town council is going to meet with Frontier Railroad this week."

Hank sighed. "The railroads like to play fast and loose with the towns they pass through. They know how economically important a train depot is to a small town. Danbury is going to make his case for why Shady Bluffs should throw its hat into the ring. It will come down to which town can come up with the best incentive for the railroad company — and its shareholders. I hate bidding wars.

"My question is, 'Why is it just coming to light now?' Until Greg Collins met with Adam in Garfield, Shady Bluffs wasn't even being considered. That makes me think it's more than money," Hank said.

He tapped his fingers on the kitchen table as he considered the situation. "You know, I think I'll have another talk with Collins. There's got to be more to the story. But for now, I'd better work for my meal." He covered his face as if he were going to rob a bank, ventured outside, and headed to the barn.

Max woke up and, having seen that chocolate cake was on the breakfast menu, helped himself to a generous slice. Lizzy just shook her head at the two males in her household.

Lizzy finished blocking the drafty window frames. She moved on to wiping down the counters, tables, and other surfaces when Hank literally blew in from chores.

"We can't let the cows out to graze until the dust clears," he said. "The pigs are smarter. They were already in the barn when I got there. But don't ask me about those dumb chickens." He unloaded only a handful of eggs from his coat pockets to prove his point.

To pass the time, Lizzy read while Hank played checkers with Max.

Noon came and went. By late afternoon, the winds calmed enough for Hank to saddle his horse and ride back to Shady Bluffs.

Lizzy noticed the house felt a little empty with Hank gone. She knew the house would feel even more empty tomorrow when Max returned to school.

Monday morning, Lizzy hitched up the wagon and drove her son into town. She brought along the letter from the Chicago lawyers. They arrived at Charlotte's house well before the school bell rang. Max knew the routine. He carried his bag of clean clothes into Aunt Charlotte's house, and then he and Will walked to school.

Lizzy tapped on the door to the kitchen. "Char, do you have a minute?"

Charlotte was tying on her full apron in preparation for her day at the doctor's office. She waved her sister into the kitchen and immediately saw something was amiss.

"What's wrong?" Charlotte asked.

"This." Lizzy handed her sister the letter.

After Charlotte read the letter, she blew out her breath. "Luke and I were afraid that we hadn't heard the last of the Pinkertons."

"Now it's escalated to a law firm. That means legal action."

"Oh, there was always a law firm involved with *these people*," Charlotte replied. "Luke, are you still here?"

Luke Jameson entered the kitchen, and Charlotte handed him the letter. He read it and said, "We'll be ready."

"What does that mean?" Lizzy asked.

"We'll watch Max at all times while he's in town. We'll walk the boys to and from school, and they won't be allowed to wander far from home. School will end in a couple of weeks, and then he'll be at the farm.

"And, as the town blacksmith and livery stable owner, I see everyone who comes and goes in Shady Bluffs. I'll be on the lookout," Luke said. "We're with you in this, Lizzy."

Lizzy had always been a planner. When facing a crisis, she made a plan, and then she worked the plan. She just needed a plan to face this current crisis. She thought about that on her ride back to the farm.

On a whim, Lizzy decided to stop at Elias Crawford's farm. She hadn't seen Elias since the blizzard. It made her wonder what her neighbor was doing. It turned out that Elias hadn't been doing much of anything. When Lizzy drove into the farmyard, she saw that Crawford's cattle and hogs were gone. No chickens were pecking for bugs in the yard.

Elias was sitting in a rocker on his porch, a jug of moonshine in his lap.

"Elias, I stopped by to see how you're doing," Lizzy said from the seat in her wagon.

"See fer yerself." He waved a hand toward the empty feedlot. "I'm done with Dakota."

"I see you've sold your livestock," Lizzy said.

"Sold what didn't die last winter. I kept back my horse and a mule. I'm pulling up stakes and heading West. I heard there's a silver bonanza out in Nevada. Men are getting rich from the Comstock Lode."

"When are you leaving?" Lizzy asked.

"As soon as I can be shed of this dern farm. I proved my claim, so the land's mine. I'm gonna sell it and head West."

Lizzy did some quick calculations. She had wished to be rid of Elias Crawford when he dammed up the creek last year. Lizzy might be able to make good on that wish thanks to her harvest last fall.

"What are you asking for it?" Lizzy inquired.

"Land's going a buck twenty-five an acre now. That's two hundred dollars for 160 acres," Elias said.

He eyed Lizzy. "Nothing but bad memories here. Looks to be another drought this year, too. No reason to plant crops that ain't gonna grow. I'll sell the farm to you for half of what it's worth: one hundred dollars. But it's gotta be cash on the barrelhead."

Lizzy got off the wagon and strode over to where Elias was sitting. She stuck out her hand. "It's a deal, Elias. I'll have the cash for you this week."

News of the Day

The Daily Press and Dakotaian, **Yankton, Dakota Territory, October 12, 1878**

Headline: Local Laconics

A dust storm of huge proportions, and provocative of unbounded profanity, is a prominent feature of today's weather. Weather indications for the upper Mississippi and lower Missouri valleys, are stationary or falling barometer, southeast to southwest winds, warmer, hazy and partly cloudy weather.

The Daily Press and Dakotaian, **Yankton, Dakota Territory, October 12, 1878**

Headline: Personal

L.B. Partridge returned this forenoon from a trip to Swan Lake. His ride was in the face of the prevailing dust blizzards, and he says it was, well, that it wasn't a very pleasant day.

Chapter 19 – Spring 1873
Town Meeting

The day after Lizzy agreed to buy Elias Crawford's farm, she rode into Shady Bluffs to talk to her banker. Hank was dusting the teller counter when Lizzy entered the Savings and Loan.

"I see I'm not the only person fighting a losing battle against the dust," Lizzy said.

"No, ma'am, you're not," Hank replied. "So what brings you to town two days in a row?"

"I need some financial advice," she said.

"You've come to the right place," Hank said. He motioned to Lizzy to sit and then took his place behind the desk.

"Elias Crawford is selling his farm," Lizzy said. "He's heard the Comstock Lode siren song calling him. He'll sell his farm to me for half of what it's worth: one hundred dollars."

"Doesn't sound like you need any advice, Lizzy. You've made up your mind."

She smiled her dimpled smile that she knew Hank loved.

"You're right about that. I just need to know how much money I have in my account. I bought three windmills last year with a bank loan. I don't want to get too far into debt."

"Thanks to the water those windmills are pumping, your farm had one of the only good harvests in the Territory. The loans aren't paid off entirely, but other farmers have seen the benefit of windmills and are taking out loans for windmills now. That's generating a lot of goodwill for your Medicine Creek Farm," Hank said.

"How much can I afford to withdraw to pay Elias?" she persisted. "How much is in my account?"

Hank checked his ledger."You've got just under seventy dollars in your account."

"That's not enough," Lizzy said with disappointment. "Elias wants 'cash on the barrel head.' I need to come up with thirty dollars more."

Hank cleared his throat. "I don't make a habit of it, but in this case, would you consider taking on a partner?"

"A partner?" She narrowed her eyes in confusion. "What do you have in mind?"

"I'll go fifty-fifty on the purchase with you — my money, not a bank loan. And we'll own the land together, for now."

"Why would you do that?" Lizzy asked.

"You're good for the loan. and you're a successful farmer," Hank said. "But mostly because I love you."

Lizzy didn't pause to think. She knew a good deal when she heard it. "I've always wanted a partner I could do this to." She kissed Hank right there in his bank.

Hank enthusiastically returned the kiss. Afterward, he said, "I've never sealed a deal with a kiss. I think I like it."

As he counted out the cash to Lizzy, Hank said, "We should celebrate. Let's have dinner at Betsy's Place. Fair warning, though. I have to be back here for the town council meeting at seven o'clock."

"I'm liking the partnership even more. I'll meet you at Betsy's at five-thirty. I have some other business to attend to."

She started with a visit to Doctor Charlie.

Charlotte was also dusting shelves when Lizzy entered the doctor's office.

"Good morning, Char," she greeted her sister.

"Lizzy, I didn't expect to see you again this week. Are you feeling alright? Did you hear something more from the lawyers?"

"Can't I just pay a friendly visit to my favorite sister?" Lizzy asked.

Charlotte wiped her hands on the apron covering her day dress. "Of course you can. But if I know my favorite sister, she has an idea up the sleeve of that pretty blue dress."

"Actually, I've been thinking about our conversation regarding Mother's Friend. It might be wise to take precautions," Lizzy said.

"There's the Lizzy I recognize. Always thinking ahead and making plans." Charlotte went to a cabinet on the back wall. Taking a key from her apron, she unlocked the cupboard and selected a small cardboard box from the top shelf.

Charlotte handed the box to Lizzy and explained how to use the medication. "Keep in mind, it's not foolproof — nothing is. But it worked for me before Luke and I married."

Lizzy suspected Charlotte might be relying on Mother's Friend to space the births of her children. Still, ladies, even sisters as close as Char and Lizzy, didn't talk about such things.

"Are you staying for the town council meeting tonight?" Charlotte asked.

"I didn't realize it was open to the public," Lizzy said.

"Frontier has the townspeople all riled up. Promises made and promises broken," Charlotte said.

"As I understood it, Adam said the land survey was to provide the railroad with options. Yes, he implied that Shady Bluffs was on the route, but..." Lizzy said, trying to defend her friend.

"That might be," Charlotte conceded, "but when Mr. Danbury left for Garfield without a backward glance... Well, people want to know how that decision came about."

"It could be the terrain," Lizzy replied. "Adam showed me the survey maps and what the railroad is looking for."

"I guess we'll find out tonight," Charlotte said.

"Are you going to the meeting?" Lizzy asked.

"I'm part of the business community here. Both Luke and I will be at the meeting."

Lizzy gave that some thought. "I guess I'll go to the meeting too."

"Excellent. Will you be staying at my house, or is that an inappropriate question? Let me rephrase that: you're welcome to stay at my house if you wish."

"Thank you. I accept your invitation," Lizzy replied.

Having some time to fill, Lizzy strolled down to the mercantile. She didn't need to purchase anything, but it didn't hurt to browse, she rationalized.

Vaughn's Mercantile smelled of coffee beans and candle wax. Barrels of flour and cornmeal were stacked against one wall. The adjoining wall held bolts of fabric and notions such as thread, needles, and such. Tools and small farm implements hung on the far wall.

Lizzy wandered over to the fabrics and began examining the pretty cotton calicos.

"We've switched out the winter wools for lighter-weight summer fabrics," Isabell said. "If you're interested in something heavier, I have some in the back."

"Not today, Isabell. I'm just browsing. I don't need anything new right now, and Max can make do with what he has for the summer. I expect he'll have outgrown all his school clothes by fall."

"Hmmm," Isabell agreed. "Max is what, eight, now?"

"Yes, can you believe it?" Then, her heart ached with the thought of losing Max. What if she didn't get to see Max turn nine? Lizzy pushed that thought out of her mind for now.

"Are you in town for the meeting with the railroad?" Isabell asked.

"No, I had other business, but Charlotte convinced me to stay for the town council meeting."

"It could get fiery," Isabell said. "There are a lot of agitated people who don't like the games these railroads are playing."

"That's what I'm hearing," Lizzy said.

She continued browsing the fabrics for a while, then drifted over to a shelf of books. "You have the new Jules Verne book! Max loved *Twenty Thousand Leagues Under the Sea*! And here's another Jules Verne adventure!"

Lizzy pulled *Around the World in Eighty Days* from the shelf and brought it to the cash register.

She walked back to the bank where her horse was tied and led it to the livery for the night. Then Lizzy walked to Charlotte and Luke's house to welcome the boys home from school.

Max and Will were debating the best fishing spots when they entered the Jameson house.

"Ma! You were just in town yesterday. Is something wrong?" Max asked.

"Why does everyone think something's wrong just because I've come to town two days in a row?" Lizzy replied.

"Because it's spring planting time," Max replied. "You don't stop planting until all the seeds are in the ground!"

Lizzy laughed. "You've got me there, Maxie. Actually, I had some banking to do. Aunt Charlotte convinced me to go to the town meeting, so I'm staying the night."

"Hunky dory," Max declared.

Lizzy laughed at the new slang. "What an odd saying," she said.

"All the kids are saying it. It's not a curse word, Aunt Lizzy," Will assured. "It means 'great.'"

"I've heard it before. It's just an odd combination of words." Then she remembered the book in her handbag.

"While I was shopping today, I found this at Isabell's." Lizzy handed *Around the World in Eighty Days* to Max.

"This *really* is hunky dory," Max said with a grin. "Thanks, Ma!"

Charlotte arrived home with the two younger Jameson children. Eliza and Linc spent their days at a neighbor lady's house. Charlotte began making dinner for her hungry family.

"Goodness, look at the time," Lizzy said. The wall clock struck five-thirty. "I'm meeting Hank at Betsy's Place for dinner. Then I'll go directly to the town council meeting."

"All right," Charlotte said as she stirred gravy in a cast iron pan. "I'll see you at the meeting."

When Hank saw Lizzy enter Betsy's Place, he rose and pulled out the chair for Lizzy to sit.

"Thank you," Lizzy said. She looked around the restaurant. "It's busy here tonight."

"Lots of people are staying in town for the meeting. In fact, I don't think the Savings and Loan can accommodate the crowd they're expecting. The pastor offered the church for the meeting," Hank said. "After dinner I'll put a sign on the door to direct people to the church."

"Isabell said it might be unruly," Lizzy said.

"It could. Hopefully they'll behave in God's house."

Over dinner, Lizzy talked about her plans for the new farmland. "I'll put a windmill up next year. For now, I'll put my cattle on Crawford's farm — I need a better name for that land, I guess."

"That's a good use of the pastureland," Hank agreed. "Are you going to plow and plant the pastures by Nellie's claim?"

"That's the plan," Lizzy said. "With the windmill down there, it makes sense to plant more corn and wheat. I'll just have to be mindful of the rocks in that field."

After dinner, Hank and Lizzy stopped at the Savings and Loan. He posted a note on the door that the town council meeting had been moved to the Lutheran church. Then they headed to the church.

Many townspeople apparently knew about the change in location because citizens were streaming into the white, clapboard building. Hank said hello to several of his customers and nodded to others.

A small table had been moved to the front of the church, and Mayor William Bartholomew was arranging papers at the table. Lizzy spotted Adam Danbury in the front row. Other members of the town council were taking their seats in the front pew, as well. Gregory Collins sat in the second pew with his reporter's notepad at the ready.

At last, Mayor Bartholomew called the meeting to order. He thanked everyone for attending the meeting.

"We can follow the usual agenda, starting with last month's minutes and treasurer's report, old business, and then new business, or we can jump to the main event. Do I have a motion?" the mayor announced.

"So moved," said one of the council members.

"Second," another council member agreed.

"All right then," Mayor Bartholomew said. "Mr. Adam Danbury has asked to address the town council and the rest of you, about Frontier Railroad's planned route through Dakota Territory."

He motioned to Adam. "Mr. Danbury, the floor is yours."

Adam rose and walked to the front of the church.

"My genuine thanks to the people of Shady Bluffs," he began. "Building a railroad is a complex undertaking. As the Chief Survey Engineer for Frontier Railroad, it's my responsibility to manage the survey crew and to analyze all possible routes carefully. Many of you met those crewmen when we surveyed routes in and around Shady Bluffs last year.

"As I've explained to many of you, it comes down to topography and terrain. Before coming to Dakota, I surveyed routes for the Northern Pacific in Minnesota. That's lake country for those of you who aren't familiar with northern Minnesota. Railroads up there have to work around lakes, bogs, and swamps. That makes laying track a lot more difficult.

"Dakota Territory, on the other hand, was made for railroads. The land is mostly flat, and that's good for Frontier Railroad. We'll still need to build bridges over the creeks and streams and, of course, the Missouri River."

Gregory Collins asked the first question. "Garfield has the same creeks as Shady Bluffs. You haven't explained the change in routes."

Adam cleared his throat. "Yes, the terrain is similar. But as I've explained to the mayor, there are incentives to consider when choosing a route. Yes, the U.S. government grants the railroads parcels of land in remuneration for the expenses involved in laying track, building bridges, and such, but local incentives are also part of that package."

"Local incentives such as…" someone at the back of the church called out.

"Additional land grants, use of office space, and monetary inducements," Adam answered.

"You mean bribes," someone else in the crowd yelled.

"Building a railroad includes transactional incentives," Adam tried to explain.

"By 'transactional,' you mean cash under the table," another angry man shouted.

One of the town council members spoke up. "So we come up with enough money, I mean 'incentives,' and Frontier will route the train through Shady Bluffs."

Adam winced. "Incentives are helpful, but, as any businessman understands, decisions can also depend on relationships," he said.

"So it's a 'who you know' type of thing," Mayor Bartholomew clarified.

"In this case, one of our stockholders suggested we meet with a former Union Army colonel who now resides in Garfield," Adam admitted. "Those Army relationships are strong."

"Who is the stockholder?" Hank asked Adam.

"That would be Joseph Hanover," Adam replied.

"Joe Hanover? He's a New York boy, just like I am. We served together in the Union Army's Engineer Battalion," Hank said. "Joe's one of your stockholders?"

"Mr. Hanover is Chairman of the Board," Adam said.

"Well, I'll be," Hank exclaimed. "I think I'll send good ol' Joe a telegram tomorrow. Maybe we can straighten out this...I'll call it a 'misunderstanding.'"

"That is certainly your prerogative," Adam said. "Keep in mind, there were other incentives offered by the Garfield business community."

"Let's get a list of those incentives, Mr. Danbury," said Mayor Bartholomew. "Just like you prefer level terrain for your railroad tracks, we want to be on equal footing for a decision as important as this one."

"You shall have that list, Mayor," Adam promised.

There was some grumbling and mumbling among audience members.

Mayor Bartholomew addressed the crowd. "Speak up now, if you have something to say or a question for Mr. Danbury."

Gregory asked when the tracks would begin to be laid, how many trains would come through Shady Bluffs each week, and other questions that assumed Shady Bluffs would be a Frontier Railroad town.

At night's end, Adam thanked the mayor, the town council members, and the townspeople who attended the meeting.

Adam got Lizzy's attention, and she walked over to say hello while Hank was in discussions with the mayor.

"I thought that went well," Adam said to Lizzy.

"There were some angry people in the crowd," Lizzy said. "I think you handled it well."

"How long will you be in town?" Adam asked.

"I've been away from the farm longer than I planned. I'll ride back tomorrow morning."

Adam's face fell. "And I need to return to Garfield regardless of tonight's outcome."

"Next time, then," Lizzy said.

They both heard a woman's voice calling Adam's name.

"Adam! I've finally found you!" The woman speaking to Adam was a small, compact woman. Her brown serge traveling suit was dusty and wrinkled. A flat pork pie hat trimmed with a dark brown velvet ribbon covered her light brown hair.

"I decided it was time that I joined you out West," she said as she removed her cloak.

"Margaret, this is a surprise," Adam said. "I didn't receive any notice that you were coming. I would have made accommodations for you."

The woman tilted her head as if considering this happenstance. "Really? I sent a letter a fortnight ago. Aunt Suzanne's health improved, and I was no longer needed there. I assumed the letter would arrive before I did, since I had to travel by train and then stagecoach. I arrived in Garfield yesterday only to discover you were here, in Shady Bluffs."

"And how did you get here?" Adam asked.

"One of your crewmen was kind enough to bring me by wagon," she answered.

Lizzy stood silently throughout this conversation between Adam and the woman in brown. She was about to excuse herself when Adam remembered Lizzy's presence.

"Margaret, may I introduce you to one of the many kind people in Shady Bluffs. This is Lizzy, er, Miss Elizabeth Ward. She owns a large farm east of town."

He turned to Lizzy. "Lizzy, this is my wife, Margaret Danbury."

Lizzy was dumbstruck. To her credit, Lizzy cordially greeted Margaret. "Welcome to Shady Bluffs, Mrs. Danbury."

She pretended to search the crowd, and then Lizzy said, "I must take my leave. I see my friend is preparing to leave."

Lizzy made her escape with grace and dignity. Still, her head was reeling from the revelation that Adam Danbury was married!

Finding Hank at the front of the church, Lizzy slipped her hand into the crook of Hank's arm. When Hank saw the queer look on Lizzy's face, he quickly finished his conversation with William Bartholomew.

Hank covered Lizzy's hand with his and asked, "Is something amiss?"

"I would like to leave now," Lizzy said as she drew her shawl around her shoulders. "If you need to stay, don't worry about me. I saw Char and Luke leave just moments ago. I can catch up with them."

"No, no, no," Hank said. "I'll escort you to Jamesons' house."

The fresh spring air helped to revive Lizzy. "Let's take the long way to Char's house," she suggested.

"You don't have to ask me twice to take my favorite gal for a moonlight walk," Hank said.

They strolled down Shady Bluff's boardwalk until they reached the end of town. "We can keep walking," Hank said.

"Yes, please. It was stuffy in there, and the night air feels good."

"There's something bothering you, Lizzy," Hank said. "Were you unhappy with the outcome of the meeting tonight?"

"Oh, no. If we can — if you can convince the Frontier shareholders that Shady Bluffs is a better option, that would be wonderful. Papa always said, 'it's not what you know, it's who you know.' I guess that certainly applies in this instance."

"Then what's bothering you?"

Lizzy stopped walking and looked into Hank's face. "I met Adam Danbury's wife tonight."

"What? Danbury is married? He sure didn't act like there was a wife back home. So she showed up tonight at the meeting?"

"Yes, just after the meeting concluded, actually," Lizzy replied. "Adam seemed quite surprised at her presence."

Hank started chuckling. "I bet he did!"

"I thought I knew him," Lizzy said. "But in all our conversations, all the time he spent at the house while Bill Anderson was dying, he never mentioned a wife. He didn't lie…but he didn't tell the truth, either." She shook her head in disbelief.

"A wife," Hank said with a chuckle. "Just another reason not to trust that dandy."

They had reached the edge of town. Beyond lie the endless prairie, dotted here and there by occasional red cedar trees.

"You know, it's taken me a while to appreciate the Dakota prairie," Hank said. "I was born in upstate New York. It's thick with trees back there: white pine, Norway maples, sugar maples, pin oak, and, of course, cottonwoods. At first, I thought the plains were empty. I had that wrong. Seeing the horizon gives people perspective…a vision, you might say.

"I came out here for a fresh start, just like a lot of folks are doing. Like you and Char did."

Lizzy caressed Hank's cropped beard. "Why *did* you come west, Hank?"

"There was nothing...no one to go home to." He paused, then said, "I guess this is a night for confessions...for revelations."

Lizzy was still, not sure what Hank was going to confess to. "You don't have to tell me if you don't want to."

"It's nothing to be embarrassed about," Hank assured her. He took a deep breath and began.

"War makes men consider their mortality. It makes us uncertain. Like a lot of men, I wanted a reason to return home after the War. So, I proposed to a young woman I'd known for years. Her name was Abigail Edison. That was right after the attack on Fort Sumter. We were married, and I went off to fight.

"I never expected that I would be the one to survive and that Abigail would die."

Lizzy gasped. "Oh, Hank. I am so sorry." She squeezed his hand.

"She died in childbirth in the spring of 1862. If I'd returned home after the War, people would have treated me differently. I didn't want their pity. Dakota Territory gave me a chance to start over."

Lizzy nodded. "A new life."

"I've wanted to tell you for a while, but the time just didn't seem right. I don't know if tonight was the right time, but you asked why I came here. Lizzy, I've never looked back. I love it here."

He pulled her into an embrace and covered her mouth with his. Lizzy's arms circled Hank's broad shoulders. Under the skylit prairie sky, they kissed. Hank's kisses trailed down Lizzy's throat, stopping at her heaving breast. Her fingers wove through his thick, golden brown hair as she revelled at the touch of his mouth on the crest of her bosom.

News of the Day

Dakota Dispatch, **Shady Bluffs, Dakota Territory, April 20, 1873**

Headline: Frontier Railroad to Choose Between Garfield and Shady Bluffs

The First Lutheran Church was standing room only to hear from Frontier Railroad's Chief Survey Engineer Adam Danbury regarding the railroad's planned route. As reported by this newspaper in previous issues, it was discovered that Frontier Railroad planned to lay tracks through Garfield, Dakota Territory, some forty miles north of Shady Bluffs. This was after the survey crew had spent months measuring and studying the lay of the land around Shady Bluffs. In an exclusive story, the Dakota Dispatch traveled to Garfield to investigate the railroad's seeming lack of interest in Shady Bluffs. This reporter learned that financial incentives offered by Garfield town fathers had enticed Frontier Railroad to abandon plans for a route through Shady Bluffs. In response to further investigative reporting in Dakota Dispatch, Frontier Railroad representative Adam Danbury agreed to reconsider the Shady Bluffs route. He intended to meet with town council members to discuss options and incentives. The town council meeting was subsequently opened to the public.

At the public meeting, Mr. Danbury outlined the reasons for moving the route to Garfield. Through questioning at the meeting, Mr. Danbury admitted that the Frontier Railroad Chairman of the Board Joseph Hanover was doing a favor for a former war buddy. Apparently,

Shady Bluffs' own Hank Johnson is also a friend of Joseph Hanover, Frontier's Chairman of the Board.

Dakota Dispatch will keep readers informed regarding updates to this changing situation.

Chapter 20 – May 1873
Brindle Colt

After the town council meeting, Lizzy kept busy on the farm. Spring was her favorite time of year. Lizzy loved the earthy smell of a just-plowed field. She said it smelled like hope. That's how she thought of spring on the prairie: it was a season of hope.

In addition to planting, it was also a season for planning. Now that Lizzy had 160 acres more to farm, she planned to expand her cattle herd and move it onto the Crawford land. She decided the land to the north was rocky and would be much better used for grazing.

Ted Nesbitt continued to work for Lizzy part-time. Together, they completed the planting, including the new fields watered by the windmill on Lizzy and Nellie's border.

Lizzy was pleased that her farm was growing. But that meant more work to do. At least Max was home from school for the summer. He had inherited his mother's love of the land and the livestock. Now eight years old, Max was growing into a tall, sturdy boy. He still had a sprinkling of freckles across his nose and big ears, but much to Max's pleasure, his ginger hair had darkened to an auburn color.

Like most farm boys, Max had daily chores. Each morning after breakfast, Max worked in the barn, gathering eggs, milking the cows, and cleaning the horse stalls. After he had fed the hogs in the pen, Max was free to do what boys do best: fish and explore. Will Jameson and Bear Walker often accompanied Max on those adventures.

It wasn't unusual for Hank to show up at the farmhouse on Friday evening, so Lizzy always set a third plate just in case.

It was a warm May evening when Hank trotted into the farmyard. Lizzy had just finished working in her kitchen garden. She carried a wicker basket of strawberries, rhubarb, radishes, and early peas to the house. In the distance, she could see Max meandering toward the farm with a stringer of shiny fish.

"You're just in time to help with dinner," Lizzy said to Hank.

"What's for dinner?" he asked.

She pointed to Max's catch. "Looks like perch and bass. While you help Max clean the fish, I'll start the rest of the meal."

"Can't say 'no' to fresh fish," Hank said. He led his mount to the barn, where he unsaddled and groomed the horse.

By the time Hank had finished tending to his horse, Max entered the barn with his stringer.

"That's a mighty nice catch today, Max," Hank said. "Bring them over to the bench and we'll clean them."

Together, Hank and Max filleted the fish.

"Hold the perch like this," Hank instructed the boy. "After you've sliced down one side of the dorsal fin all the way to the tail, turn it and slice along the other side. Then, pull off the dorsal fin and the skin. It's ready for the pan."

"That's hunky dory, Mr. Johnson," Max said. "Let me try."

Hank handed the fillet knife to Max but watched carefully to make sure the boy did not hurt himself. Max's first attempt was not quite as clean as Hank's fish, but it was a start.

"You're getting the hang of it, son," Hank said to Max.

"Thanks, Mr. Johnson."

"Why don't you call me 'Hank,'" the big man said as he tousled Max's unruly hair.

Both of them smiled.

That evening, they enjoyed a dinner of fried fish and potatoes, fresh peas, and greens. Lizzy said, "Unless you two gentlemen are determined to empty the creek of every perch and bass tomorrow, I'm wondering if you'd like to ride over to Nellie's ranch and see her new foals."

"Can we, Ma?" Max asked eagerly.

"The fish will still be there the next day," Hank said. He rose to help clear the table.

"Who wants dessert?" Lizzy asked.

Max's eyes lit up. "Yes, please!"

"I have a treat for you tonight," she said. "The first fruit of the season."

Lizzy brought a bowl of fresh strawberries and a pitcher of cream to the table.

Later, after Max had gone to bed, Lizzy and Hank sat in the rocking chairs on the porch. At first, they sat in companionable silence, enjoying the night sounds of crickets and owls.

"I like it when you come out to the farm," Lizzy said. "Max does, too. He asked me today if you'd be visiting."

"The feeling's mutual," Hank said. "Coming out here seems so peaceful. Besides, bachelor life in town can be lonely."

Lizzy made a sound of disbelief. "Lonely? You're the most eligible bachelor in Shady Bluffs. Char told me there's a widow in town who's set her cap for the town banker."

"Mabel Thompson?" Hank laughed. "She's not my type. Besides, I have my eye on a pretty farmer." He reached out to take Lizzy's hand.

After some time, Lizzy asked, "How are the railroad negotiations going? Have you heard back from your Army buddy?"

"Joe Hanover and I have been trading telegrams regularly," Hank replied. "I've been extolling the fine economic climate of Shady Bluffs. I believe with the right financial incentives…"

"You mean 'bribes,'" Lizzy interjected.

"They're not bribes. They're part of a financial package. At least that's what I'm told by our esteemed town council," Hank replied.

"Fine. But what about your Army buddy?"

Hank exhaled. "I'm not ready to tell the mayor, but I think ol' Joe is coming around to my way of thinking. Frontier's decision is coming down to 'who you know,' and Joe and I were pretty good friends during the War."

"That's good news," Lizzy said.

"I think I deserve a reward."

"What do you have in mind?"

Rather than telling Lizzy, Hank rose and gathered Lizzy into his arms. She leaned in and kissed the big man.

"My place or yours?" Hank asked.

"Your room," Lizzy answered. "It's on the other side of the house."

Hank chuckled. "You do make a fuss when I'm loving you."

"You're a scoundrel, Hank Johnson."

"That's what attracted you to me," he said.

Hank carried Lizzy into the guest room on the far side of the house, where they could celebrate in private.

After chores were done the next morning, the three rode south from Lizzy's farm. Lizzy and Max rode on Lizzy's mare. Hank accompanied them on his gelding.

It promised to be a warm day. Red hawks were already weaving in and out of the fluffy, white clouds. Occasionally, one of the raptors would dive into the prairie grass and emerge with a small rabbit or gopher.

"Those hawks are good hunters," Hank said. "I bet they have a nest nearby."

Eventually, the birds disappeared into the distance. But there was still plenty to watch. Max spotted a mother fox teaching her kits how to hunt.

"Look," he said in a low voice. "She's found a mouse."

They watched as the mother fox pounced on the mouse and then presented it to her babies.

"Spring is about new babies," Lizzy said.

There was a breeze sweeping across the prairie, and when they reached the border to Nellie's land, the windmill's blades were spinning. Water was flowing into the tank.

"That's a sound I like to hear," Hank said.

"Yes, I'm already using the water for my crops in these fields," Lizzy said. "Nellie is using the water for her horses. Look, there's a mare with her baby."

They watched as a buckskin mare and her foal grazed in the lush field of bluestem grass. In the distance, two foals frolicked in the prairie grasses while their mamas concentrated on eating their fill of the tender bluestem grass shoots.

"They're beauties, aren't they," Hank said to Lizzy and Max.

"Nellie always had a way with horses," Lizzy said. "And speaking of Nellie, here she comes."

Nellie galloped up to the trio on the buckskin mare she rode from Missouri to Dakota Territory eight years ago.

"Spring is in bloom, isn't it," Nellie said. "These are just a couple of the new foals. Remember Thunder, that stallion I bought last year? His first foal was born last week. You should see him!"

"That's why we're here, Nellie," Lizzy said. "We took the day off to visit the best and fastest growing horse ranch in the Territory."

They followed Nellie south to her ranch. More than a dozen horses grazed in a fenced paddock by the barn.

"There he is," Nellie said with pride. Thunder, an impressive bay stallion, trotted around the paddock as if he owned it, daring anyone to challenge his rule.

"There are more horses in the barn. I had three mares foal yesterday," Nellie said. She jumped off her horse, threw the reins around a nearby fence, and motioned to her visitors to follow her into the barn.

Lizzy, Max, and Hank followed eagerly.

Sun shone through the loft windows in the barn, providing plenty of light to see the newest members of Nellie's ranch. The horse barn had a dozen stalls, most of which contained a mare and a newborn foal.

The first stall held a flaxen chestnut mare and bay colt with a dark brown mane and tail. The foal had a distinctive white blaze that ran from his nose to just above his eyes.

"He's a looker," Max said. "Is he from Thunder?"

"You're a good judge of horses, Max," Nellie said. "Yes, this one is the first foal from Thunder."

"The first of many fine horses," Hank said in appreciation.

"Max, would you like to name him?" Nellie asked.

"Thanks, Miss Nellie," Max said. "I'd call him Blaze."

Nellie patted Max on the shoulder and said, "Blaze is the perfect name for this one. Let's go look at the other foals."

Every stall had a mare and foal in it. As they walked through the barn, Lizzy saw a roan mare and filly, a dapple gray mare with a smoky black colt, and a dun mare with a red dun foal; the combinations went on.

"This is the promise of a bright future for you and your ranch," Hank said. "You're building an impressive stable of horses."

"Thank you, Hank," Nellie said. "But you know, I might be growing a bit too fast. I'm looking for new owners for a couple of my two-year-olds." Over Max's head, Nellie winked at Lizzy.

"Let's take a look." Nellie continued walking toward the paddock.

Outside, Nellie climbed up to perch on the fence around the horse enclosure. Max followed her example. Ten or twelve two- and three-year-olds frolicked in the pen.

"See that brindle colt by the feed bunk, Max?" Nellie said. "His mama has a new filly inside, and he's feeling a bit lonely. Let's go say 'hello.'"

Max and Nellie hopped off the fence and approached the brindle colt. She scooped up some grain and held it out to the horse to eat. Then Nellie took another handful of grain and handed it to Max.

"I've been hand-feeding him since he was born. Just remember to keep your fingers together and your hand flat when you offer the grain. It's easier for him, and you'll keep all your fingers."

Max did as Nellie instructed, and the colt nibbled at the grain.

"He's hungry! What's his name?" Max asked.

"I've been calling him 'boy,' but he needs a proper name, doesn't he?"

Max nodded.

"What would you name him if he were yours?" Nellie asked.

"Well, he's got these dark stripes over a lighter coat...kind of like a tiger," Max said. "I'd call him Tiger."

"That's an excellent name for this horse," Nellie agreed.

By then, Lizzy and Hank had joined Nellie and Max. Nellie looked at Lizzy and said, "I think it's high time this son of yours had his own horse, Lizzy."

"Once again, I agree with you," Lizzy said.

Max's eyes grew large as saucers. "My horse?"

"Max, I was riding bareback when I was your age," Nellie said.

"Well, you were an exceptional child, Nellie," Lizzy said, with just a little teasing in her voice.

"I was," Nellie replied. "But I believe I'm looking at a fine horseman right here."

She pursed her lips. "Tiger here is a three-year-old. I've been working with him and he's pretty good with a saddle. In fact, I believe there's a saddle in the barn that I used when I was your age, Max. It's in the tack room. Look for the one with the blue leather seat."

Max took off in a dead run.

"That is one happy boy," Lizzy said in amusement.

"I assume you two have been cooking this up for a while," Hank said.

"I wouldn't dream of offering a horse to Max without Lizzy's consent," Nellie said. "But I did suggest it to her. Every eight-year-old should have their own pony."

"Pony," Hank snorted. "The colt is going to be a full-size stallion in a year or two."

"And Max will be growing with Tiger," Lizzy said.

Max returned with the small saddle, a saddle pad, a bridle, and a cinch.

"I know you know how to saddle a horse, Max," said Nellie. "But this is your first time with Tiger. Let's do it together."

Nellie and Max spent the afternoon with Tiger. By the end of the day, Max was able to ride with Nellie leading the colt by the reins.

While Nellie and Max worked in the corral, Lizzy and Hank worked in the kitchen.

"I didn't know you were a baker," Lizzy said as Hank pulled a loaf of bread and a pan of muffins from the oven.

"There's a lot we don't know about each other," he said. "Tell me something about you that I don't know," Hank challenged Lizzy.

"Have I told you about the times that Frank James stopped by my house in Missouri?"

"THE Frank James…from the James Gang?"

"The very same," Lizzy confirmed.

"I want to hear this story," he said.

"The first time I met Frank was," Lizzy paused to count the years. "In the fall of '61. He'd deserted from the Confederate Army and was walking back home. The James family lived in the next county. He was looking for a hot meal and a place to sleep for the night."

"Well, I'll be," Hank said. "Frank James. And then what?"

"Then he left the farm the next morning. I didn't see him again until he showed up a few months later. He'd joined up with William Quantrill," Lizzy said.

"Wait! You met William Quantrill?"

"That was quite an encounter," Lizzy said. "Captain Quantrill and his men were looking for a meal. They needed to hide out from a group of Jayhawkers. They ended up in a gun battle. Between Quantrill's Bushwhackers and the Jayhawkers, my house was never the same. There were bullet holes in every wall, and they shot out all the windows."

"And where were you during this gun battle?" Hank asked.

Lizzy could laugh about it now. "I hid in a closet. Afterward, I patched up the men that could be helped. We buried two men in the orchard."

"That's quite a story, Lizzy."

"Oh, there's more," she said. "A few months after that — Charlotte was home from the War by then — Frank rode up to the farm in panic. Char and I greeted him with shotguns leveled at him. It was after Missouri's First Battle of Independence. Frank had come to fetch me to help nurse the wounded. When he found out that Char had been a medic, well, she volunteered herself to go."

"How long was Charlotte there?"

"A week or so," Lizzy replied. "It was quite the adventure. While Char was there, she 'ran into' Luke at that field hospital. I think that's when the real love affair between those two started, even if they didn't know it at the time," Lizzy confided to Hank.

"And have you seen Frank James since then?" Hank asked, expecting an answer in the affirmative.

"No, and I hope I never see him or his gang of bank robbers again."

"Speaking as the town banker, I say Amen to that," Hank agreed.

Dinner was almost ready when Nellie came to the door and called Lizzy and Hank out to watch Max ride his new horse.

"He's a natural, Lizzy," Nellie said. "I don't know why we didn't think to get him a horse before this."

"Because he's eight years old, Nellie! But I can see that he's a good horseman. Thank you for suggesting this. How much do I owe you for the horse?"

Nellie waved her hand. "You don't owe me a thing. I lived with you for four years after I came here. Tiger is my thank you to you and Char."

"You know that means that Will is going to want a horse, too," Lizzy said.

"I know. I have just the filly picked out for him."

Over dinner, they talked about the railroad, and Hank filled in Nellie on the latest news from Frontier's shareholders.

"I knew some of that," Nellie said. "Gregory has been covering this story pretty closely."

As if he heard his name, Gregory Collins knocked on Nellie's door.

"Am I too late for supper?" he asked.

"There's plenty to go around," Nellie said.

"You probably know more about what's happening with the railroad route," Hank said to Gregory. "What have you heard?"

"Mayor Bartholomew thinks Frontier will be laying track through this part of Dakota Territory within the month," Collins said.

"Yes!" Hank said enthusiastically.

"Do you know the route?" Nellie asked. "Will it use the water stop route between Lizzy's land and mine?"

"I heard they're planning to move the tracks to the north," Gregory said. "The land north of Lizzy's farm."

Lizzy tilted her head. "Are you talking about the farm that Elias Crawford had?"

"Maybe," Gregory said tentatively, fork in midair. "I don't know if they've decided on the exact route yet, but that sounds right." He continued eating.

The sun was hanging low on the western horizon when Lizzy, Hank, and Max mounted their horses and rode back to Lizzy's house. Gregory and Nellie waved goodbye from her front porch.

News of the Day

Daily Press and Dakotaian, **Yankton, Dakota Territory, September 2, 1878**

Headline: The Dakota River Valley

The Dakota Valley Homestead, published at Olivet, devotes considerable space in its last issue to the discussion of its favorite theme – the construction of a railroad from Yankton up to the valley of the Dakota river, and the grand opportunity which Yankton possesses for acheiving [sic] future greatness. As this is a subject which Yankton must seriously act upon, we quote largely from the Homestead's article:

There is probably no city in the northwest having better advantages to lay a foundation for prosperity and future greatness than Yankton; and whatever disposition congress may seem pleased to make of the territory, those advantages still remain if they are properly fostered by its inhabitants. It would be quite simple to suggest the idea of Yankton losing the Missouri river trade if reasonable care is taken by her citizens to retain it and that reasonable care is all that is necessary to hold the growing trade of the Dakota valley. But the very act of negligence that may forfeit to her the latter will just as surely in time cut off the upper Missouri and all its present and future advantages to Yankton leaving her at best but a poor imitation of Sioux City and a shadow only of the greatness and power promised to her by the natural position she occupies connected with the overtures extended by the outstretched hand of fortune.

We learn that the Dakota Southern railroad would have been extended beyond Yankton long ago had the extension not been opposed by her people.

Chapter 21 – June 1873
Railroad Town

Hank's wartime friendship with Joe Hanover proved advantageous for Shady Bluffs. Hank called in an old favor, and gangs of railroad laborers began arriving in the Dakota Territory in June to work on the railroad's new route. The men laying track and pounding spikes were called "gandy dancers" because of the synchronized rhythm as they pounded the spikes along the "lining" bar, called a "Gandy," that aligned the tracks.

The work was hard and dangerous, but Irish immigrants and former slaves lined up to be part of the railroads' westward expansion. Frontier's workers laid two to ten miles of track a day, depending on the terrain, the weather, and the delivery of iron rails to the worksite.

It was a warm June morning when Lizzy and Max drove the cattle into the new pasture to the north.

"What's that sound?" Max asked his mother.

"I don't know. Let's check it out," Lizzy replied. She made a clicking sound and spurred her horse toward the unfamiliar noise.

Lizzy eyed a heifer that had broken away from the herd amid the cacophony of clanging metal. She told Max, "Make sure that heifer stays with the herd."

Max and Tiger pushed the heifer back toward the herd, and they continued on. Just beyond the land that used to belong to Elias Crawford, Lizzy spotted the railroad crew. Men armed with picks, sledgehammers, and shovels toiled over a ribbon of steel that ran to the eastern horizon. Other men laid heavy wooden ties in parallel rows at the front of the steel rails. Supervisors and surveyors rode horses up and down the line, ensuring the ties and the rails were laid correctly.

One of the men on horseback was Adam Danbury. He noticed Lizzy and Max and cantered over to them.

"It's happening, Lizzy," Adam said when he reached them.

"I see that. So the railroad will run just north of my land," she said. "Max, stay with the herd, please."

Lizzy watched as Max trotted off toward the herd of cows and calves.

Adam continued, "The tracks are on public lands. We're not trespassing on private property."

"Oh, I'm not accusing you of that," Lizzy said. "I was just thinking my cows and your trains are going to be neighbors. And I'm wondering how that will turn out."

"Our trains are equipped with cowcatchers. Shouldn't be a problem," Adam said.

"Shouldn't be a problem for your trains, but what about my cattle?"

"Well, I heard ranchers down south are using wire fencing to keep their cattle in pastures."

"So much for open grazing lands," Lizzy said. She frowned.

"I didn't realize this land was part of your farm," Adam said. "The plat maps said that someone named Crawford owns the land south of the tracks."

"That was Elias Crawford. His wife died last winter, and Elias wanted to sell out. I made an offer, and he left for the silver mines in Nevada. Not much of his farm was planted. It was too rocky to plow, so I'm moving my cattle up here for grazing."

A wistful look washed over Adam's face. "How have you been, Lizzy? I haven't seen you since…"

"Since your wife came to town," Lizzy completed his sentence. "That was a surprising evening, Adam." She narrowed her eyes. "I think you were just as surprised as I was."

"Margaret and I have been apart for so much of our marriage that oftentimes I didn't feel married. There were times when I wanted to tell you about Margaret," Adam said. "I thought we — you and I — had something."

"For a while, I did too. But I was wrong. A lie of omission is still a lie."

"Can we at least be friends?"

"Not yet. Give it time."

"Fair enough. I wish you happiness, Lizzy," Adam said. He turned the palomino back to the work crews and started to ride away.

"One more thing, Adam," Lizzy called out over the din of the workers.

Adam reined in his horse, turned around, and looked hopeful.

"Yes?"

"How long will it take for the tracks to reach Shady Bluffs?"

"We're averaging five miles a day, give or take," Adam said. "We should be in Shady Bluffs sometime next week."

"And then where?"

"We keep going West," he said.

"You'll pass through Lakota lands," Lizzy observed.

"Maybe. Maybe not. We're considering moving the route further north, away from Indian lands."

"Take care, Adam," Lizzy said. She waved as he returned to the work site.

Well, that went better than I expected, Lizzy thought. She sat on her horse and watched Adam ride off.

Adam's estimation that the track would be completed to Shady Bluffs in a week was correct. While his crew laid tracks, another construction crew built a depot building and water tank on the eastern edge of Shady Bluffs. The depot was large enough for passengers to purchase tickets, wait for their train, and disembark with their baggage. A large tank on the opposite side of the tracks provided the water to power the locomotives' steam engines.

The day finally came when the first Frontier Railroad locomotive steamed into Shady Bluffs. It was a day of celebrations for the railroad company and the town.

Red, white, and blue bunting banners decorated the buildings on Main Street. Townspeople and homesteaders from nearby farms and ranches gathered to celebrate. A podium had been erected in front of the new train depot. Mayor William Bartholomew, dressed in his Sunday best coat and trousers, stood on the podium along with Adam Danbury.

Cheers went up, and the crowd began applauding when the first passenger, Joseph Hanover, Chairman of the Board, disembarked. Hank Johnson waited on the train platform and was the first to shake hands with Hanover.

"Joe, it's been too long," Hank said as he slapped Hanover on the back. "Looks like the years have been good to you, my friend."

Hanover smiled and looked Hank up and down. "Maybe a bit too good. You're still in fighting form, Johnson, while I've grown soft. Too much time sitting in board rooms, I'm afraid."

Although he wasn't as tall as Hank, Joseph Hanover probably weighed fifty pounds more than the banker. Hanover had dressed formally for the celebration. He wore a dark gray frock coat and trousers of paler gray. A tall, black top hat completed Hanover's fashionable look.

"They're waiting for you on the podium," Hank said. The two men made their way through the crowd to the speakers' platform.

"Danbury, it's good to see you," Joseph Hanover said.

"Thank you, sir," Adam said. He extended his hand to shake his employer's hand. "I'd like to introduce you to Mr. William Bartholomew, mayor of Shady Bluffs.

"Good to meet you," Hanover said to the mayor.

While the men exchanged pleasantries on the podium, a brass band assembled on a nearby stage. The band consisted of trumpet, trombone, bass players, and a drummer. All the band members were dressed in military-style uniforms with high-collared navy jackets that were trimmed in double rows of gold buttons.

The band kicked off the festivities with a popular march tune. After that, Mayor Bartholomew stepped up to the podium.

"The day we've been anticipating and have worked for has finally arrived," the mayor said. "It was touch-and-go at first, but thanks to our esteemed banker, Hank Johnson, Shady Bluffs is the latest Frontier Railroad town!"

The crowd erupted into applause and shouts.

"Hank assured me that he did not want to speak today," Bartholomew continued, "but when you see him on the street, give him a hardy 'thank you.' Now, without further ado, I'd like to present Frontier Railroad Chairman Joseph Hanover."

Hanover replaced Bartholomew at the podium. After the crowd settled down, Joseph Hanover said, "Frontier Railroad is pleased to include Shady Bluffs as one of our railroad towns. To memorialize this event, we will pound a special brass spike into the tracks right here, in front of the depot."

Hanover held up a shiny spike. "Just like the golden spike at Promontory Point, Utah, this spike signifies the completion of a promise."

The crowd roared in approval.

Joseph Hanover and William Bartholomew stepped off the platform and onto the actual tracks in front of the depot. Adam Danbury was waiting there with two brand-new sledgehammers. Hefting the hammers, Hanover and Bartholomew took turns pounding the brass spike into the rail. When the spike was flush with the rails, the two men shook hands.

Bartholomew addressed the crowd, "This is an occasion to celebrate! Gentlemen, strike up the band!"

Tables on Main Street were covered with roasted meats of all kinds and a variety of baked goods, from breads and muffins to pies and cakes, as well as lemonade and iced tea. Bartenders from the Four Aces Saloon and the Prairie Rose Saloon rolled out barrels of beer for thirsty patrons.

Hank found Lizzy and Max at the far end of Main Street near Jameson's Blacksmith shop.

"There you are," he exclaimed. "This is a great day for Shady Bluffs."

"Yes, thanks to you," Lizzy said.

Luke, Charlotte, and their three children joined them.

"Ma, can Will and me get something to eat?" Max asked Lizzy.

"I'm surprised you waited this long," Lizzy said with a laugh. "Off with you. And take the little ones with you."

They all watched as the cousins ran or skipped toward the tables filled with sweets.

"I'm so glad that Max and Will are friends," Lizzy observed.

"They're more like brothers than cousins," Char said.

Luke turned to Hank and said, "That must have been quite the favor you called in to get Frontier to change the route. You've been pretty mum about it."

Hank shrugged. "You were in the War, Luke. Soldiers watch out for each other. Joe and I were like Max and Will over there. We were like brothers."

"I get it, you don't want to talk about it," Luke said. "Sometimes things happen in war that need to remain unsaid."

"Oh, it's not that," Hank said. "It was at Gettysburg. My god, that was a time." He paused, memories of the bloody battle flooding back. Hank shook his head as if clearing the memories.

"It was near nightfall on the second day of the battle," Hank said. "Joe was walking the perimeter when a couple of Johnny Rebs caught him off guard. They were going to take Joe prisoner then and there. I saw it happen and came up from behind, surprising the Confederates. They skedaddled.

"Joe always said he owed me after that. He'd have done the same for me," Hank said with another shrug. "When he got my telegram about Shady Bluffs, he was more than willing to move the route back here. Enough talk about the war, let's dance, Lizzy."

Hank crooked his arm for Lizzy and led her to the temporary dance floor by the band. After the dance, Hank introduced Lizzy to Joe Hanover.

"I am pleased to make your acquaintance, Miss Ward," Joe said. "I'm even more pleased that Hank has found someone as delightful as you. Hank tells me that you own a farm not far from town."

"I do, Mr. Hanover," Lizzy said. "Your tracks are just north of our land."

"Our land," Joe said with a questioning tone. "Hank said you are a single lady. And please call me Joe."

"I am, indeed, Joe," Lizzy replied. "But this farmland was owned by a neighbor. He wanted cash, and Hank offered to partner with me on this land. So it's *our* land."

They chatted a while about Joe and Hank's time in the Army and how the men needed to stay in touch.

As Hank walked Lizzy back to where the Jamesons stood, Lizzy watched as her friends and neighbors enjoyed the potluck banquet while young people danced to the songs played by the brass band. *This is a much better sight than that terrible day when the buffalo ran through Main Street,* she thought.

Then she shook off that memory and focused on what Hank was saying.

"You and Char called your claim 'Medicine Creek Claim.' I'm thinking we need a name for the new parcel of land. What do you think of 'Iron Horse Claim'…what with the Frontier tracks just to the other side of the boundary?" Hank said.

"Frontier Railroad will play a big role in the success of Shady Bluffs. I think that's a grand name for *our* farm," Lizzy agreed.

Soon, Frontier Railroad's steam locomotives brought new settlers and goods and supplies to the town. Frontier's passengers arrived from towns and cities to the East. Many had been lured to Dakota Territory with promises of fertile land and temperate climates. Others were escaping their hard-scrabble existence in big city factories. Others came West to find family members who had already settled in Dakota Territory.

George and Clarice Weston were looking for a particular family member: their grandson.

The Westons' son, James, had quarreled with his father after returning home from the War. James had seen the horrors of war and the inequities caused by speculators during the conflict. Rather than work in the family business, James and his wife, Sandra, set out for Dakota Territory shortly after their son was born in the spring of 1865.

George Weston, who had made his fortune in Chicago's livestock packing houses, hired the prestigious Pinkerton Agency to find his wayward son and, more importantly, his lost grandson.

The Pinkerton Agency's job was to track James and Sandra Weston's journey from Chicago to the Dakota frontier. Detective Josiah Chatton picked up the family's trail in Galena, Illinois. Further west, a Cedar Falls, Iowa, hotel guest registry included an entry for the couple in March 1865. Another hotel, this one in Fort Dodge, Iowa, also recorded the stay of a Mr. and Mrs. James Weston just a few days later.

From there, the trail went cold until someone at the Pinkerton Agency saw Gregory Collins' story about Lizzy Ward's windmills. Detective Chatton connected the dots and headed to Shady Bluffs to learn what he could about Max Ward. James Weston's parents were now disembarking from Frontier Railroad's Dakota Express train. Unlike the other passengers leaving the train, the Westons traveled in the luxury of a private car.

A porter unloaded several trunks on the boardwalk in front of the train depot. George Weston disembarked and stretched his legs after two days on the train. Clarice Weston, dressed in the height of fashion, followed her husband. Yards and yards of fabric and flounces covered a full hoop skirt, making it difficult for Clarice to navigate the narrow steps of the train car. Once on the boardwalk, she opened her lacey parasol and critically surveyed the dusty Main Street of Shady Bluffs.

Josiah Chatton met the Westons on the boardwalk. Chatton had traveled First Class, which afforded more comforts than the Second and Third Class Cars, but did not have the luxury of Weston's lavish private car.

"I trust your journey was pleasant, Mr. Weston," Chatton said.

"It was sufficient, although Mrs. Weston was hinting that we need to upgrade our car if we are to travel by rail again," George replied.

"It was noisy and smokey," Clarice complained. "I much prefer travel by ship."

"If only we could find a sea or ocean to accommodate you, dear," George said. Through the years, he had learned to soften his wife's petulance with humor.

"It appears there is only one hotel in town," George said. Using his walking stick, he pointed to the Prairie Palace down the street.

"Shady Bluffs is a small town, but it's growing thanks to the new railroad," Chatton said. "There's a passable diner, Betsy's Place, next to the hotel."

George held out his arm for Clarice and said, "My dear, our lodging awaits at the Prairie Palace. It's just a short walk from here."

After making arrangements for the trunks, the Westons and Josiah Chatton made their way to the town's lone hotel. Fortunately, the Westons were able to secure the hotel's only suite — the same one Adam Danbury had stayed in when he was in town. But unlike Adam, the Westons chose to have dinner in their hotel room. Betsy Tomlinson delivered dinner for three to the Westons' suite.

Clarice unpacked her clothing without the assistance of a lady's maid. "What was I thinking, George? I should have insisted that Alice accompany me on this trip. Who will help me dress?"

"I will make inquiries at the front desk, my dear," George replied.

Over dinner, the Westons and Josiah Chatton discussed the next steps in their search.

"I believe we should begin with the newspaper reporter," Chatton said. "He will jump at the chance for a story about a long-lost grandson. And he can provide valuable background information."

"I thought you said he came to town only recently. He wouldn't have been here when my son passed through," George said.

"Yes, but this is a small town, and Collins is close to the Wards and Jamesons," Josiah said.

"The name 'Ward' was in your report, but who are the Jamesons?" Clarice asked.

"Luke Jameson owns the blacksmith shop and livery stable. His wife, Charlotte, is the town doctor," Josiah explained.

"The town doctor is a woman." Clarice frowned slightly. "How unusual."

"You'll find the Wild West is much different from the genteel society you're used to, Mrs. Weston."

"Indeed," Clarice sniffed.

"Go on, Chatton," George said.

Josiah cleared his throat. "Charlotte Jameson is Elizabeth Ward's sister. Miss Ward, you'll recall, is the woman who found your grandson after the stampede — if he is your grandson," Josiah corrected. "That brings us to the proof you alluded to. Did you bring pictures of your son?"

Clarice rose from the small dinner table and went to her valise. She retrieved a small, silver-framed portrait of a young boy from the suitcase. She handed the photo to Josiah.

"A Daguerreotype! This is much better than a painting," the detective said. "How old was your son in this photo?"

"It was taken in 1849," George said. "James was nine. It's an excellent likeness of him."

"I also brought a portrait," Clarice said. "The Daguerreotype doesn't show Jamie's bright red hair like this painting does." Clarice found the painting she had unpacked earlier and displayed it for the men. The painting showed a young, red-haired boy holding a cap. Standing on the top step of a grand staircase, the boy leaned against the railing. He wore a short, collarless jacket and navy blue knickerbocker pants that stopped just below his knees.

"Excellent," Josiah said as he studied the portrait and the photograph.

"Does this boy named Max look like the boy in these pictures?" George asked.

"I can't say," Josiah said. "I tried to find him when I was in Shady Bluffs last winter. When I visited Lizzy Ward's farm, she said the boy was away at school. I have no reason to think she was lying to me."

"They sent him away to boarding school?" Clarice asked.

"I'm not certain," Josiah said.

"What did we pay you for, Chatton? I would have expected better from Pinkerton," George said.

"Apparently, some schoolchildren stay in town during the winter if they live too far from town. Even if I had located the lad, I would not have been able to confirm that he was your grandson," Chatton replied. "That is why you are here. If the boy resembles your son James, we can begin proceedings."

"Humph," George muttered. "Well, let's meet with this newspaper man of yours tomorrow."

News of the Day

The Montana Post, **Virginia City, Montana Territory, Friday, May 14, 1869**

Headline: Completed at Promontory Point, Utah

Yesterday, May 10, at high noon, the last rail was laid and spiked, connecting the Union and Central Pacific railroads. It was the completing of an enterprise fraught with more interest than the tunneling of Mount Cenis or connecting the Red and Mediterranean seas by the Suez Canal. Exchanges and telegrams inform us that on the Pacific and Atlantic coasts it was to be celebrated with becoming ceremonies and popular demonstrations.

Success to the great enterprise and volunteer toast from Montana. May the ties between East and West never be lessened.

Chapter 22 – June 1873
Visitors from Chicago

The Westons and Josiah Chatton entered the newspaper office the following day, only to find the office deserted. They could, however, hear the clunk-clunk of metal meeting metal in the press room beyond the front office. Josiah took the initiative to peer into the press room.

When the printing press paused momentarily, Josiah called out, "Good morning, Mr. Collins. May we have a moment of your time?"

"Of course, Mr. Chatton. Make yourself at home in the office. I'll be out when this page run is complete."

When he emerged from the press room, Gregory was surprised to see three visitors in the front office. Josiah Chatton stood while a distinguished older man sat behind Gregory's desk. A well-dressed woman of the same age sat in the visitor's chair.

Gregory wiped his inky hands on a somewhat clean towel before shaking hands with Chatton. "Good morning. What brings you back to Shady Bluffs? I thought you had concluded your investigation."

Josiah Chatton said, "I'm seeing the investigation through to the end, Mr. Collins. May I present Mr. and Mrs. George Weston."

George Weston extended his hand for Gregory to shake. Mrs. Weston nodded her head in acknowledgment.

"Nice to meet you, Mr. and Mrs. Weston," Gregory said. "I assume this is regarding Max Ward."

"We have reason to believe that the infant Miss Ward found eight years ago is actually our grandson," George Weston said.

"We've come to take our grandson home," Clarice said.

"Whoa," Gregory said. "How can you be sure that Lizzy's son is the boy you've been searching for?"

"I have a paper trail of the family's journey west," Josiah said.

"And I have," Clarice began to say, but before she could divulge that critical proof, George held up a hand and said, "And we have certain documents that will prove our claim."

"I see," Gregory said. "And why are you talking with me? I'm just a newspaper reporter. Shouldn't you be talking to the sheriff…or to Miss Elizabeth Ward?"

"In due time," George said. "We wanted to hear your background information about the stampede and the day that we lost our son."

"That was eight years ago. I wasn't in Shady Bluffs when the stampede happened. I can only give you second-hand accounts of the day," Gregory said. "You should talk with," he paused to consider his recommendation. "You should talk with Hank Johnson, our town banker. He was there when Lizzy rescued little Max."

Gregory calculated that Hank would play his cards close to the vest and would get more information than he would reveal.

George Weston nodded. "Where do we find Mr. Johnson?"

"Across the street to the east. The Savings and Loan is next to the post office," Gregory said.

Hank was helping a customer when the three Chicagoans entered the Savings and Loan. George Weston cleared his throat to get Hank's attention. The banker nodded and said, "I'll be with you as soon as I'm done assisting my customer. Please help yourself to a cup of coffee while you wait." Hank indicated the coffee pot on the small table by the front window.

"How soon can I get the windmill kits, Hank?" the customer asked.

"Lizzy's kits arrived three weeks after we ordered them, Stan. That was before the railroad came to town. I'm guessing you'll have the equipment in half that time."

"Can't be too soon," Stan Walker replied. "It's promising to be a hot, dry summer. Where do I sign for the loan?"

"Right here, on the dotted line," Hank said. He handed Stan a fountain pen. "I'll take care of ordering the Eclipse kits for you."

Stan Walker made his mark on the bank loan document. "Lizzy's windmills made a world of difference for her crops. She's a smart farmer, and I aim to follow her example. I appreciate your help, Hank."

After the banker and the farmer completed their business, Stan Walker picked up his broad-brimmed felt hat, nodded to Gregory, and left the office.

"Now, how can I help you, Mr. Chatton?" Hank asked.

"Good day to you, Mr. Johnson," Josiah said. "I'd like to introduce Mr. and Mrs. George Weston."

The men shook hands, as was the custom. Hank waited for Chatton or Weston to explain their presence.

"Mr. and Mrs. Weston are in Shady Bluffs in response to my investigation last winter. We've come to you because Mr. Collins said you were here when the buffalo stampede occurred."

"That's right. I'd been in town a couple of weeks when the Bushwhackers stampeded the buffalo and robbed my bank," Hank said.

"And you saw Miss Ward rescue the baby," Josiah prompted Hank.

"No, I was busy helping other victims when Lizzy found Max under the rubble," Hank said. "Lizzy said she found the baby underneath his mother's body. The mother was gone, but she'd protected Max from getting hurt."

"And where was the baby's father, if I may ask?" George asked.

Hank understood the purpose of the Westons' visit. He chose his words carefully, "As I recall, the body of a man that no one could identify was found down the street — or what was left of the street. Most of Main Street was destroyed by the buffalo."

"Did you find a Conestoga wagon that might have belonged to this couple?" Josiah asked.

"The buffalo broke up most of the buildings. A wagon would have been kindling in that stampede," Hank answered.

He turned to address the Westons. "We searched for the baby's family, Mr. and Mrs. Weston. You should visit with the Sheriff. He'll tell you that we printed posters asking for information about the family. We tried to find Max's family. When no one stepped up, Lizzy adopted the baby.

"What's your intention regarding Max?" Hank asked.

"We want to take Max home," Clarice spoke for the first time.

"I see. And how do you know that Max is your long-lost grandson? Eight years is a long time — a lifetime for Max," Hank said.

Clarice looked at her husband. George nodded and said, "We might as well show our hand."

Clarice drew the Daguerreotype of James Weston from her handbag. She handed the photograph to her husband, and George held it up so Hank could see it. "This is a photograph of our son James. He was about the same age as the boy we're seeking."

"May I get a closer look?" Hank asked. George handed the silver-framed photo to him.

"Hmmm, it's hard to say from a black-and-white photograph," Hank said, trying to sound unconvinced.

"I also have a color portrait of our son," Clarice said. "It's at the hotel."

"Mr. Johnson, we're not asking you to identify our grandson," George said. "Our reason for meeting with you was to learn more about the day of the stampede. Is there anything else you can tell us about that event?"

"The stampede was like nothing I've ever experienced — and I was in some of the worst battles of the War. I was at the Siege of Yorktown and at the Battle of Gettysburg. But when those buffalo went through this town, they flattened buildings, leaving piles of wood and bodies in their wake. Yes, I was there that day. Finding Max…finding him alive…well, that was a miracle."

No one spoke for several moments.

"I'm sure it was horrible, and we're grateful that our grandson was spared," George said.

"You don't know that Max is your grandson," Hank corrected him.

"We have good reason to believe that the baby found in the rubble is, indeed, James Weston's son," Josiah said.

"I reckon that's for the Sheriff to determine," Hank replied.

"I spoke with Sheriff Wilson when I conducted my investigation last winter," Josiah said. "The Sheriff's Office is our next stop."

"Thank you for your time this morning, Mr. Johnson," George Weston said.

Hank nodded and wished them a good day.

The sheriff's office was on a side street, around the corner from the bank. Chatton and the Westons found Sheriff Ben Wilson sorting through new Wanted posters.

Wilson looked up and recognized Josiah Chatton. "Chatton, I heard you were back in town. Still looking for that boy?"

"Yes, Sheriff. I've brought the boy's grandparents. This is Mr. and Mrs. George Weston. The Westons arrived from Chicago yesterday."

"Heard that too," Sheriff Wilson said. "So you think you've found your boy?"

"We believe that Max Ward is the Westons' grandson, Sheriff," Josiah said.

"What's your evidence?"

Josiah Chatton recounted the trail of hotel stays across Illinois and Iowa.

"And you are aware that we made a good-faith effort to locate the baby's family?" Sheriff Wilson began. "Posters and newspaper stories carried the news of the baby found in the rubble. Why didn't you step up then, Mr. Weston?"

"We would have, if we had seen any of those news stories or posters," George replied. "When James left, he made it clear he was cutting ties with his mother and me. I didn't expect to hear from him. Then, by chance, we saw the newspaper story about Miss Ward's windmills. We thought — we hoped — there was a chance that the baby was James' son, our grandson."

Then George Weston retrieved the framed photo of their son. "Our son, James, was approximately the same age as Max is now. Can you confirm that this is a good likeness of Max Ward?"

The sheriff studied the photograph. "Hmmm, there are some similarities. But I'm not certain I could make a confirmed identification on the basis of this old photo." The sheriff handed the photo back to George.

"I believe our next step is to meet with Miss Ward and her son," George said as he handed the photo to his wife.

"Sheriff, I think it would be wise for you to contact Miss Ward," Josiah said. "I wouldn't want any misunderstandings to arise from the meeting."

"Yep, I can do that. I suppose you are staying at the Prairie Palace," Ben Wilson said. "I'll ride out and talk with Lizzy."

While Josiah Chatton and the Westons were in the Sheriff's office, Hank hurried over to the blacksmith shop.

"Luke, did you know that Pinkerton agent is back in town?" Hank asked as Luke plunged a red-hot horseshoe into a tub of water.

"Damn it. Why is he still poking around?"

"This time, he's got his clients with him. They claim to be Max's grandparents."

"They can claim all they want, but it's their word against Lizzy's," Luke said.

"They've got a photo of their son, who they say is Max's father. And, Luke, the boy in the photo — he's about Max's age — looks a lot like our Max."

"That will kill Lizzy," Luke said. He removed his heavy leather work gloves and pulled off the leather apron. "Let's go talk with Charlie."

Hank and Luke found Charlotte in her office. She was unpacking a box of medical supplies that had just arrived on the morning train.

Charlotte frowned at the looks on the faces of Hank and Luke. "What's wrong?"

"The Pinkerton agent is back, and he brought the couple who hired him," said Luke. "They claim to be Max's grandparents, and they have a photo of their son when he was Max's age. They plan to take Max home with them."

"Have you seen the photo?" Charlotte asked.

"I have," Hank answered. "It's a good likeness of Max. The boy's eyes, the shape of his face, his nose, his ears. It could be Max."

"Oh, no," Charlotte said. "Where are they now?"

"They're talking with Ben Wilson," Hank said. "We need to get to Lizzy before the Westons — that's the name of the couple looking for their grandson."

"I'd go, but if I close the bank, Chatton will know I've gone to warn Lizzy," Hank said.

"I'll go," Charlotte said. "She should hear this from me anyway. What else do I need to know?"

Hank repeated his conversation with the Westons. While he talked, Charlotte closed her office for the day. "Luke, please saddle my horse. I'll take the children to…"

Luke interrupted her, "I'll tend to the kids after I bring your horse around."

"What should I do?" Hank asked.

"Pray," Charlotte said.

Charlotte had always been a good rider, but she rode to Lizzy's farm like she had the devil on her tail. She didn't see anyone in the farmyard when she reined in the horse. Then Ted Nesbitt emerged from the barn.

"Howdy, Doctor Charlie," he said. "You look like you're here for a medical emergency."

"It's an emergency of sorts, Ted. Do you know where my sister is?"

"She and Max were moving cattle in the north pasture. That's the old Crawford place," he clarified.

"Then that's where I'm headed. If she gets back home before I catch up with her, please tell her to wait for me," Charlotte instructed the hired man.

Nesbitt tipped his straw hat at Charlotte in understanding.

Lizzy and Max were on the far side of the herd when Charlotte spotted them. They appeared to be examining something on the ground, but Charlotte couldn't make out what it was. She called out to Lizzy.

Seeing the trail of dust Charlotte had left in her wake, Lizzy was alarmed. Quickly, Lizzy mounted her horse and rode to intercept her sister.

"What's happened? Is someone hurt…or worse? Is it Hank? One of your children? Luke?" Lizzy peppered her sister with the rapid-fire questions.

"No one is hurt," Charlotte assured her. "But something has happened that you need to know about. It's about Max. That Pinkerton man is back in Shady Bluffs, and this time he brought the people who hired him. They think Max is their grandson."

"Oh, no," Lizzy groaned.

"They've spoken with Ben Wilson, and he's on his way out here to update you. But I wanted you to hear it from me. You need to be prepared for the news."

"Do they have proof that Max is their grandson?"

"Hank says they do," Charlotte replied.

"Hank? They've spoken to Hank?"

"Yes. Gregory directed them to Hank because he was in town the day of the stampede," Charlotte explained. "And Gregory knew that Hank would get whatever information he could to prepare you."

"Is Ben bringing the detective or the people who hired him?"

"Luke and Hank told me it was just Ben," Charlotte said.

"What's the evidence?" Lizzy asked.

Charlotte closed her eyes and took a deep breath. "They have a photo and a portrait of their son when he was Max's age. Hank said it's a good likeness of Max."

Lizzy's head was spinning. Then she started making plans. That's how Lizzy dealt with adversity.

"Well, Max and I best get back to the house," Lizzy said. She called to her son, and he trotted over on Tiger.

"We'll need to bury that heifer," Max said as he reached his mother and aunt. "I can come back here with Mr. Nesbitt if you want me to, Ma."

Lizzy nodded distractedly. "Yes, we should bury her before it attracts wolves and coyotes to the herd."

"What happened?" Charlotte asked.

"One of the heifers must have been on the tracks when the train came through," Max said.

"Yes, well, let's get back to the house. You and Ted can return with shovels," Lizzy said. She was relieved Max wouldn't be present when Ben Wilson arrived.

She hadn't calculated that Ben Wilson would be as prompt as he was. The Sheriff was waiting on the porch when Lizzy, Charlotte, and Max rode into the farmyard.

"Hello, Ben," Lizzy greeted her visitor. "I have something to attend to, and I'll be right with you."

"Max," Lizzy said to her son, "Tell Ted about the accident. The two of you can bury her." Max went in search of the hired man. Lizzy and Charlotte joined Ben on the porch.

The words "accident" and "bury her" got the Sheriff's attention. "What's going on, Lizzy?" Ben Wilson asked. "Who are you burying? Sounds like something your Sheriff should know about."

Lizzy waved her hand as if it were of no importance. "One of our heifers was hit and killed by the train. We need to bury her before the predators find her."

Ben Wilson blew out a sigh of relief. "You should place a claim with Frontier for the loss," he suggested. "Lizzy, I have some news for you, but I'm guessing Charlotte has already filled you in."

"She has, and I'm thankful she was the one to tell me," Lizzy replied. She reached out for her sister's hand.

"I think it's best if you meet with the Westons, Lizzy," the Sheriff said. "I can arrange the meeting at the Sheriff's office."

"No, I think it would be better to meet somewhere less public," Lizzy countered. "Not their hotel room — a neutral space."

"That makes sense," Ben agreed. "What do you have in mind?"

As Lizzy mentally reviewed potential meeting places, Charlotte said, "How about the church? We can ask the pastor to close the building for the meeting."

"That's an excellent suggestion, Doctor Charlie," Ben said. "I'll speak to Pastor Hess when I get back to town. We'll schedule the meeting for tomorrow afternoon. That gives you time to get to town."

"Yes," was all Lizzy said.

Charlotte and Lizzy watched Sheriff Wilson ride toward town.

"Now what?" Charlotte asked.

"I've had a long time to think about this," Lizzy said. "Eight years, in fact. If Max is their grandson…if he is a member of their family…well, I guess they have a right to bring him home."

"Oh, no, Lizzy!"

"On the other hand," Lizzy continued, "Max has been my son for eight years. I found him, nursed him when he was sick, taught him how to read, how to milk a cow…I've been the only family he's known for eight years. Is it fair to tear him away from everything he knows?

"But, if they can prove that Max is their grandson, they have a legal right to him," Lizzy concluded. "Tomorrow will be an important day for all of us."

"Do you want me to come with you to the meeting?" Charlotte offered.

"I'm not sure," Lizzy said. "Let me sleep on it."

The sisters sat in silence on the porch for a space of time. Lizzy considered all the obstacles she and Charlotte had faced over the years, either together or separately. Ultimately, however, they had always been there to support each other.

Finally, Charlotte rose, brushed off her riding skirt, and tied on her broad-brimmed sun hat. "I'd best get back to town," she said. "You'll stop at my house before the meeting." It was a statement rather than a question.

They hugged, and Charlotte said, "We'll get through this just like we've gotten through the deaths of Mama, Papa, our brother, and the cursed War." She patted Lizzy on the back as she hugged her younger sister.

When Max returned from burying the heifer, Lizzy explained the situation to him. Her son reacted much as Lizzy had expected.

"You're my Ma. This is my home. I don't want to go with some strangers." He spoke with a tremor in his voice. Then he started crying.

Lizzy took Max in her arms, stroked his auburn hair, and rubbed his back.

"Shh, Maxie. We'll get through this. I can't imagine life without you. You're my heart."

Lizzy didn't sleep much that night.

When the sun rose on that warm June morning, Lizzy wished she had gotten more sleep. But she rose from her bed and peeked in on her sleeping son. It might be the last time she would see him sleeping in her house. But Max was lying awake in his bed.

"Morning, Ma," he said. "I've decided I'm not going to town."

"Maxwell Ward, you're not in a position to decide that. We will go to town and meet these people.

Now, get washed up, then put on your church clothes. I'll make breakfast after I get dressed."

Lizzy took extra care with her appearance today, too. She chose a pale blue dress with white pearl buttons down the bodice. White lace peeked out from the elbow-length sleeves. She knew it wasn't what women were wearing back East, but in the West, practicality outweighed the bustles and flounces that were currently in fashion. She plaited and pinned her blonde hair into a style she had seen in *Godey's Lady's Book*, wishing she had a stylish hat like the one Mrs. Danbury had worn.

Squaring her shoulders, Lizzy looked in the mirror and said, "Elizabeth Ruby Ward, you are ready for this."

Ted Nesbitt arrived for work just as Lizzy and Max were hitching the horse to the wagon.

"Ted, we have business in town today. I'll see you tomorrow."

They arrived in Shady Bluffs by mid-morning. "Max, take the horse and wagon to Uncle Luke's livery. Then, meet me at Aunt Charlotte's house. I'm going to the train depot to place a complaint about our dead heifer."

News of the Day

The Semi-Weekly Republican, St. Francisville, Louisiana, May 21, 1872

Headline: Agricultural Column – Wire Fences in Texas

Mr. R.E. Tallbot, Georgetown, Williamson county, Texas, describes a new wire-fence which has been extensively introduced into that section, which, it is claimed, can be built for less than $1.25 per rod. It has been fully tested by wild Texas cattle, and is perfectly hog-proof. It consists of eight wires, No. 9 size, passing through cedar posts a rod apart. The lower four wires are 6 inches apart, and the others 9 inches. This will give a 5 foot fence. Between the posts weave in three sawed or split pickets, which should not reach the ground. Staple the wires to the pickets.

Chapter 23 – June 1873

Lizzy's Plan

At the Jameson house, Charlotte poured tea for Lizzy and herself. "It's my own blend of mint tea. Very soothing."

"It better not put me to sleep, Char," Lizzy said. There were dark circles under her eyes. "I didn't have a 'good night.'"

"I can only imagine, Lizzy. What's your plan?"

"You know, for the first time I can remember, I don't have a plan. And that scares me."

"Did you want me to come to the meeting at the church with you? I can be there for moral support," Charlotte said.

"I'd like that," Lizzy said. "And I'm thinking I'd like Hank in the meeting, too. There will be three people on the other side."

"See, you do have a plan," Charlotte countered. "I'll let Hank know."

"No, I'll go there," Lizzy said.

When Hank saw her enter the Savings and Loan, he opened his arms, and Lizzy folded into his embrace. Hank kissed the top of Lizzy's head and made soothing sounds while she sobbed in his arms.

"I'm sorry I couldn't have been the one to tell you about the Westons," Hank said.

"No apology is necessary," Lizzy said. "If you'd left after meeting with them, it would have been a red flag. But I'd like you to be at the meeting this afternoon. One o'clock at the church."

She sniffed and dabbed at her eyes. "Enough crying. Whatever happens, I will face it," she said with steel in her voice.

Hank pulled out a clean, white handkerchief and handed it to Lizzy.

"You can and you will."

Lizzy, Charlotte, and Hank entered the church on the hill at one o'clock. Sunlight streamed through the stained-glass window above the altar, spilling a rainbow of colors into the church's sanctuary.

Pastor Hess was waiting for Lizzy and her group. "I wish this were a happier occasion, Miss Lizzy," the pastor said. "I thought you could meet in my office. I've added extra chairs to accommodate everyone." He showed them into the office and returned to the sanctuary to wait for the other attendees.

Sheriff Wilson was the next to arrive. He joined Lizzy, Charlotte, and Hank in the pastor's office.

"Lizzy, I sure wish I didn't have to be here. But as the only law in town, it's my duty to make sure everything is done fairly and lawfully."

"I understand, Ben," Lizzy said.

"You're a fair man," Hank agreed.

They heard a commotion in the outer area. Then, Pastor Hess ushered Josiah Chatton and the Westons into the office. Hank and Ben Wilson rose when the newcomers entered the office.

Ben Wilson made the introductions. "Miss Elizabeth Ward, this is Mr. and Mrs. George Weston. And I believe you've met Mr. Chatton."

"Yes, Mr. Chatton visited my house last winter," Lizzy said. She nodded to the Westons and said, "Hello."

Ben Wilson continued the introductions. "This is Miss Ward's sister, Doctor Charlotte Jameson. And you met Mr. Johnson yesterday."

"Hello, Mr. Johnson," George Weston said. "Pleased to make your acquaintances, Miss Ward and Mrs. …er…Doctor Jameson."

"With that out of the way, let's get down to the purpose for this meeting," the Sheriff said.

"May I begin," Josiah said before the Westons could stir up emotions. Sheriff Wilson nodded in agreement.

"I'd like to start by recounting the events that have led up to this meeting," Josiah said. "The Westons engaged the Pinkerton Agency after reading an article from the *Dakota Dispatch* that had been picked up by the *Chicago Tribune*. The newspaper article told of Miss Ward's windmills. The story mentioned Miss Ward's adopted son. That piqued the Westons' curiosity.

"Until that time, Mr. and Mrs. Weston had assumed their son and his family had arrived safely somewhere out West. It was the timing of the events that caused the Westons to hire me. It was my task to discover if their son, James Weston, and his wife, Sandra, had perished in Shady Bluffs' stampede in April 1865.

"I conducted a thorough investigation," Josiah continued. "picking up the trail in Galena, Illinois. In Cedar Falls, I found a hotel guest registry that included an entry for the couple in March 1865. I tracked them to a hotel in Fort Dodge, Iowa, later that month. Then the trail went cold."

"This seems very circumstantial," Hank said. "You're making assumptions."

"Normally, I would agree with that, Mr. Johson," Josiah said. "I laid out the facts to Mr. and Mrs. Weston as I had uncovered them. I cautioned them that hotel registries do not provide strong proof that their grandson was the boy in the newspaper article. Then they showed me the photograph and the portrait of their son. I believe the next step is to compare the images of their son with Miss Ward's son."

"Did you bring the photograph and the portrait?" Ben asked the Westons.

"We did," George Weston replied and motioned to his wife. From her handbag, Clarice Weston took out the silver-framed black-and-white Daguerreotype of James Weston at age nine. George opened a small valise and retrieved a painting of the same boy standing on the top step of a staircase. The painting showed the boy's coloring: red hair, green eyes, and freckles.

Charlotte's face was unreadable, but Lizzy bit her lip.

"We've produced our evidence," George Weston said. "Now, we'd like to see our grandson."

Charlotte looked at Lizzy and said, "I'll fetch Max."

A short time later, although the time dragged for Lizzy, Charlotte returned, holding Max by the hand.

Clarice Weston gasped. "That's our boy!"

"I am not," Max said defiantly.

Lizzy rose and went to her son. She whispered in Max's ear, "Be respectful, sweetheart."

Josiah held up the portrait near Max's face. The resemblance was undeniable. The boy in the painting had redder hair than Max had, but both boys had green eyes, a sprinkling of freckles, and ears that stuck out just a bit too far.

Max looked at the painting, and his face crumpled. Then he buried his face in the skirt of Lizzy's dress. Lizzy rubbed his back as she had when he was a fussy baby. The gesture seemed to soothe him.

"I believe this proves our case," George Weston said. "Sheriff, do you believe this boy is the son of our son? Our grandson?"

"The boy in the picture looks a lot like Max," Sheriff Wilson admitted. He turned to Lizzy. "Miss Ward, I'm afraid I will have to ask you to surrender Max into the custody of the Westons."

"I don't wanna go with them," Max protested. "I want to stay with you, Ma. You're my mother. Some dumb painting doesn't change that."

Lizzy knelt down and looked Max in those green eyes. "I'll always be your mother, Maxie," Lizzy said in a calm voice.

Gathering her strength, Lizzy stood up and addressed the Westons. "This is very difficult for *my son*," she said, emphasizing the words "my son."

"I understand that he may be your blood relative. And I understand you will be taking him back to Chicago. But I have a proposal that I believe would be in the best interest of Max…of *our* boy, Max."

"A proposal?" George Weston repeated as a question. "What would that be?"

"That we share Max," Lizzy said. "Max has grown up in Dakota Territory. Fishing in the creek, riding his horse, even working on the farm. He loves this life."

"Absolutely not," Clarice Weston said. "We need to get him into a good school immediately."

"Let her speak, Clarice," George said to his wife. "Go on, Miss Ward."

Lizzy cleared her throat, hoping it would help her speak with more strength.

"He would attend school in Chicago, Mrs. Weston. I propose that he spend several weeks with me in the summer. The train service would make this an easy trip for him.

"His friends, his cousins, everyone he's ever known is here," Lizzy continued. "Spending a few weeks in the summer would allow him to keep those relationships."

"Miss Ward," George said, "I would like to discuss this with my wife before we give you an answer."

"That is all I can ask," Lizzy said.

"My sister and her son will stay in town with my family," Charlotte spoke up for the first time. "Let's meet here again tomorrow."

That night at the Jameson house, Lizzy, Charlotte, and Hank updated Luke on the outcome of the meeting.

"When I saw that portrait, I knew that Max was their grandson," Lizzy said. "The resemblance between James Weston and Max is undeniable. He's a Weston. But he's also a Ward. I just hope they'll understand how important it will be for Max to come back to his Dakota family in the summer."

"It's a good compromise," Hank agreed. "And it gives the Westons something to think about tonight. Let's just hope they understand that it will make Max happy."

"I don't think Mrs. Weston liked your plan, Lizzy," Charlotte said. "But then, I don't think that woman likes much of anything. I heard from Betsy Tomlinson that Clarice Weston is a very 'difficult' guest for the folks at the Prairie Palace. Nothing is good enough for her."

"I think I ruffled her feathers," Lizzy admitted. "She didn't expect me to make a counteroffer. Her husband, on the other hand, is a businessman who is used to negotiating for what he wants. He may see it as a way to make Max more amenable to moving to Chicago."

"Did Ben Wilson say anything to you after the meeting, Hank?" Luke asked.

"He thought it was a good compromise. Truth be told, I don't think Ben realized how much Max looked like James Weston until they were side-by-side."

"Let's get some sleep, everyone," Luke counseled the group.

In the morning, Charlotte and Lizzy made breakfast for the extended family.

"It's just like old times," Charlotte observed. "I miss our early years on the claim. Life was simpler then."

"Those were good times," Lizzy agreed. "But I wouldn't trade my time with our children for anything." And then the reality of her words struck her.

"Oh, Char, what if I lose him forever?" Her voice wavered in grief.

Charlotte hugged her. "I don't think that will happen. Remember what Mama used to say about worrying: Ninety percent of what we worry about will never come to be, and we can't do anything about the other ten percent."

"I told Max that just the other day. I miss Mama and Papa."

After breakfast, Max and Lizzy went for a walk. Lizzy wanted to spend as much time with her son as possible before he left for Chicago.

"But I don't want to go with those people, Ma," Max said. "I'll run away and come back here to be with you."

Lizzy knelt down to look Max eye-to-eye. "That would be fool-hardy and dangerous, Max. Besides, they would know where you had disappeared to. I'm hoping that they'll agree to let you spend summers here. We can be together then."

The boy collapsed into Lizzy's arms. "Don't let them take me, Ma."

"Shh, Maxie. You were theirs before you were mine. You're part of their family, too."

"Will you take care of Tiger while I'm gone?" Max asked.

"Of course! I'll make sure he gets ridden regularly and has plenty of time in the pasture. Say, maybe cousin Will would take care of him. What would you think of that?" Lizzy suggested.

"Will really likes Tiger. And his parents haven't given him a horse yet."

"I bet Will could write you letters about Tiger."

"You think so, Ma? That would be hunky dory."

Lizzy promised that she would write to Max every week. Max promised to write regularly but weekly seemed a stretch for him.

After lunch, Lizzy and Charlotte stopped at the Savings and Loan and waited as Hank closed the office so he could accompany them.

This time, the Westons and Josiah Chatton were waiting when Lizzy, Charlotte, and Hank arrived at the church.

Lizzy wasn't sure how to read the sour look on Clarice Weston's face. She hoped it meant that Clarice hadn't gotten her way and that the compromise had been accepted.

"Good day, Miss Ward, Doctor Jameson, and Mr. Johnson," George Weston said. "My wife and I have had time to consider your suggestion. It's a highly unusual arrangement, you understand. Still, it may be in the best interest of the boy."

A spark of hope began to grow in Lizzy's heart. Maybe Max wouldn't be cut off from her forever!

George Weston continued his monologue. "My wife is not completely comfortable with this arrangement, but I think it's worth a trial run."

Lizzy's heart nearly exploded. "Oh, Mr. Weston, thank you."

"We intend to return home on the afternoon train tomorrow, Miss Ward. Please see that Max is packed and ready to accompany us."

Lizzy nodded dumbly. She didn't trust her voice to respond. Charlotte took Lizzy by hand, and they left the church office. Lizzy's mind was spinning. How would she tell Max that he would be leaving the only home he'd ever known?

Charlotte and Lizzy found their sons at the blacksmith shop, watching Luke repair a harness for a team of plow horses. The boys were fascinated with Luke's attention to detail. He had stripped the leather straps and collar off the harness, along with other parts that were not made of metal.

"There's not much left of the bit," Luke said to the boys, "so I'll have to build a new one for these harnesses."

Luke's artistry mesmerized Max and Will as the blacksmith fashioned a new bit out of a length of metal.

Charlotte cleared her throat to get the boys' attention. "I'm afraid the blacksmithing lesson is done for the day. Will, you're needed at the house." She and her son left.

Lizzy held out her hand for Max. They walked to the edge of town while Lizzy outlined the arrangement.

"You love summer on the prairie, Max. It's the best time of year. And I'll plan to make trips to Chicago to see you when I can."

Tears streamed down Max's face. "I don't want to go, Ma."

"And I don't want you to go, but I don't have a legal claim to you, sweetheart. We need to ride back to the farm and pack up some things for you — although the Westons said they would be purchasing all new clothing for you."

"Hmmph," Max said disagreeably. "Those fancy-pants clothes that I see in your magazine?"

Lizzy smiled and patted Max on the shoulder. It would do no good to argue with him about the clothes "city boys" wore.

"Let's just make the best of it," Lizzy said. "Would you like to have a picnic supper tonight? We'll stop at Betsy's and get a basket of fried chicken and one of her pies."

"Yes," he said enthusiastically. "Can we invite Hank?"

Lizzy's eyes sparkled, both from Max's happy response and perhaps from tears she was holding back.

Back at the farm, Max asked to ride Tiger one last time before he left. Lizzy was glad to spend time alone with Hank to discuss the events.

They sat together on the porch bench. "Where did you come up with the idea for summer visits, Lizzy?" he asked.

Lizzy shook her head. "It just came to me while we were talking. I tried to put myself in Mr. and Mrs. Weston's shoes. What if they had to leave Max with me?"

"It's the best of both worlds," Hank said. He put his arm around Lizzy. "He's lucky to have you as a mother." She leaned her head onto Hank's shoulder.

"I've watched you raise Max since he was that tiny babe you found in the rubble. You've been a good mother to him," he said. "But, as boys get older, sometimes they need the steadying hand of a father."

He turned Lizzy to face him. "I'd like to be that father. But more than that, I'd like to be your husband. Will you marry me, Lizzy Ward? I know this has been a long time coming, but I love you, and I want to spend our lives together."

Lizzy gasped. "Well, that wasn't something I was expecting to hear today."

"It's a lot to take in. and I probably shouldn't have popped the question today, but I want you to know that I'll be here for you."

"I always knew that, Hank." She put her hands on the sides of Hank's face and kissed the big man. "That's my answer. Yes, I'll marry you. But, let's not tell Max just yet. He's got a lot to deal with right now."

"I've always said you're a smart lady, Lizzy." He returned Lizzy's kiss with passion.

When Max returned from riding Tiger, they walked to the west pasture near the first windmill. Hank spread a quilt on the grass while Lizzy unloaded the picnic basket's contents.

"This is one of my favorite views," Lizzy said. "You can see the setting sun in all its glory." The summer sun, glowing in shades of pink, orange, and golden yellow, slowly dipped into the horizon.

"Thank you, Ma," Max said.

Lizzy looked puzzled. "Thank you?"

"Thank you for the life you've given me. I love this land. And having supper here tonight with you and Hank, well, it's the memory I'll hold on to the hardest."

"Oh, Maxie," Lizzy said. She gathered the boy into her arms, speechless at her son's heartfelt sentiment.

The next day was hard for Lizzy and Max. Hank had ridden back to town to allow them some time to themselves.

"I don't think you'll need a lot of clothes for the trip," Lizzy said as she folded several shirts and packed them into a carpetbag. "I'm sure your grandmother will take you shopping for clothing that will be appropriate for Chicago."

Max didn't respond, so Lizzy continued. "Do you want to pack anything else?"

Max scanned the shelves by his bed. "Yes," he said. He pulled the two Jules Verne books and put them in the bag with his clothing.

Lizzy nodded in approval.

They climbed onto the buckboard wagon, and Lizzy snapped the reins.

Lizzy tried to make small talk on the ride, but Max responded in monosyllables, so she gave up. They rode in silence, listening to the calls of prairie chickens and songbirds.

Arriving in town well before the afternoon train, Lizzy tied the wagon to the hitching post in front of Charlotte's house. When they entered the Jameson house, it seemed that no one was at home.

"Charlotte," Lizzy called out. "Charlotte, are you at home?"

"Surprise!" The three cousins burst out from hiding places behind the sofa, a large chair, and the window curtains. Each cousin was holding a wrapped package.

"We wanted to give you something to remember us," Will said. "Even though you'll be back every summer." He handed Max a brown leather pouch. "I wanted to get you a rolling hoop, but Ma said that was too big for the train."

Max opened the pouch and poured out a handful of glass marbles.

He grinned at his cousin. "Thanks, Will."

It was little Lincoln Jameson's turn to present his gift to Max. When Max unwrapped it, he found a wooden top. The pointed end and the handle were painted red. The body of the top had a series of red and blue stripes on it.

Max gave the top a couple of spins. "This is hunky dory, Linc. Thank you!"

Finally, Eliza stepped forward. "I didn't get you a toy, Max." She handed him a wooden box with a clasp on it.

When Max opened it, he found sheets of writing paper and two sturdy pencils.

"Thank you, Eliza," Max said. "I will write to all of you and tell you about Chicago."

Then Max kissed Linc and Eliza. Rather than kissing Will, the two boys shook hands like men.

"And I have a treat for Max, too," Charlotte said. She brought out a beautifully frosted chocolate cake. "This is for dessert. Lunch first, then cake."

"This is better than a birthday," Max asserted.

Soon — too soon Lizzy's opinion — it was time to meet the Westons at the train station.

The Westons' ornate private railcar had been coupled to the Frontier Railroad's afternoon train. Clarice and George Weston stood outside the depot as half a dozen trunks were loaded onto the train.

As the Jamesons, Lizzy, and Max approached the depot, George Weston collapsed. Charlotte and Luke helped George onto a nearby bench. Charlotte called to Will, "Fetch my medical bag."

"How are you feeling, Mr. Weston?" Charlotte asked. She listened to his heart with her stethoscope and counted heartbeats.

"Diffy," he responded.

"He hasn't been making sense all morning. I think he means 'dizzy.'" Clarice told Charlotte. "He sounds inebriated, but I know he has not been drinking alcohol."

"Do you have a headache?" Charlotte asked him.

He put his hand to his temple and said, "Hurts."

Then George Weston vomited.

"Oh, dear. What is happening?" Clarice Weston said.

"I can't be sure," Charlotte said, "but I believe it may be apoplexy. Let's get him to my clinic."

Hank and Luke put George Weston's arms around their shoulders and assisted him to the doctor's office down the street. Charlotte, Lizzy, and Clarice followed in their wake.

News of the Day

The Charlotte Democrat, **Charlotte, North Carolina, December 22, 1880**

Headline: Sleep, Fainting, Apoplexy

What is apoplexy? From the suddenness of the attack and the apparent carelessness of it, the Greeks connected it to their own minds with the idea of a stroke of lightning as coming from the Almighty hand it literally means "a stroke from above." As instantaneous as the hurling of a thunderbolt in a clear sky, there comes a loss of sense, and feeling, and thought and motion: the heart beats, the lungs play but that is all – they soon cease for ever.

Chapter 24 – June 1873

Change in Plans

Now, in her clinic, Char had changed from her role as a loving wife and mother to that of a skilled doctor and surgeon. George Weston was her patient.

She directed Luke and Hank to lay George Weston on the table in the exam room at the back of the doctor's office. Clarice Weston followed her husband into the room. She seemed to be in more distress than her husband, who was experiencing the actual medical emergency.

"Apoplexy!" Clarice Weston echoed Charlotte's potential diagnosis. "Martha Talbot's husband had a seizure and never recovered. What shall I do?"

"Mrs. Weston, may I prescribe a sedative for you? That might help calm your worries."

"Yes. Yes, that would be appreciated," Clarice replied.

"Lizzy, please brew a pot of that special tea for Mrs. Weston," Charlotte instructed Lizzy. Then Char mouthed the word "mint" to clarify her instructions.

"Of course, Doctor Jameson," Lizzy replied. She disappeared into an adjoining room that served as a small kitchen for the clinic.

Charlotte loosened George Weston's cravat and collar, which seemed to give the man some relief. Her immediate thought was to reduce George's discomfort. The man was shaking and thrashing in violent seizures.

"Luke, please make sure that Mr. Weston remains on the table. I need to prepare medication for him," Charlotte told her husband.

While Luke stabilized George Weston, Charlotte administered a dose of laudanum to her patient. The tincture of opium seemed to give George some relief.

Clarice re-entered the exam room and saw that her husband's seizures had subsided.

"Martha Talbot's husband benefited from bloodletting," she said. "Will you be doing that?"

"I don't believe in bloodletting," Charlotte said flatly. "I believe the body needs all its resources to fight disease. What I saw in the War was that bloodletting simply weakened patients."

"Well!" sniffed Clarice. "That is the preferred treatment in Chicago."

"We're not in Chicago, Mrs. Weston," Charlotte said with authority. "You are welcome to bring him home for that treatment. While your husband is in my clinic, I am in charge."

"When can I bring him home?" Clarice persisted.

Charlotte listened to George's heart and lungs. "He needs to rest. I would like to keep him in the clinic overnight. We can reassess his condition tomorrow."

Charlotte eyed Clarice Weston's demeanor and decided to take a softer approach. "Mrs. Weston, apoplexy can be as trying for the family members as it is for the patient. May I suggest that you return to your hotel and rest? I can prescribe some laudanum for you, as well."

"Laudanum, yes, I would like that," Clarice replied. "Thank you, Mrs. — er, Doctor Jameson."

Charlotte plucked a small bottle of laudanum from the top shelf of her locked cabinet and handed it to Clarice. "One drop twice a day, Mrs. Weston."

Clarice Weston nodded and tucked the blue glass bottle into her handbag. During the medical examination, Josiah Chatton arrived at the clinic. He thanked Charlotte for her attention to Mr. Weston and announced that he would escort Mrs. Weston back to the Prairie Palace Hotel.

With Clarice and Josiah gone, Charlotte dropped into a large, cushioned chair in the waiting room. Lizzy paced the room. Hank and Luke watched as their women coped with yet another life-changing crisis.

"What happens tomorrow?" Luke asked both women.

"It's my medical opinion that George Weston is not strong enough to take on the responsibility of an eight-year-old boy," Charlotte said. "And don't start me on Clarice Weston."

"I don't wish ill health on anyone, but perhaps the Westons will realize that they should not take Max away to Chicago," Lizzy said. "Perhaps," she paused to consider her idea, "I can offer a new plan."

Lizzy outlined her plan to Charlotte, Luke, and Hank. The four agreed that Lizzy may have a solution that everyone would accept.

"We should know more about Mr. Weston's recovery tomorrow," Charlotte said.

"I really need to get back to the farm," Lizzy said. "I know that Ted has been tending the livestock, but it's not fair to him or his children. I'll tell Max that I'll return tomorrow."

Max, it turned out, did not want to stay in town, away from his mother — and his horse. Privately, Lizzy thought Max's yearning to return to the farm had more to do with seeing Tiger.

"It may appear that you're planning to run away with Max," Hank warned Lizzy. "Before you leave town, let's apprise Ben Wilson of the situation."

"That's a sound idea," Luke agreed.

The sisters updated the Sheriff on George Weston's condition.

"I'm keeping Mr. Weston in the clinic overnight for observation," Charlotte said.

Lizzy explained that she was returning to the farm to give Ted Nesbitt a reprieve but would return the following day. Then she said that Max wanted to go to the farm with her.

"Lizzy, I know you would never do anything illegal, but it just wouldn't look right if I let you ride off with Max on the day he was supposed to go to Chicago with his grandparents. I'm afraid Max will have to stay in town."

"I understand, Sheriff," Lizzy said.

"Lizzy, why don't you bring Tiger to town tomorrow? There will be time for Max to ride the horse then," Charlotte suggested.

"As my son would say, that's a hunky dory idea." Lizzy smiled.

Lizzy found Ted and three of his eight children weeding the kitchen garden when she drove the buckboard into the farmyard.

"I see you brought reinforcements today, Ted," Lizzy said as she climbed off the wagon.

"The oldest two are watching the three young'uns," Ted answered. "Chores keeps 'em busy and out of trouble."

"Eight children! I don't know how you do it," Lizzy said. She made a mental note to put something extra in Ted's weekly pay.

"Each and every one of 'em is a blessing, Miss Lizzy. I was sorry to learn that Max is leaving us."

"There have been some developments. Mr. Weston has taken ill, and that might change their plans," Lizzy said. "I've returned home for a change of clothing and to help with chores. I'll be riding back to town tomorrow."

Ted gestured in understanding, then went back to supervising his children.

345

Lizzy looked on, wondering what having a houseful of children would be like. *It would be wonderful,* she concluded.

She rode out to the north pasture to check on the cattle, then turned south to verify the watermill by Nellie's land was still pumping water. The windmill and the water pump were working as intended.

A good investment, Lizzy thought.

The Nesbitts had finished their work for the day by the time Lizzy returned to the farm. The garden had been watered from the nearby windmill and pump. Baskets of peas, beets, green beans, and carrots were waiting for her on the front porch.

Hiring Ted Nesbitt was one of the best things I've done, Lizzy thought. She would split up the produce and leave a note for the Nesbitts to bring home some of the bounty from the garden.

The house felt empty to Lizzy. Even though Max had spent weeknights in town during the school year, this felt different. Despite her plan, Lizzy had misgivings about its outcome tomorrow.

She thought again of Mama's saying that ninety percent of her worries would never come to be. Lizzy hoped her Mama was right.

The July morning dawned hot and dry.

Not a cloud in the sky, Lizzy observed as she gathered eggs. Knowing that droughts could persist for several years, she wondered how long this one would last.

A breeze moved the vanes of the windmill; water trickled into the holding tank.

Lizzy tied Tiger to the back of the wagon and started out for Shady Bluffs. From her perch on the wagon bench, she scanned the Dakota prairie. It was brown and lifeless. Where she should be seeing purple clover, pink coneflowers, and golden sunflowers, she saw plants that had wilted from lack of rain. Even the lush prairie grasses, usually waist-high by now, were struggling to survive.

At last, she arrived in Shady Bluffs and drove directly to Charlotte's house. Max ran out to greet Lizzy — and Tiger — as soon as they arrived.

"You brought him! Thanks, Ma," Max said. "Can I take him out? Will wants me to give him a ride."

Lizzy laughed at her son's enthusiasm and agreed. "Tiger's saddle and tack are in the wagon bed."

While the boys saddled Tiger, Lizzy joined Charlotte for a cup of coffee.

"How is Mr. Weston?" Lizzy asked.

"He's better. The seizures have subsided for now, but he's far from recovered. He appears to have some paralysis on his right side. That's concerning," Charlotte answered.

"I'm so sorry to hear that."

"Mrs. Weston will be at the clinic in about an hour," Charlotte said.

"I'd like to meet with them," Lizzy said. "Is it appropriate...do you think I could meet with them today?"

347

"Mr. Weston is mentally alert even if he has some physical impairments," Charlotte said.

Lizzy agreed to wait until Charlotte had spoken with the Westons about George's prognosis.

Clarice Weston was weeping inconsolably when Lizzy entered the clinic. She knocked on the private examination room and announced herself. George Weston invited her into the room.

"I'm glad to see that you are recovering, Mr. Weston," Lizzy began. "This was certainly an unforeseen situation."

She took a deep breath and continued. "This may not be the time to take on the added responsibility of an energetic eight-year-old boy. I have a proposal for you. It's still a 'sharing' agreement, but instead of Max staying with you most of the year with a visit here in the summer, I'd like to suggest that he stay in Dakota Territory with an extended visit during the Christmas holidays. We could arrange for other visits as you feel fit."

Clarice and George Weston looked at each other. George began to talk but had difficulty finding the words.

"George," Clarice said, "let me speak for both of us."

George nodded and waved his hand for Clarice to proceed.

"My husband and I have discussed this very thing, Miss Ward. While we would love to spend more time with our grandson, we are not in the position to raise a youngster at this time."

She looked at her husband to confirm his agreement. George gave Clarice a partial smile — the best he could do with his current medical condition.

Clarice continued. "Your proposal is similar to what George and I discussed before your arrival today. We will not be bringing Max to Chicago at this time."

Lizzy clasped her hands in muted joy.

George said, "More."

"Yes, dear," Clarice said. "We would like to spend more time with our grandson and look forward to visits both in Chicago and here in Dakota Territory."

"There is nothing I want more than for Max to know and love his grandparents," Lizzy replied.

Everyone smiled in agreement and relief.

"I think the first thing to do," Lizzy said, "is to let the boy in question know. With your approval, I'll fetch Max so we can all tell him."

When Max entered the clinic, Mr. and Mrs. Weston were seated in the waiting room. While he knew that his grandfather had suffered an apoplexy, Lizzy had not let on that there was a change in plans.

"Good morning, Mr. and Mrs. Weston," he said.

"Grandfather and grandmother," George corrected him.

"Yes, sir," Max said.

"Max," Clarice said, "your grandfather's health has changed our plans. Your mother and we have decided that you will stay in Dakota, with occasional visits to Chicago."

Max beamed, but he controlled his urge to shout in happiness.

"Doctor Jameson," Clarice looked at Charlotte, "is it your medical opinion that Mr. Weston can return home this week?"

"I would recommend a longer recuperation, but…" Charlotte began.

"We have telegraphed our family physician, and I believe Doctor Summers should arrive here in two days. He will accompany us back to Chicago."

"That is an excellent plan," Charlotte said.

"And that will give you time to get to know your grandson," Lizzy suggested.

George and Clarice held out their hands for Max. He responded by reaching out to them.

Max stayed with the Jamesons for the next two days. During that time, he spent time learning about his father, James Weston. George and Clarice regaled Max with stories about Jamie: his favorite activities, misadventures, and life growing up in Chicago.

They had fewer anecdotes about Sarah Weston, but they were able to provide Max with some background on his birth mother and his parents' courtship. Unfortunately, Sarah Weston's family had perished during the war, so there were no living relatives to supplement these recollections.

News of the Day

The Chicago Daily Tribune, Chicago, Illinois, July 9, 1874

Headline: The Drought – Special Dispatches to The Tribune from Seven States

New Jefferson, IA, July 8 – The small grain in this section is suffering badly for want of rain, especially wheat, which will not be half a crop, unless we get rain inside of five days. Early corn is beginning to suffer, but there is no material damage yet. The weather is intensely hot, the mercury going to 104 yesterday.

Kansas City, MO, July 8 – In this vicinity and south of here, corn and oats are badly affected and will not yield much. Northeast and west the corn is not suffering, but will after this week if there is no rain.

Chapter 25 – July 1873

Where There's Smoke

The second summer of drought continued unabated. Dakota Territory's rich, black soil collected in drifts and piles like a winter snowfall. Those farmers who had optimistically planted wheat or corn crops in the spring looked to the skies for relief. But there was nary a promise of rain or rain clouds in the sky.

For Dakotans like Lizzy Ward and Stan Walker, who had built windmills, the lack of rain was a painful reminder that this would be a poor harvest for many of their neighbors.

Lizzy and Ted were working in the west section of the farm, manually watering the fields from the storage tank attached to the first windmill she had erected. The windmill and water tank had been built on a small rise in the land. The irrigation system used gravity and moveable pipes from the water tank to feed water into the furrows. Moving the pipes was back-breaking work, but the result was worth the labor.

"I'm moving the watering pipe to water the corn, Miss Lizzy," Ted said.

Lizzy picked a stalk of wheat and examined it. The plant was now flowering. Soon, the kernels would develop. Nodding in pleasure, Lizzy imagined an entire field of golden wheat waving in the breeze.

The corn in the east field, where Ted was moving the pipes, was surviving thanks to the regular watering. Lizzy knew that the corn crop was entering a critical stage in its development. The plants needed adequate moisture in order to develop the kernels and the size of the cob. It would be a few weeks before the plants reached their full height and began to tassel. And that brought her to harvest time.

But it all depended on the weather. Timely rains — without hail — would see the corn and wheat safely into Lizzy's harvest wagons and on to the mill.

"Ted," Lizzy called out, "when you finish watering that field, let's set the pipes in the far field and let the water just flow as it will."

"Yes, Miss Lizzy," he replied.

Lizzy's other windmill, the one the Frontier Railroad crew built next to Nellie's land, was less productive than the western windmill. Still, it was a good source of water for Nellie's horses and Lizzy's nearby fields. Lizzy rode to the southeast section of her farm to ensure the windmill was working.

The "Frontier Windmill," as Lizzy referred to this structure, was producing a trickle of water. She saw that the windmill's vanes were turning, but not much water was pumping into the water tank. Lizzy made a mental note to check the well next week. Maybe it needed to be deeper.

There's always something to fix or repair on a farm, Lizzy thought. She smiled. That was what made farm life rewarding. Farmers made a positive difference.

Lizzy decided that the well was a project for another day. It was time to get back home.

As she rode up to the farmyard, she envisioned a proper farmhouse replacing the long sod house that straddled the border of Lizzy and Charlotte's original claims.

That soddy allowed the sisters to meet the Homestead Act's requirement that homesteaders build a dwelling on their claim. Now it was time to put the sod house to use for other purposes. Just what that would be, Lizzy still needed to work out.

Lizzy's mind was on her two-story dream house when she noticed clouds in the distance.

These were the wispy clouds that she was accustomed to seeing — insubstantial clouds that did not bring a promise of rain.

I wish that was a rain cloud, she thought.

After she had unsaddled and groomed her mare, Lizzy went to her garden and picked fresh vegetables for dinner. On her way into the house, she thought she smelled smoke. Thinking it was the cookstove, Lizzy checked the oven for smoldering embers. It was cold.

She began to panic. If the smoke smell wasn't from the cookstove, it must be outside. Racing to the porch, Lizzy scanned the distant horizons. Then she saw it — a growing billow of smoke to the north, near Stan Walker's land.

Ted returned from the west fields as Lizzy ran to the barn to resaddle her mare.

"What's wrong, Miss Lizzy?" he asked.

"Smoke…fire!" She pointed to the smudge in the blue skies to the north. "I'm riding up there to help, but I don't know where Max is. Can you find him?"

"Sure thing," he replied as he galloped toward the creek.

In the past, Lizzy had faced small prairie fires — fires that could be quenched with buckets of water or smothered with wet blankets and rugs. This looked much larger, and it was growing by the minute.

When she reached the land Hank called Iron Horse Claim, Lizzy got her first look at the blaze. The fire ran the length of the railroad tracks on her side of the line. The train bed, filled with gravel and rock, seemed to slow the spread of the fire on the ground. Still, the wind could catch an ember, and the fire would be on both sides of the track and would move toward Stan Walker's farm.

As she was sizing up the fire, Stan Walker appeared through the smoke.

"Miss Lizzy," Stan called. "This is too big for buckets. I'm gonna move the pipe from the water tank over this way. Bear is at the windmill now."

"I'll help," Lizzy said. Finding a break in the fire line, Lizzy and her horse jumped the tracks, landing on Stan Walker's land.

Stan's wife, Clara, and their eldest son Bear, were adjusting the pipe attached to the water tank. Lizzy and Stan hurried up to help.

"Let's point it in the direction of the fire," Stan directed the crew. "Bear, ride up to the barn and fetch all the buckets, blankets, grain sacks, and anything else that will hold water. And pack some shovels if there's room."

John Running Bear Walker hightailed it back to the farm on his father's horse.

"What started the fire?" Lizzy asked Stan and Clara.

"Best as I can tell, it was sparks from the afternoon train," Stan said. "I've seen sparks fly from the metal wheels on the tracks. It's tinder dry out here. That would have been enough to start a blaze."

Lizzy had seen those same sparks and thought about the danger they presented. And now they were dealing with it.

The three adults positioned the pipe in the direction of the fire. Through the smoke, Lizzy saw two more figures racing toward them. It was Ted and Max. Both of them were riding at a full gallop. They didn't stop when they reached the tracks. Instead, both riders jumped the railroad tracks just as Lizzy had.

"We saw the smoke, Ma," Max yelled. "Me and Mr. Nesbitt are here to help."

"Every hand is needed," Stan said to the newcomers. "Bear is bringing buckets and blankets to fight the fire."

Moments later, Bear returned with as many firefighting supplies as he and his horse would carry. Stan motioned to the end of the water pipe, and Bear deposited the buckets, blankets, and rugs at that point.

"Grab a bucket and start dousing the fire where you can," Stan said. "Clara, get those blankets and rugs soaked in water. You and Miss Lizzy can use them to smother the fire."

"Boys," he looked at Max and Bear. "You are the runners. Keep refilling those buckets for Ted and me."

The six firefighters worked tirelessly until the sun was low in the western sky.

Because of the billowing smoke, Lizzy couldn't see the gathering clouds on the horizon. She, along with the other homesteaders, continued to fight the blaze. Just when it seemed they were getting ahead of the fire, another finger of flame would ignite farther down the tracks.

"Stay at it, Nesbitt," Stan called out. "See that lick of fire there?"

"Got it," Ted replied, tossing another bucket of water on the blaze.

They were all startled by the explosive sound to the west. Lizzy's heart sank, thinking that the fire had jumped far ahead of their efforts. Then, the sound boomed again. Looking up, Lizzy saw heavy, dark clouds. That sound was the wondrous boom of thunder.

After another crack of thunder and lightning, the heavens opened up.

"Rain! It's raining," Lizzy said more as prayer than an observance.

Both the boys threw down their buckets and began to dance.

Ted looked into the rain and said, "Thank you, Lord."

Stan and Clara Walker hugged each other.

"It's an answer to a prayer," Stan said.

"It's an answer to so many prayers," Clara corrected him.

"Rain," Lizzy said again. "Healing rain."

She lifted her face to the life-giving rain and let the drops wash off the soot. Blonde tendrils of hair, drenched in the shower, framed her face. When she opened her eyes, Hank was gazing down at her.

"You! How did you…," Lizzy said in wonderment.

"I could see the smoke from town. I knew it was coming from your place. I rode out as fast as I could. Luke and a few others are behind me."

Lizzy could see a party of riders galloping toward them.

Hank took Lizzy's face in his hands, leaned down, and kissed her soundly. She put her arms around his neck and held him tightly.

When they pulled apart, Hank surveyed the wreckage left behind by the fire. The Walkers joined them, and Stan said, "Miss Lizzy, you're the reason we were beating the fire."

"I don't know what you mean, Stan," she said.

"If we hadn't built that there Eclipse windmill this spring, we wouldn't have had the water to put out the fires," Stan said. "When I saw your harvest last fall, well, I knew I had to build a windmill for my crops. It's because of you that we had the water we needed."

"My Lizzy's a smart one," Hank said. "I'm betting more farmers are going to follow your lead and put up windmills. You can't count on the rains to come when you need 'em."

"But thank goodness they came today," Lizzy said. She lifted her face to the rain again and savored the waters from heaven.

Luke and the other men from town reined in their horses and surveyed the scene.

"Looks like we're too late," Luke said. "You folks took care of the fire."

"We had a little help from above," Stan said. He pointed to a few smoldering fires. "But there's still work to do if you want to pitch in. Grab a shovel or a bucket."

Together, the homesteaders and the townspeople stopped the fire from spreading.

"They've got this handled, Lizzy," Hank said. "Let's go home." He called out to Max to follow them back home.

The rain continued through the night and into the next day. It was a steady rain. A soaker, the old timers called it. The greedy, bone-dry earth welcomed the rains.

Holding hands like young lovers, Lizzy and Hank sat on the front porch and watched as the prairie transformed before their eyes. Wildflowers bloomed again. Grasses stood tall on the plains and rippled in the wind.

For the first time that she could remember, Lizzy felt complete. She didn't know what the future would bring, but she knew that Hank would be there, by her side.

"This," Lizzy said as she gazed out on the prairie, "this is why I love the land. It's the promise of a better tomorrow."

The End

Newspaper Citations

The historical newspaper articles cited at the end of many of the chapters were researched and accessed through the Library of Congress' *Chronicling America* collection. The text of these articles, typos and all, appeared as is in the cited newspapers. The Library of Congress states that the newspapers in *Chronicling America* are in the public domain or have no known copyright restrictions. Newspapers published in the United States more than 95 years ago are in the public domain in their entirety.

The *Dakota Dispatch* newspaper stories are original to *Iron Horse Claim.*

Chapter 1

"Western Patents." *The Chicago Tribune*, 15 Jan. 1868, p. 1.

Chapter 2

"Selection of Depot Grounds – What Has Been Done." *The St. Cloud Journal [St. Cloud, MN]* 4 January 1872, p. 1.

Chapter 3

"Wapello County Agricultural Fair." *The Ottumwa Courier* [Ottumwa, IA], 22 Aug. 1872, p. 1.

Chapter 4

"Stock Horses." *The Advertiser* [Brownville, Neb. Territory], 11 Apr. 1872, p. 1.

Chapter 5

"Dexter Windmill" (advertisement). *The Oskaloosa Herald* [Oskaloosa, IA], 31 July 1873, p.1.

Chapter 6

"Hydrophobia." *Nashville Union and American* [Nashville, Tenn.], 5 July 1874, p. 1.

Chapter 11

"Minnesota News." The St. Paul Daily Globe, 12 Apr. 1879.

Chapter 12

"The West." *Marshall County Republican* [Plymouth, Ind.], 12 Sept. 1872, p. 1.

Chapter 13

"Offering a Reward." *The Weekly Miner* [Butte, MT], 24 June 1879, p. 1.

Chapter 14

"The Credit Mobilier and Old Tammany." *The Chicago Tribune*, 17 Sept. 1872, p. 4.

Chapter 17

"State News." *The State Journal* [Jefferson City, MO], 14 Aug. 1874, p. 1.

Chapter 18

"Local Laconics." The *Daily Press and Dakotaian* [Yankton, Dakota Territory], 12 Oct 1878.

"Personal." The *Daily Press and Dakotaian* [Yankton, Dakota Territory], 12 Oct 1878.

Chapter 20

"The Dakota River Valley." The *Daily Press and Dakotaian* [Yankton, Dakota Territory], 2 Sept. 1878.

Chapter 21

"Completed at Promontory Point, Utah." *The Montana Post* [Virginia City, MT], 14 May 1869, p. 1.

Chapter 22

"Agricultural Column - Wire Fences in Texas." *The Semi-Weekly Republican* [St. Francisville, LA], 21 May 1872.

Chapter 23

Hall's Journal of Health. "Sleep, Fainting, Apoplexy." *The Charlotte Democrat* [Charlotte, NC], 22 Dec. 1880, p. 1.

Chapter 24

"The Drought – Special Dispatches to The Tribune from Seven States." *The Chicago Daily Tribune,* 9 July 1974, p. 8.

About the Author

CK Van Dam is a daughter of the Dakota prairies. With degrees in History and Journalism, she has embarked on a second career, creating stories about the strong women who built our nation and our world.

Her debut novel, *Proving Her Claim*, received two Spur Awards from Western Writers of America: Best Western Romance and Best First novel. The inspiration for the book came from historical records that found 42 percent of women homesteaders successfully proved up their claims, while only 37 percent of the men received title to their lands.

Lone Tree Claim, the second book in the "Claim" series, tells the story of a Civil War widow who comes to Dakota Territory after the devastation of war. As a woman alone on the frontier, she fought nature as well as powerful cattle ranchers.

The inspiration for *Medicine Creek Claim* and *Iron Horse Claim* came from the story of two sisters, Mary Ida and Edith Ammons, who homesteaded in Dakota Territory in the early 1900s.

Learn more at ckvandam.com

www.ingramcontent.com/pod-product-compliance
Lightning Source LLC
Chambersburg PA
CBHW061937130726
47909CB00013B/2027